Praise for C.C. Wiley's
Knight Dreams

"Ms. Wiley has perfectly captured the feel of the era she's chosen, her story is rich and detailed."
~ *The Good, The Bad, and The Unread*

"C. C. Wiley enchants with admirable imagery and a compelling writing style... This is a wonderful 15th century romance with a touch of history and imagery that thrills the senses."
~ *The Long and the Short of It*

Rating: 5 Nymphs "This is my first book from C.C. Wiley, but if Knight Dreams is any indication, it won't be my last."
~ *Literary Nymphs Reviews Only*

"This is a must read for those who love historical romances."
~ *The Pen and Muse*

"The plot keeps moving along with action and intrigue, and her writing makes you feel as if you are right there."
~ *Two Lips Reviews*

Knight Dreams

C.C. Wiley

A SAMHAIN PUBLISHING, LTD. publication.

Samhain Publishing, Ltd.
577 Mulberry Street, Suite 1520
Macon, GA 31201
www.samhainpublishing.com

Knight Dreams
Copyright © 2010 by C.C. Wiley
Print ISBN: 978-1-60504-789-8
Digital ISBN: 978-1-60504-674-7

Cover by Angela Waters

First Samhain Publishing, Ltd. electronic publication: October 2009
First Samhain Publishing, Ltd. print publication: August 2010

Dedication

I couldn't have written this story without my darling husband's love and support. My family almost always understood that when I was writing, they needed to give me room to create. They cheered me on, even in the tough times. Thank you, my sweet family.

I want to thank my writing friends in the Solvang Writing Group. In particular, my heartfelt thanks goes to Cynthia who brings laughter wherever she goes; to Janie, whose brilliance with the English language keeps us sane; and to Trudy, whose spirit lights up the room and warms our hearts.

Many thanks to my critique partner and friend, Kimberley Troutte, who always reminds me to breathe while I hyperventilate over changes. And to my fabulous editor, Deborah Nemeth, I thank you for helping make this story shine.

Lastly, thank you, God, for hearing my whispered prayer and bringing it to reality. I am forever grateful.

Chapter One

Valley Wye, Wales, 1409

All day, Terrwyn tried to peel away the ache that burrowed deep into her young bones. In spite of her efforts, the heavy residue from last eve's dream weighed on her mind. She had hoped the mountains and rugged Welsh countryside would clear her thoughts. Even the four gray rabbits, bound and hanging from her saddle, were not enough to lift her spirits. Instead, her thoughts dashed back to worry her even more.

Her nursemaid had called her dreams the gift of night visions. Terrwyn remained unclear whether the gift was a blessing or a curse.

A flash of movement caught her eye. Her brother rode toward her on his little pony, his legs dangling over its round belly. Had their father still been lord of the valley, Drem would have already traveled to another household. There his duties as squire of the body would teach him all that was required of a knight. One day, his skill with sword and arrows might have earned the king's favor.

That opportunity had been lost when the rebel Owain Glyndwr attempted to take the Welsh throne by force from England's own Prince of Wales.

She wished for a way to share her night vision, her fears for her brother. But her pride remained bruised from the last time he scoffed at her warnings.

Reining in her mount, she called out, "We dare not travel farther. The English soldiers may be near."

Although one year younger than she, Drem sat taller on his

mount. He leaned down to yank a strand of her hair. "Afraid, are you?"

Terrwyn shook her head. "You know I'm not. But Mam and Father will wonder where we are."

He pulled a face and frowned. "Not likely. Too busy crooning over red-faced babies."

"Drem," Terrwyn scolded, "the twins require their attention."

"They near killed our mam," he grumbled. "They aren't even boys. At least then it would be but a few years until they lend a hand with the lambing—instead of being yet another burden."

"Burden, is it?" The terse words barely hissed through her teeth. Squaring her shoulders, she edged her pony away. "I'll be sure to relay your sentiments to Catrin."

"What do you mean?"

"When the cold mountain air cuts against your bare skin, you'll be wishing our sister does not know you count her darning skill among the *burdens*." With a quick snap of the reins, she pointed the pony's head down the hill. "Since you fill the valley with your importance, I find it too crowded for my taste. I shall leave you to yourself."

Drem grabbed the halter and coaxed her pony close.

"Terrwyn, I didn't mean to hurt your wee feelings. Nor do I close my eyes to Catrin's skill with a needle. Thank the saints I have at least one sister who can sew a straight line. Mayhap the others will find a skill that will bring a blessing to our door."

"Think you I've no skill to offer?"

That same question had burned often enough in her heart. Lacking the talent of plying needle to cloth was certainly a nuisance at times. However, the inability to stir up something edible in a cook pot was swiftly becoming a festering thorn in her pride.

After great thought, he gave his answer with a shrug. "None which adds value to a female."

"You, a young boy of ten and two years, counts himself an authority on the fairer sex?"

Drem's lips curled into a smirk. "I've more knowledge of fair damsels than you could ever imagine."

8

Terrwyn swatted at his hand with the little riding whip she kept tucked in her boot. It whistled through the air, missing his knuckles by a faerie's hair. Hearing him utter a curse under his breath, she crowed with glee. "Ha-ha! Instead of cabbage and broth, it will be your words you eat tonight."

"Better my words than your cooking." Ducking another swat, he moved his mount out of reach and yelped.

"Enough of this foolery," Terrwyn said. "It will soon rain and I don't want to be caught in the downpour. Let's find the last lamb and be on our way home."

Straightening in his saddle, he scoured the horizon with an intense scrutiny worthy of a sheepherder's hound. "Look. Over there." He pointed to the shelf of rocks jutting out from the hillside.

Terrwyn let the hood of her cloak fall back and leaned into the raised leather ridge of her saddle. Even if she squinted, she barely made out a movement. Trusting in her younger brother's keen eye, she nodded in agreement. Letting him lead the way, she followed as he edged the pony around the patch of wide stone.

Drem dropped from his mount. Crouching low, he moved into the ravine. Moments later, he crawled out. His face was white as the craggy tops of a mountain in winter. A sheen of tears glittered from his eyes. He motioned for her to move down the hill.

"Where is the lamb?" Terrwyn asked.

"It didn't make it," Drem choked out. "Too little to live through the chill in the air."

"That makes two lambs this day."

She did not have to say what was on both their minds and would soon be on the minds of the villagers. It was an omen of bad things to come. Someone was bound to point a finger to their newly arrived twin sisters and announce they were the harbingers of more evil to befall their tiny village.

The heaviness from last night's dream resurfaced. "We best return home," she said.

Drem gave a quick nod and moved his mount next to hers. He pulled out his finely made bow of dwarf elm and carefully readied the arrow in the notch.

"What is it, Drem? What do you see?"

"Mounted riders."

The guilt of her silence pressed down. She should have made him listen to what she saw in her dream. The single word rushed out in a whisper. "English."

"Warn the village." Drem whacked the back of her mount with the flat of his hand.

"Nay!" she cried out.

The pony's rump twitched before it set off down the hill. Heart beating in her throat, Terrwyn gripped the reins as she righted her seat. Gaining control of the mountain pony, she ignored her brother's orders and whirled around to race back to his side.

The little pony trembled under her thighs. The ground shook with the pounding of hooves as the English soldiers raced after Drem. The air echoed with the sound of heavy leather and metal slapping against horseflesh. The glint of swords flashed in the daylight.

Her eyes widened. The men raced toward her brother just as they had in her dream. Unable to leave him behind, Terrwyn pulled out her bow. Bracing her heels in the wooden stirrups, she stood up from the saddle. The arrow placed in the notch, she aimed at the advancing men. The feather-quilled weapon screamed into the air.

She heard the horse's panicked whinny, the soldiers' angry shouts. Her aim had succeeded in turning them from Drem. The soldiers reined in and brought their mounts about. Relief for her brother's safety flooded through her. It would not be long until he left the slab of stone and circled around for her. She prayed he did not take his merry time.

She looked toward the sound of hoof beats thundering nearer.

Her little pony pranced and blew out a nervous breath. Its muscles bunched and flinched. Terrwyn swung the bow over her shoulder. Dropping into the well of the saddle, she slapped at her pony's flank with the riding crop. Her fingers tightened on the reins as the pony shot off down the hill toward the wooded glen.

The limp rabbits beat against her thigh, leaving streaks of bloodied fur upon her skirt. Green leaves of the great oaks blurred as she dashed past. She ducked under a low branch and narrowly missed taking off the top of her head. Mouth dry, her breath came in a ragged draw. She gripped the reins with one hand and leaned forward, stretching over the pommel of her saddle.

"Come on!" she urged the pony. "A few more steps. We'll lose them by the falls."

She needed only to round the bend to see the waterfall straightaway. The water would shield her from the men until Drem joined her. Reining in, she slowed her pace and maneuvered around a felled tree. She looked over her shoulder to scan the tree line, then heard the hiss of an arrow.

A frantic whinny erupted as her pony shied to one side. Its footing wavered. Terrwyn's seat began to shift. Kicking out of the stirrup, she rolled away from flailing legs, narrowly dodging a sharp hoof. The pony grunted and fell to the ground. Its ragged breaths filled the glen.

Terrwyn sucked back the pain that threatened to break apart her chest. Anger burned in her throat. Her darling pony lay next to her. Gently sliding a palm over its velvet nose, she felt the soft blows of air, each breath coming slower, shallower. Until finally they diminished and Terrwyn knew its life lingered no more.

Flattening her body into the loam of the forest, she dug her fingers into the earth and did her best to squash the fear leaping in her throat. Her mind was a hive of questions. How close were the English? Had they seen the spot where she fell? Where was Drem?

Before she moved, she had her first answer.

The toe of a thick wooden-soled boot caught her in the ribs and rolled her over. Terrwyn clamped her lips together and kept from crying out. She stared openly at the ugly pale-skinned men and their long faces, weak chins, pale blue eyes and hair the color of gruel.

A great brute bent over her and poked at her chest. "Here now! What do we have?" He moved the veil of dark hair from her face with the tip of his sword. "She's small enough to be a woodland faerie."

The other soldier dismounted and spoke over her as if she had no mind. "Don't touch her," he warned as he shoved the brute aside. "Me mum did say, if you had a taste of faerie, then your fella would fall off."

Terrwyn stared at the mottled sky overhead. Tears burned her eyelids and her ears still rang from when she hit the ground. Her stomach twisted with concern for Drem. If he had escaped their trap, then he would have been there by now. She feared her ruse had not been enough to draw all the soldiers away from him.

She heard the creak of leather accepting the shift of weight. A horse nickered softly, mouthing the bit with its tongue. The sound of twigs crushed under heavy footsteps drew near. She blinked. An English soldier towered over her.

His scowling visage was flushed red with anger. "I don't fear the Welsh tales," he said as he pushed the men out of the way.

Grabbed by her tunic, Terrwyn was lifted from the ground. Her back slammed against the base of a large oak. The palm of his hand pressed against her shoulder, grinding her flesh into a ridge of rough bark.

"Be this your errant arrow?" The bloodied shaft he held under her nose was tipped by a wedge of dull gray iron just as any arrowhead might be. She shook her head.

Squinting, the cow-faced man looked as if he did not believe her. "You there," he ordered one of the men, "bring that quiver to me."

He poured out the contents on the ground and crushed her bow with his heel. Upon hearing her hushed gasp a smile of satisfaction lifted his lips.

"I knew I would find a lying Welshman. Just not a wench, young and tender as this one." He licked his big lips and trapped her against the tree with a ham-sized hand on each side of her head. He moved closer, grinding his groin into her hip. "Aye, you'll thank me for what I'm about to give ya."

Unable to stand the sight and smell of the soldier, she turned her head. She squashed the whimper that threatened to bubble in her throat and gripped the tree, her nails digging into the bark. Her eyes squeezed tight, she began to whisper a prayer to the saints. As she ended her prayer, a yelp rang out.

Terrwyn opened her eyes to see why the soldier was now howling like an injured cur. A familiar arrow, its shaft marked with colored thread, impaled his hand. A volley of arrows shot through the air. Two more soldiers hit the ground, burrowing their stomachs into the leaves.

Attempting to drop to the ground, Terrwyn found her cloak gripped by the impaled soldier. She kicked out at his knees and felt the impact of her heel against his flesh right before she fell to the ground. His weight against the tree, the man cursed as another shaft narrowly missed his wrist, striking his sleeve instead.

"Do as I say this time," Drem called out. "Run while I hold them here."

Eager to put distance between herself and the soldiers, Terrwyn moved to do as she was told.

Her steps faltered. There, in the trees, the English soldiers stood behind her beloved brother. An uncontrolled shiver ran through her body as she reluctantly bent her knee and knelt on the ground.

One of the soldiers grabbed Drem, trapping his arms. Another soldier bound his wrists together. They ignored Drem's thrashing legs and twisting body, lifted him up onto the destrier's wide saddle and shackled his legs under the beast's belly.

Drem aimed his elbow at his captor's face. With a gruff warning, the soldier made a point to look toward Terrwyn. Satisfied she understood his threat, the soldier swung up behind Drem and motioned to his companions to prepare to leave.

Terrwyn stared intently, memorizing what she could. The stocky, brown-haired young man spoke tersely to the men. The soldiers did not seem to notice their orders came from one so young. Her stomach knotted. When he turned his mount, she saw a mottled scar running along the left side of his nose and cheek. Could this be Henry of Monmouth, England's Prince of Wales?

A young man about the same age as the prince rode up on a fine warhorse. Though he wore a soldier's garb of leather jerkin and padded leggings, the badge on his chest displayed the red Lancaster rose. He tipped his head to show respect to the royal sitting beside him. Given leave to speak his mind, he leaned forward, resting his forearm on the pommel of his saddle.

Though Terrwyn could not hear his comments, she knew their conversation did not go well when the prince shook his head in denial at the lanky soldier's request. The Prince of Wales's unyielding visage darkened. Their conversation came to a swift end when the prince nudged his mount and rode away.

The young man's perfect posture remained rigid as his stallion pranced under his grip. He swept the chain-mail hood off his head. Two red splotches colored his high cheekbones as he tugged his long fingers through his coal black hair.

Terrwyn wondered at his bravery. Perhaps madness. No matter, she thought dejectedly, whatever his objections, they were lost on closed ears.

As the small band of men rode past, their leather boots blurred in front of her face. She blinked away remnants of dust and tears. Despite her struggle, hope slipped through her fingers as if it were silk from a milk thistle.

"You cannot do this," she cried out. "He is but a child."

The dark-haired soldier stopped his mount in front of her. He held out his hand.

Terrwyn stared at the simple chain-link gauntlet and could not force herself to rise. She lifted her head, fixing her eyes on his face. "Please. Release my brother."

His eyes shimmered with concern before he shamefully turned his face away and rode on.

Drem's mount drew near enough that Terrwyn thought she might reach out and touch his leg. His face was pale. Anger bloomed over his cheeks.

He shook his head violently when he saw she meant to go to him. "Nay," he hissed. "'Tis naught you can do."

She gripped the soldier's boot and pleaded through tears. "Stop! I beg you."

"Listen to the lad." The cow-faced soldier tapped her shoulder with the flat of his blade. "Mind you, you'd have no troubles if not for Owain Glyndwr's band of mischief makers."

Drem looked back once more and shook his head. Helpless, Terrwyn watched the soldiers leave the glen. She swallowed her tears and vowed her first bitter taste of defeat would be her last.

Chapter Two

Southeast Wales, a small village near Abergavenny (Aber-uh-vennie) Spring, 1415

Terrwyn slapped the cleaning rag on the trestle table and scrubbed at the congealed oats and puddles of stale ale. Tonight the Sheep's Glen was nearly bursting. The villagers had crowded into the tavern when word came that strangers rode the hillside. Fear, swift as the river Usk, poured through the smoke-filled room.

"We know how the English soldiers work," one of the men shouted.

"Aye," agreed Smithy, a barrel-chested man. "They already took everything of value. What have they come for this time?" He turned toward the crowd of villeins, pumping his fist in the air. "I say we meet them with force, turn them away before they set foot in our village."

Her father, Dafydd ap Hew, once lord of the lands, stood beside the great hearth, weariness on his face. The upheaval of hearth and home had marked his shoulder-length hair with gray streaks, and the salting of gray brows and beard heightened the depth of his solemn dark eyes. His stature bent with the weight of responsibility, belying his thirty-eight years. He raised his arm to gain their attention. His voiced boomed over the heated voices. "Good people, we've known one day the English king would send his soldiers again to us."

"What do you intend to do?" yelled Smithy. "Drop your chausses and bend over as you did six years ago?" Encouraged by a few sniggers, he continued, "Do you aim to stand by and let the English king have his way again?"

His thick neck swelled with indignation, but Dafydd did not dignify the insult. He held his eyes on the crowd. A quiet, knowing smile lifted the corner of his lips as he let his gaze touch each and every man.

"Aye," he said softly, "six years ago my lady wife and I paid the greatest price of all. If our first son yet lived, he would have reached ten and eight year." He looked about the room, letting his eyes fall where Terrwyn stood. "Too late, I learned my error in judgment. Today we do not join forces with the rebel Owain Glyndwr. This time, we show the English soldiers we intend obedience to King Henry's crown." Dafydd's voice grew despite the flutter of uncertainly in the room. "We will let them draw near. Encourage them to raise a horn of ale. Then we will know their intentions before they take place."

The crowd erupted with alarm. Angry slurs turned into pushing and shoving until there was no safe place to stand.

"Silence!" Dafydd shouted. "My decision is made."

He turned to leave and stopped.

"Dafydd." Smithy gripped his shoulder, stalling him from vacating the tavern. "You cannot mean for us to dine beside them." His hold tightened. "We've lost too much, man."

"Would you have a better solution?"

"You ask too much from us," Smithy said.

"'Tis the only way to learn what brings them here and what will make them leave. We must know their purpose before it is too late to change it."

Terrwyn shoved her hair from her face. The questions leapt from her mouth before she had time to stop them. "What would you have us do, Smithy? Fight them with pitchforks and hoes?"

Stunned, the men spun to look at her. Their glances shifted between father and daughter.

Terrwyn walked away from the table, the cleaning forgotten. "I, too, desire the English to keep to their own land. Just as I desire Owain would put a stop to his raids into the English holdings. You've heard the rumors, same as I. He hides close by. Each attack led by that devil and his band of followers brings more sanctions against us."

Smithy thumbed his chest. "I say we send them on their way tonight."

She smiled, willing her lips to hold firm. "I acknowledge, 'tis a brave and brawny group of men I see before me. But listen to my father. Our numbers are too small to raise a hand against English rule. Even now, they know 'tis lambing time. Already they wait with the temerity of slavering wolves for their share of the flock. Would you rather they take them all? You dream of a time when our children forget the ache of an empty belly." She paused, letting her words sink in. "Peace is what we desire. Peace is what we'll have if you listen to your lord and do as he says."

Glancing up, Terrwyn met her father's gaze and nodded encouragement.

Dafydd stepped up beside her and clasped her hand. "'Tis nothing you can do to stop Owain from stirring their English blood for revenge. But you can join us. 'Tis only for a short time. The soldiers will move on when they discover there is nothing more for them to seize."

The heavy door swung open. As if one accord, the men lifted their heads and a hush settled over the smoke-filled room.

"Good wife," Dafydd said, "what brings you here?"

Terrwyn's mother squared her jaw and grasped the coarse woolen cloak tight around her middle. The men sat in uncomfortable silence, casting their eyes at the knots in the trestle table.

"Isn't there a place for a woman filled with child to sit and rest?" She purposefully patted her rounding belly, pointing out the fullness of her own breeding time. A slight smile lifted the corner of her lips as a row of male backsides shuffled over.

Dafydd nodded toward the vacant spot on the bench closest to the hearth. "Gwenhwyfar, sit and be silent if you are able."

She nodded in obedience and moved to squeeze in between the two brothers, Bran and Maffew. "Good eve, Bran." She splayed her fingers over her cloak and rested her cupped hands upon the crest of her protruding belly. "Maffew, be certain to tell your mother I believe it will soon be time for her services."

Bran cleared his throat. "We swear, my lord, to tell our

mam when she returns from the mountains."

Gwenhwyfar straightened her spine. The bulge under her cloak stretched the woolen material until the weave was about to split. "'Tis I, not Dafydd ap Hew, who is in need of a midwife." Her words nipped at him as if she were a corgi after the heels of a wayward sheep. "I do not mince my words. 'Tis near a fortnight since your mother walked into the wooded hills. Find her and bring her back. I will need her skill before the end of tomorrow."

Worry marked Dafydd's face. "Go, do as she bids."

Bran and Maffew nodded their obedience and stumbled out the door.

The silence in the tavern was stifling. The men shifted their seats. Throats cleared uncomfortably. They kept their heads down, entranced with the workmanship of their boots. Their deep frowns revealed that their trust had wavered.

Dafydd jerked his chin toward Gwenhwyfar, silently pleading for assistance.

Terrwyn edged toward the bench and touched her mother's shoulder. "Come home to the cottage. Warm your insides with Catrin's mulled cider."

The bench creaked as Mam pulled away. Her glare bounced off Terrwyn, ricocheting to Dafydd. "I've heard the talk, my lord. The village is bursting with fear, wondering what you will do to save them this time."

"Mam." Terrwyn bent close. "You do not want to do this."

"Aye, daughter, I do." She rose from the bench, one hand supporting her back, the other gripping the edges of the cloak together. "You will not place yourself between your father and me."

Shrugging, Terrwyn stepped back, her palms up in surrender. She would know the breadth of her mother's wrath before she closed her eyes for the evening. There were no secrets between father and daughter to keep. It was the residue from last eve's dream that had brought her to the tavern. The feel of change in the air rubbed her senses raw.

"Well, Dafydd." Gwenhwyfar motioned with a flip of her wrist, covering the span of the room. "What fine Welshmen do you intend to send to the English wolves this time? Whose heart do you intend to break tonight?"

"Gwennie." Dafydd moved toward his wife. "Look about you. I assure you, they don't come for the boys but for the mutton."

Gwenhwyfar grasped the sleeve of Dafydd's tunic. "Then why do they set up their camp outside the village? Archery targets are being set for competition as we speak. Which flock of wee lambs do you think they intend to take from us this day?"

୧୫୭

Terrwyn could not shake the heaviness from her shoulders. The dream the night before gnawed at her head until she could not stand the feel of her mattress anymore. She rose from the bed she shared with her sisters. Moving quietly, so as not to rouse them, she dressed in the shadow of the morning light.

"And where do you think you are going?" her sister Catrin asked.

Terrwyn pressed a finger to her lips, motioning for quiet. "I need to prepare for the birth."

"'Tis today?" Startled, Catrin began to sit up and stopped. The young twins, Glynis and Adain, slept on each side of her. During the night, the girls had draped their arms around her shoulders as if clinging to her for support. "You've had a dream," she said, working to keep the fear from her voice so as not to awaken her bedmates.

Terrwyn nodded. She did not know how to put the feeling into words. Nevertheless, the feeling was there. She must heed the dream or receive another hour of sleepless thoughts. Mam would need all the faith their prayers could muster. "I will fetch Isolde and send her here."

"And if the midwife has not returned from the mountains?" Catrin peeled the twin's fingers from her hair and propped her head with her arm.

Terrwyn knelt to touch Catrin's smooth cheek. She forced her own fears away and smiled confidently. "This is Mam's seventh birthing. When it happens, it won't be as long as the last time. She has been eating well and, up until the soldiers came, her thoughts have been light."

"And if it is not a boy?" asked Catrin.

"Then our mam will ignore Isolde's wisdom and try again for a son."

"What did you see in your dream? Is it a fine healthy boy?"

The air caught in Terrwyn's throat. She nodded. "Aye, a fine, healthy boy." She rose from where she knelt beside Catrin's crowded bed. "Dawn will soon be upon us. Keep an eye on the girls. I must find the herbs that will help Mam until Isolde returns."

With Catrin's simple nod, Terrwyn was free to leave and turn to the task of repairing the tranquility torn apart by her dream. After nineteen years, she knew well enough not to ignore the night visions. However, they were only a window to the future and could be altered if you were determined to see it done.

At least that was what she liked to tell herself.

Once outside the family cottage, she took in a deep breath. The sound of the English encampment tore into the quiet fabric of the gray-misted valley. A voice, so out of tune it would shame the singer's own mother, sang a battle song glorifying the English crown. Someone cursed the minstrel and the song was forgotten as the soldiers' argument filled the air.

Terrwyn cinched in the strap to her quiver and drew it snug across her back. Pulling her cloak tight, she hastened her pace. The path meandered past the small church building. The chapel's wooden shutters remained closed to the heavy air. Pale stones, marking the loss of loved ones, stood erect in the burial garden behind the simply constructed building.

Outside the village circle, smoke swirled up from the thatched roof of the watermill. Tawny light filtered through the cracks of the sheep byre as herders prepared for another day of birthing lambs into the world.

Terrwyn twitched the edge of her skirt, saving the hem from a mud puddle. With her empty basket held tight to her side, she marched past the alehouse and did not look to see if a familiar figure stumbled out of the building. Ignoring the damp chill eating its way through the soles of her shoes, she headed to the outer edge of the village.

A small garden, readied for the spring planting of herbs and flowers, lay beside Isolde's cottage. The doors and windows were shut snug and tight. Terrwyn eyed the chimney, searching for signs of the morning fire. Not a wisp of smoke curled up to the heavens. Nor did a light shine under the door.

Worry began to knot her stomach. The night hours had passed and still Bran and Maffew had not returned with their mother. Surely Isolde would come back as soon as she received Mam's message. The midwife had to be there to change the outcome of Mam's fate. Pounding on the doorframe until her knuckles were raw, Terrwyn glanced at the nearby rolling meadow. Dew on the new grass shimmered under the dawning light. No sign of fresh tracks marked the lush hill.

Forced to change the fates herself, Terrwyn searched her memory for the lesson in healing Isolde had recently given her. She turned from the cottage and began the climb toward the glen that held the early flowers that might ease her mother's pain.

The sun moved higher, burning the mist out of the sky. Refusing defeat, she clung to the hope of Isolde's imminent return and pulled up a few timid shoots of wild onions. They would serve well as a token gift for the midwife's wisdom. And still, she did not find the herbs Isolde had used in the times before. Nor did she find the flowers she saw in her dream.

Hearing her name, Terrwyn straightened and quickly abandoned her search for hidden balls of spring mushrooms. Her little sisters ran toward her as fast as their legs could carry them.

Their errand so urgent, Adain failed to notice when her hair caught on a bramble bush. It was only when the thorn scraped against her scalp that she stopped with a yelp.

Following a few steps behind, Glynis yanked her twin's long brown strands from the snare. "Come quick, Terrwyn! Mam is hurting."

Terrwyn's heart pounded savagely against her ribs. She could not help casting a desperate glance to the horizon. Surely Bran and Maffew were only on the other side of the knoll.

"Terrwyn," Adain urged. "There is no time to waste!"

Terrwyn nodded. Grabbing up the hem of her skirts, she lifted it above her knees and hurried down the hill. Near the village, she stopped to catch her breath. "Where is Father?"

Glynis and Adain looked at each other.

Terrwyn captured Glynis by the sleeve and shook her arm. "And where is Catrin? Why isn't she by Mam's side while I am out?"

Adain answered before Glynis opened her mouth. "He is with the English soldiers. They came for him early this morn. Catrin went to fetch him home but has not returned."

Terrwyn smoothed Adain and Glynis's hair and offered them a brave smile. "All right then." She kissed their cheeks. "I know that you are weary, but I ask you to scamper back to Mam. I will be there as soon as I am able."

Tears welled up in Glynis's dark brown eyes.

"Hurry now!" Terrwyn said. "I've a stop to make at the midwife's before I return home. Then I'll be there straightaway."

"But, Terrwyn," Aiden asked. "What are we to do?"

Hearing the catch in Aiden's words, Terrwyn spoke gently. "Not to worry. Babies have a time all to themselves. They will be here when they are ready. While you hold Mam's hand and smooth her brow, Glynis can sing her a song or two. That will surely bring a smile to her face."

The twins nodded in unison, then ran hand-in-hand in the direction of their cottage.

Terrwyn headed back to the midwife's home. Drem's disappearance had taken a toll on their mother's health. Everyone in the village knew this pregnancy was against Isolde's advice. The twins had been Mam's last successful birthing. And the stillbirths of the two babes after them had forged a determination in her mother that would not allow failure. She would birth another son for her Dafydd. A son to carry the land in his name. Even if it took her last breath.

Terrwyn could not imagine how she was to guide mother and baby through the valley of life. She had been by her mam's side when the little ones were delivered, still and lifeless. She had seen the torment of yet another loss to both her parents. And she had no idea how to make this one any better than the last two.

Not if her night visions were true.

Terrwyn paused. A horseshoe hung over the door, promising luck to those who entered. She touched the smooth iron, praying its force would spread through her and pass onto her family.

Knocking twice, she stepped inside the cottage. The last time she and Isolde met had ended in frustration. The midwife had taken the notion in her head that she could not count on Bran and Maffew to succeed her in the skill of healing. To Terrwyn's dismay, Isolde looked upon her to take up the role. At the time, Terrwyn thought faeries had touched the old woman's mind in the middle of the night. Now she thanked the saints for their hand in fate.

Casting a hasty look about, she found the saltbox on the shelf. Beneath it was a bottle of holy water to keep Isolde's home pure. Underneath the shelf was a willow basket filled with red woolen yarn and matching flannel. Isolde swore red brought luck and would not only restrain the faeries' mischief but also keep sickness at bay. Terrwyn did not know if she put much stock in that notion, but the flannel cloth had helped Glynis when she last had a sore throat.

Terrwyn pulled out the soft material from the basket. She filled it with the herbs the midwife had pointed out to her on her last visit. Crushed motherwort, raspberry leaves for tea, and oil infused with rosemary were added to the pile. Just as she was leaving, she realized she had nearly forgotten the most important item of all.

The large wooden birthing chair sat in the corner waiting for her to figure out how she would move it without a lot of fuss. Father was a proud man and would not take kindly to the notion of having his private business bantered about the village, but Mam needed that chair.

Someone was whistling a song outside the window. It was an old tune her brother used to sing to her. When she was a young child. When life was pleasant.

She looked out the doorway and saw a tall stranger, a man strong of arms and straight of back, walking down the path with apparently no rush in his step. He carried himself with pride. She hesitated. The cut of his tunic was rough and serviceable. He had a look about him that caused a person to think he could handle whatever befell him. Sure as the saints lived, he could not be an Englishman. Yet there was something oddly familiar about him. Perhaps he traveled from the North Country.

Without another thought, she waved him over. "You there. Pick your feet up and bring yourself here."

The man paused. The morning breeze ruffled a tuft of his black hair. He turned to look over his shoulder and then to the right. His face flashed a moment of surprise as he seemed to finally notice her. Thumbing his chest, he pointed at himself.

"Aye, you." Terrwyn nodded. "Hurry!" Relief lifted her spirits. Although the man appeared to be simpleminded, it did not matter so long as he had a good strong back and carried the chair without complaint.

As the stranger closed the distance between them, Terrwyn noticed the red rose badge of the English king sewn on his tunic. Relief fled as quickly as it came. Oh, how could she have been so foolish? She felt the blood drain from her cheeks. Her mouth went dry. She thought of nothing but running behind the safety of the door.

"Is there something amiss?" His deep voice trailed over her skin.

Terrwyn grasped the leather handle, tugging to pull the door shut. "Forgive me. 'Twas a mistake."

"A mistake?" Concern darkened his eyes. Reaching over her head, he pushed on the edge of the door. It swung easily on well-oiled hinges. He looked about the room and glanced down. "My own mother would cuff my ears if I didn't help a healer."

"Oh, no, I am not—" Terrwyn began.

"Have you a bug in your head? You called me over and none too quietly. Do you require my help or not?"

Terrwyn squared her shoulders and pushed against his chest with the flat of her hand. "I don't require anything from an Englishman."

"And would you accept my help if I were Welsh?"

"The only thing of Welsh I see before me is the wool that

covers your legs." As soon as the words left her mouth, Terrwyn felt her face flush. She had no reason to notice how his clothing covered his limbs. She dutifully ignored the way the corner of his mouth twitched before he spoke.

"I don't think my mother would find your comment amusing. Now, heed the common sense. If you required my help minutes ago, you'll require it now."

Terrwyn wanted to deny him. The desire to slam the door on his face rushed through her veins. How could she admit he was right? "You think I don't show wisdom?"

"I think you Welsh are a prideful, stubborn lot." He took a step in, closing the gap between them. "Now use your head and let me help you."

Terrwyn's thoughts raced to her mother. She should be at Mam's side. Not arguing with this irritating stranger.

A common soldier trotted up. Breathless, he touched his forehead and bent an awkward bow. "Sir James, the villagers are waiting for your attention to the targets."

"Sir James, is it?" Terrwyn bristled. "Ah, aye, a fine Welsh name indeed."

Spying a familiar face, she shouted to the sheepherder's son striding across the path. "Gareth, come assist your lord's daughter."

With her feet planted square and firm, she nodded to the scowling man before her. "Go to your men, Sir James. I have no need for your help, nor will I ever."

Chapter Three

The birthing chair stood on the bare path in front of Dafydd ap Hew's cottage. It may as well have been a village crier, announcing the coming of their lord's child. Terrwyn felt the eyes of the villagers, who were sure to notice her cowering by the door. She cringed when she saw the gray form rush toward her.

"How fares your mother this day, Terrwyn?" Valmai called out as she shuffled across the dirt path. The smell of infused violets wafted across the yard. The combination of Valmai's last meal of onions and the scent of her favorite flower made a pungent odor often found in a moldering garden. "Your mother will be thankful she has you girls to lend a hand. I will say a prayer in the chapel for Gwenhwyfar."

"My thanks, Valmai." Terrwyn turned her head and pulled in a breath of fresh air.

"And you?" The old woman bent forward, her pointed beak almost touching the tip of Terrwyn's nose.

"Me?" Terrwyn said, barely controlling the awkward squeak in her voice.

"Aye. Have you word of your brother, Drem?"

"Nay, Valmai. I vow when we do, you would be among the first to learn of it."

Valmai's lips pursed together as if she held something distasteful on her tongue. "What of your night visions? Have you seen him?"

"Hush." Terrwyn glanced back at the cottage, hopeful no one heard what Valmai said. "You know we don't speak of such things."

The old lady pulled her gray shawl tight around her thin arms. Her glare flashed and then passed as quickly. "You deny God's gift? When it would lead you to what you seek?"

For six years, Valmai had asked her these same questions. Terrwyn wondered if a time would come when she could give her a different answer. It would be a fine day when she told the old nursemaid that her favorite charge was found. Until then, she would suffer Valmai's punishment.

"Hmph," the old woman snorted in response to her silence. "Shameful! A gift untended is a gift soon lost."

Terrwyn prayed Valmai's warning was correct this time. Sooner or later, the night visions had to disappear. She had tried ignoring the dreams. She had even plugged her ears with wool to keep out the sounds. Though little good it did her. About as effective as trying to keep her eyelids open with pinesap. Hope rose in her chest as regularly as the tide. Maybe today would be different.

Valmai poked a finger into Terrwyn's shoulder, effectively burrowing into her thoughts. "Tell me. What will you do without a midwife?" Her nail dug into the woolen bodice. "Of course, not that I need to tell you, but Isolde's boys are not being truthful about her whereabouts." She cast a furtive look over her shoulder. "I saw it with my own eyes, I did. Isolde didn't lose her way in the mountains. Oh no! She rode away to the great house on the hill."

Terrwyn glanced to the horizon. Her last hopes of Isolde's imminent return began to fade. "I'm certain Bran and Maffew know where to find her. They'll fetch her home in time."

"Foolish to expect them back so soon." Valmai tapped the arching back of the wooden chair. "You know the womenfolk would help if your mother would accept it. However, she was mighty clear on her wishes the last time."

"I'm sure she meant no harm by what she said."

"Understand, girl, we have no bone to scratch with you." Valmai sniffed. "Our quarrel is with your mam, not the children. Nor do the sins of the parents rest on your shoulder. As I see it, there are two ways for you to dig yourself out of this hole. Figure out a way to make the baby stay in your mam's belly. Or prepare to bring another soul into this sorry land."

With her parting advice delivered, she turned and left Terrwyn standing by herself. Alone. The weight of what was expected resting on her head.

No matter how hard she tried, Terrwyn could not bring herself to step indoors. The bundle of herbs pressed against her side. She shifted the red flannel so the hard edge of pottery no longer poked her ribs. The mouth of the doorway sealed off the unknown. It was the portal between life and death. She rested her cheek against the cool wood of the doorframe. Listening to the sounds within, she knew from the times before that the birthing would continue for quite a while.

Dafydd opened the door and stepped outside the cottage. His tight smile did not reach his eyes. He held his hand out, drawing Terrwyn from her hiding spot. His strong fingers gently squeezed her shoulder. "She needs you."

"Isolde—"

"Nay, this day you must be midwife."

"What if I cannot remember?"

Dafydd shook his head. "It matters not to that babe if he is the first child you help draw from his mother. And sooner than later, your mam will not care about anything but holding him in her arms." He paused and then added with a wry smile, "And saints help us if it is not a healthy boy."

Terrwyn gripped her father's hand, which rested on her shoulder. The weight of it felt as heavy as the mantle that had been thrust upon her. "I shall do all that I can."

"Then we shall pray that you do more than you can." He placed a hasty kiss on her cheek and turned to follow the path that led past the alehouse.

"Wait! You're leaving? Mam—"

Dafydd held his hand up for silence. "I cannot help your mam bring me a son to replace the one that is forever lost."

"Drem will return to us."

"No one knows what has become of your brother."

"I can find him." Terrwyn gripped his sleeve before he turned away. "Father, I dreamt of him. Saw him. Handsome and strong."

Dafydd smoothed her hair. The rough calluses ridging his fingertips scraped across her cheek. "Terrwyn, I cannot allow you to place your hopes on dreams. We have waited for word of your brother for so many years. How long must we hope?"

"As long as it takes!"

"Sadly, that time has passed. 'Tis the very reason your mam tries so hard to bring another son into the world. For me, there is naught I can do but spend my time with the English. I'll listen to their tales and hope the memory of your brother stands out among all the others who were taken so long ago."

Resolved to meet the task she was given, Terrwyn squared her shoulders. "Seems to me we all must look to the saints for miracles."

"Aye," he agreed. "'Tis certain we need their help."

⋘⋙

James paused beside the wooden contraption blocking the path to Dafydd ap Hew's home. Although the house was not as small as the rest of the villagers', it by no means represented the lifestyle of a Welsh lord. Instead of strong thick walls made of fieldstone and mortar, the walls were little more than stacked logs. Straw and wattle were stuffed between the cracks to keep out the cold and inevitable rodent.

He ran his hand over the smooth wooden back of the chair. The wooden hoops reminded him of the stirrups that hung from his saddle. The broad wooden seat was unpadded and stained with wear. Leather straps were knotted at the arms. God help him if he allowed his mind to unravel its use. This was not a chair to sit beside the hearth and enjoy the crackle of the fire. 'Twas furniture which earned its keep.

So why did it stand neglected outside the home? Where was the too-delicate young midwife? A knot of suspicion gnawed at his gut. Could it be a ruse to turn his attention from gathering able-bodied men?

He narrowed his eyes to discern movement from behind closed shutters. Today was not the day for the lord to keep himself hidden from sight. The archery contest, if one could truly call it so, had been an utter failure. The whole lot of them had either been too young to pull the string on their bows or too old to survive the trek to France. Only a handful held promise. And yet he overheard them discuss the skill of one remaining archer in the village. It was his hope that the famed Welshman would present himself. He did not wish to order his men to change the archer's mind.

This visit to the village wedged between Monmouth and Abergavenny awakened dark memories from his youth. Yet here he was again, six long years later. Only this time, a sworn vow to his king had brought him. If not for the message left for him in the friary at Dunstable, he would have found a means to avoid returning. The threat of imminent war had a way of helping you justify your decisions.

He glanced at the shuttered windows. Aye, he would have this fine archer added to Henry's army whether he readily showed himself or not. But how to gain his trust? Ever since he and his men set foot in this tiny village, they had been thwarted in every angle. Welsh hospitality was spread mighty thin. Even a pint of ale was hard to come by.

A keening moan slithered through the cracks between the shutters and under the door. Determined to gain an invitation to cross their cottage threshold James gripped the arms of the chair and hauled it to his chest. "What sane man would turn away a gift of help when needed?" he reasoned under his breath.

Thoughts of the proud and haughty midwife came to mind. Perhaps sanity would not be the question to examine. Another moan slid through the air.

"Ah." James advanced toward the door. "Mayhap desperation is the key."

Holding the chair as if it were a shield, James shoved through the doorway and was assaulted by the musky odor of sweat and stale air. At first glance the long narrow room appeared to be empty of its inhabitants. The flames in the hearth flickered, casting twisted shadows on the wall. The lid on a round-bottomed kettle rattled. The contents of scorched lentils sputtered and spit into the fire.

James let the chair thump to the floor. Throwing open the wooden slats that sealed the window, he let fresh air seep into the room. He grabbed the nearby poker, hooked the pot and swung it away from the flames. The lid slipped back into place and the room began to clear of the ruined meal. Satisfied the cottage would no longer burn down around his head, he approached a half-opened doorway.

"Dafydd ap Hew, 'tis I, Sir James Frost, who comes in the name of King Henry. Show yourself now."

A delicately shaped back straightened as if jabbed with a stick. A mane of brown hair drooped over the midwife's shoulders as she turned quickly from her patient. The bucket she held to her chest sloshed its contents on the floor. Her flushed cheeks reddened to a deeper hue. Dark brown eyes snapped and glittered back at him.

"You won't find him here!"

"'Tis a pity. I require his assistance. I have heard your village contains an archer who cannot be outdistanced in skill. King Henry commands his presence for the reclamation of France."

Sweat slid down her forehead and dripped off her chin. James tipped his head and attempted to ignore the young woman's dampened bodice. He knew he was staring at the *V* formed in the middle of her chest. Right there in between her rounded breasts. He licked his dry lips and searched for something intelligible to say. Shifting his eyes, he met the gaze of a female who lay upon the bed. She panted heavily, her protruding belly filled with the child fighting to be born.

"As Terrwyn told you," she said between gritted teeth, "my husband is not here."

The woman she called Terrwyn threw down the rag she had been wringing out. "Have you been banged too many times in the head? Can you not see there is a woman birthing a baby?" Her tirade was echoed by a loud groan coming from the bed. She jerked a heavy drape across the alcove to give the woman privacy.

James finally recovered. "Perhaps, if you could direct me—"

"Mindless English dog!" Terrwyn shoved the bucket into his chest. She smiled wickedly as water splashed over the rim, landing on his newly shined boots. "Find him yourself," she said as she propelled his back toward the door.

Only one other female had ever intimidated him and that was when he was eight years old. And by damn, he was not about to let it happen to him once more. He moved his feet carefully so that his boots would not suffer her wrath again. He pushed back on the rim of the bucket and watched a single drop of water land on the ridge of Terrwyn's jaw.

Giving into temptation, his thumb scraped over her smooth skin. He felt her tense before she jerked her head out of easy reach. Her eyes widened at the sight behind him.

"You," she said with a whisper. "You brought that in?"

"I did offer my assistance earlier."

"I did not—"

Emboldened by her flustered state, James pressed his finger against her lips. The heat in her glare blazed back at him. He snatched his hand away before she had a mind to take a bite. "Think nothing of it." Offering his widest smile, he added with a jest, "Where I come from, those who are gifted must offer something of themselves in return."

Anger glittered through her soot-colored lashes. "I tell you now, Sir James Frost, there is nothing of myself that I willingly give to you."

James leaned in, closing the space between them. "More's the pity. Then I shall tend to my broken heart and settle for Dafydd ap Hew's whereabouts instead."

Terrwyn's knuckles whitened as she gripped the bucket tighter to her chest. The tip of her tongue felt along her lips as if tasting where his touch had been. "More than likely you'll find my father in the alehouse. The Sheep's Glen is an easy building to spot."

James could no longer resist the urge that had been with him since the first time he set eyes upon her. Leaning in, he ignored the shield between them and brushed a kiss against her rose-pink lips.

The tips of her dark lashes fluttered over her cheeks. She took a hasty step back. The water sloshed out of the bucket, leaving a damp trail down her bodice. Her mouth moved, but no words came out.

A harsh cry from the woman in the alcove sliced through

the charged air. "I need you now, daughter!"

James turned to leave. He paused, his hand resting on the latch. Terrwyn had already returned to her mother's side.

"Until we meet again, sweet Terrwyn," he murmured softly under his breath. "Until we meet again."

∝≀⊗

Mam's lips were swollen from when she bit down to keep from crying out. The simple act of holding her son to her breast made her tremble from the exertion. She kissed his head, counted his toes and smiled. "Thank the saints, your brother's birth will hold what is left of our land. Catrin, come tuck the flannel around Padrig."

While the tiny boy grunted and rooted, searching for his mother's breast, Terrwyn tried once more to hold the wooden cup to Mam's mouth.

Mam shook her head and turned away. "Fetch your father. Tell him—tell him he has a healthy son to take Drem's place." Her breath caught, her chest rose and fell slowly. Her fingers relaxed and she wearily closed her eyes.

Terrwyn moved past the homes standing along the path. An amber glow seeped through the cracks around the windows. Behind the doors, flames flickered and wavered. One by one, doors were opened, unfurling a river of light. Faces anxious for news lingered in the shadows. They held their distance, respectfully waiting.

Had it not been for the dusk pushing away daylight, she would have never guessed the time. Nor did she know if day or night had passed since first braving the unknown and stepping over the threshold between life and death.

Raucous laughter rent the silence of the night, mocking the memory of her mother's anguish. A flute spat out a tune while someone battered an accompanying beat. Large warhorses were tethered outside the alehouse. Small mountain ponies, tied nearby, kept their distance from the monsters. She eyed the glow from within and searched out the shape of her father's shadow.

What was it the midwife once told her? With celebration came a price. Even now, she did not trust her mother had the ability to cling to life a moment longer.

Gathering what little courage she had left, Terrwyn pulled open the door and entered the overcrowded room. Tables were littered with empty pitchers and mugs half-filled with ale and watered-down whiskey. Bare heads, in various shades of brown and red locks, gathered in male revelry. Her father held court in the middle. His storytelling was known far and wide, perhaps as well as his reputation with his fists.

The man standing closest to Dafydd's side lifted his face and his head of silky black hair caught the firelight. Recalling her previous run-ins with the Englishman, she dutifully ignored the way her pulse began to accelerate. Her breath caught as his sky-blue eyes flashed with recognition. A slow smile crept over his mouth. He raised an eyebrow in her direction and bent to speak to her father.

Terrwyn's anger ignited as if her heart were dry tinder. It burned through her veins when she noticed the familiar way he placed his hand upon her father's shoulder. He whispered something, this time in her father's ear. Her father's laughter stalled and the room slowly quieted as if directed by an unseen hand.

Dafydd rose from the bench and came forward. "Terrwyn." He spread his arms wide, offering a place for her to step into. "What news have you?"

Shouts of goodwill and encouragement emptied into the room, followed by a burst of laughter. Someone pounded Dafydd's back as he made his way across the tavern. When he stumbled over an errant foot, her enemy rushed to her father's side and caught him before he hit the floor.

Dafydd brushed the helping hands away. "Enough. I have need to hear good news from my daughter." He pushed his way to Terrwyn. His flushed face and the beads of sweat over his upper lip belied his calm manner.

She was mystified by Sir James's show of concern toward her father. It was as if he sensed she carried more than good news. He cupped Dafydd's elbow, nearly lifting him above the throng of well-wishers. Keeping up the appearance of joy and impatient exuberance, he joined in the shouts of laughter and led the way outside.

Once in the fresh air, Dafydd turned to swipe James with his fist. "Enough, I say! I did not give my leave for you to handle me as if I were a bag of wool."

"Hurry, Father. 'Tis certain you'll want to see Mam before—"

Tears welled in his eyes. Joy dissolved in front of her. A shuddering breath escaped, collapsing his bravado. "Tell me," he urged. "Tell me I have a son and all is well with my lady wife."

She made a quick search of her heart and could not bring herself to voice what she had already seen with her curse. If they made haste, he might yet have time to tell his Gwennie just how much he adored her.

"Come, Father. Mam calls for you."

Chapter Four

Terrwyn shielded her eyes from the hazy sunlight peeking over the angled rise of rooftops. Shadows danced with the gentle sway of the misty morning breeze. The trees wept fat drops of moisture from their newly formed leaves.

They wept, for she could not.

A shiver ran through her body. After settling the shawl around her shoulders, she knotted the ends with a resolute snap. The list to restore what she borrowed from Isolde's cottage was cast solidly in her memory. Herbs were needed to console her father. So involved in his loss, he did not see the pain in those who remained with him.

Wearily, she left Isolde's cottage. It mattered little that she had not found sleep in the last three days. Much needed tending. As the eldest, it was her duty to see all was prepared. Someone would need to sit by her mam until it was time to say their final farewells. Coin must be found. Prayer and offering for her mother. A suitable wet-nurse must be secured. Plus there was the livestock to be fed. The garden plot hoed. Water to be drawn. Peat cut and fetched. The list was endless and did not offer her rest. She could do little but smile at her good fortune in not finding sleep for so long. At least, for now, she would avoid the night visions that haunted her dreams.

Her choice of path set, she hurried beyond the dew-covered green meadow. The field of sweet grass was already dotted with a flock of sheep.

A long shadow wavered then joined hers. Terrwyn stifled the need to smooth her hair as James appeared by her side.

Hastening her steps, she walked as fast as she could without betraying her desire to run away. She was certain the weight of her skirts had doubled since she donned them that morning. Sweat trickled a path between her breasts. Her irritation blossomed. No matter how quickly she moved her feet, his legs appeared to cover the distance with half the effort. He even had a bounce in his step. Could he not see that she wanted to be left alone? Must he be struck over the head to understand?

Casting him a swift glance, she took in the angle of his jaw, noting where to land her fist. A faint shadow of whiskers peppered his cheeks. His nose was not long and hawk-like, nor did it look as if he grew an apple shape on the end of it. Indeed, it was well proportioned to his face. She shrugged and gave up. Perhaps his face was not as ugly as she wished to remember. She peered through her lashes and let her gaze flow over the rest of his form.

His dark hair stuck out from under his cap. A forest green tunic cropped his thighs. His brown leggings were spattered with mud and bits of twigs. The hilt of a small dagger peaked over the leather belt, and he had a bow slung over his shoulder.

Terrwyn pinched her mouth into a frown. By the looks of him, he had been hunting. Well, no matter what the king's decree, he was not welcome to hunt whatever he willed.

"Good morn, Terrwyn."

Had it not been her misfortune to turn her face, her plan to ignore him would have been successful. However, hard as she tried, she could not take her eyes off the flash of blue when he winked at her.

Her mood soured further as he began to hum a light ditty. She wondered if he had learned it while gathering her countrymen for the English king. She found it difficult to believe his mother was Welsh. What woman would want her son to serve the king by harvesting men?

She could no longer bite her tongue in silence. "What is there to be joyful about on this day?"

James reached out to move a wisp of hair from her forehead. "Any day that you can feel the breeze and look upon those you love is a day to rejoice. And you, 'tis certain you have twice the reason, what with your new brother."

Terrwyn's steps faltered. The bundle of Isolde's herbs and jars of tinctures slipped from her grasp. If not for the tanned hand that caught them, they would have shattered.

"Here," he said, motioning with the bag. "Allow me to carry this."

Terrwyn blinked as sunlight caught on the intricately. woven band of silver wrapped around his finger. A heavy foreboding settled in her stomach. The sun was up and so were the villagers. She allowed a furtive glance to stretch over the village. Those who walked the path paused, frowned and shook their heads. Making a point to show their distaste in her choice of companion, they rushed to the opposite side of the path.

Terrwyn jerked the bag from his grasp and wrapped her arms tightly around it. James, so intent on commandeering it from her, did not notice the gasps of horror. Nor did he turn his face when his lips nearly touched hers. She searched the cottages that lined the path, looking for a place to hide. To her dismay, a familiar gray shawl came into sight.

Valmai rushed over, her shuffling feet and scent of violets announcing her presence. "Terrwyn, in truth, how could you? You let your dear mother slip away! Did I not tell you to call on me when her time was near?"

Terrwyn blanched. Had she misunderstood Valmai's directions? She thought it had been clear. "Deal with your own," had been Valmai's message. She felt the eyes of those around her, their silently directed accusations burrowing into her heart.

"Had you used the gift, you would have avoided your mother's death."

"Heartless," a villager joined in.

Terrwyn felt the roar of blood rush from her face. "Nay! M-mam—" she stuttered, pausing, lost for words to continue. The single name conjured up her misgivings, her fears of failure, and most certainly her loss. What more could she have done to change the fates?

"Forgive me, Terrwyn, I've been away." James flanked her side and raised his voice above the melee. "You'll give your lord's daughter the respect that is due her."

"And who are you to tell us otherwise?" another shouted.

"Enough, Sir James," Terrwyn hissed, tugging on the pack held between them. "I've enough heartache. I have no need for more."

She faced the small band of solemn villagers. "'Tis true, our hearts are breaking from our loss of a good woman. I know the loss of your lady is great. We will all miss her. However—"

Their wary glances told her that they did not listen. They were too busy noting the narrow space she shared with the Englishman. A murmur of discontent began to rustle through the villagers.

"However," she added, her voice growing with determination, "'tis your lord whose heart carries the greatest pain. He requires the strength of his people to stand for him while he is bent with grief."

Slowly, moans of sorrow began to weave into the air. The women gathered and moved as one toward Terrwyn's home.

Had it not been for the guilt that tore at her heart, she might have felt relief for their assistance. As it was, she could not rid her mind of Valmai's finger-pointing. What use was a gift if it did nothing but fulfill a curse? She should have ignored her mother's demands and searched out the women for some bit of knowledge she did not have. At least then her failure would not have been met unaided.

Without a word, James held out his hands and Terrwyn reluctantly allowed him to carry her burden. He hooked it over his shoulder. With his free hand, he slipped her fingers into his palm. He pushed through the throng of women. Gasps of outrage cut into their mourning. Yet they parted and moved out of his way.

Terrwyn felt their looks brand her with the mark of failure. Heard the whispers murmured under their breath. Saw the shock register on those they passed.

The simple thought sifted through the turmoil in her heart. It was as she'd seen it many nights before. Only this time, she was not alone.

Chapter Five

Terrwyn ran the blade of her knife around each leg of the hare. She skimmed the well-honed edge over its neck and down its soft belly. Mindful of her task, she began to peel back the fur. A flawless pelt held a chance of bringing more coin from the furrier.

Some believed the only choice of weapon against the hare was to snare it with nets. Their aim uncertain, they did not loose their arrows upon their prey. She disliked this mode of hunting and preferred to place her arrow perfectly.

Unlike the men, she had no time to sit and while away her morning. There were pelts to gather and sell to the soldiers before they took their leave. What meat her family did not eat she would cook and offer to the men for a hefty price. Sheep, they could not afford to part with. However, a few conies caught fresh from their warren might whet the men's desire to part with their money. Her family would enjoy the feel of a little jingle in their pockets.

Only yester eve she had overheard Sir James's men talk of their imminent departure. No longer would they sit on their backsides and wait for the mysterious archer to show himself. To a man, the soldiers agreed that there were no other archers in the village, nor did they hide in the surrounding lands. She had heard their grumbles, their arguments that it was more than likely the wretched Welshmen were telling tall tales to match their lies.

A knowing smile raised the corners of Terrwyn's mouth. A sharp marksman must be sure to keep his arrows from arcing in the air when English soldiers were sniffing about.

She flipped the rabbit fur onto the growing pile of pelts at her feet. Not as tender as fowl, however its dark meat would still put a glow in her father's cheeks. Perhaps today he would fill his belly with something more than strong ale.

Terrwyn looked up to see her little sisters' tawny brown heads in the distance. She took off her apron and wiped the red stains from her hands. Stretching out the kinks in her back, she waited for Glynis and Adain to reach her side.

Worry pulled at her mouth as they drew near. The cherry blossoms in their cheeks had faded. Their dark eyes were red-rimmed and swollen. Terrwyn folded her arms around their thin shoulders and held them tight. Their weeping, which had been heard day and night, was now replaced with silence.

Terrwyn was grateful for the compassion the villagers had shown her family. They had treated Mam with utmost care as they washed and prepared her body. They wept while they plaited her mane of silky brown hair. They covered her head in fine linen and wrapped a shawl woven of the purest wool around her shoulders. Finally, Terrwyn herself had placed two gold coins, payment for passage to the other side, on her lids.

Terrwyn had waited to hear the clap of thunder as her mam discovered it was an Englishman who had slipped those coins into her daughter's hand. Truth be told, her mother would probably forego entrance into heaven's gates rather than accept help from his sort. Though she hated to keep it a secret, Terrwyn dared not let anyone know of James's generosity. Still it was a wonder that her father never came to question how she had enough coin for a church burial.

While the women ministered to Mam, the men of the village had put their back into preparing the burial site. Their blades sliced through the woven mat of sod, scratching a hole into the earth. They gently peeled back the sod as one would when working the skin from an apple. Resettled over her mother's coffin, it became a blanket woven of earth and vegetation. And there, Mam rested.

A week had passed since Mam's death. One by one, the villagers had nodded and agreed that there was nothing more for them to do. Their task was finished until another life passed on to the other side. And her family was left to face the day by themselves. Life would not wait. It would move on with or without her family's permission.

Terrwyn pushed back at the heavy weight that pressed against her heart and she squeezed her sisters' shoulders. "Here now, Glynis, look at these berries. If you smile brightly, I'll wager Catrin might construct a sweet or two."

Glynis bent down to peer at the willow basket at their feet. "Do you think father will like a taste?"

"I cannot imagine our father turning down a treat such as this."

Glynis picked up the basket and held it protectively to her chest. Adain shook her head and answered the question her twin did not speak aloud. "I shall stay and help Terrwyn."

Her face solemn, Glynis nodded and set off in the direction of the village.

Terrwyn smoothed Adain's hair, reminded of the little wren that often sat on their windowsill. Small, delicate, the little bird was easily forgotten until it began its song. "You do not mind so very much?"

Adain quietly shook her head and began to gather the pelts.

Terrwyn caught her sister's hand. "Do not bother yourself with this. Take the other basket. Find a few cheery posies—"

Adain stared at the empty basket. After giving the suggestion a considerable amount of thought, she glanced up. "Mam always loved the flowers I brought."

Terrwyn's heart swelled when the cloud lifted from Adain's face.

With basket in hand, Adain squared her shoulders. "I will pick only the ones that are as beautiful as our mam."

Terrwyn matched Adain's serious tone with her own. "'Tis a difficult undertaking you have set for yourself. But one that shall make us all proud of your efforts."

Satisfied the girls were busy with their tasks, Terrwyn renewed her concentration on the last rabbit lying at her feet. She wielded her blade with precision, moving the skin away from the meat.

Her thoughts felt the familiar tug and, before she realized

43

it, she found herself lost in the vision she had seen the night before. She pushed at the shadows, holding them at bay. Instead, the shape of the black swan swam in front of her eyes. Wary of the bird's nasty disposition, she watched it draw near and had the odd sensation of wanting to stroke its feathers.

Terrwyn flinched and sucked on the blood seeping from the knick along her thumb. If not for hearing the shouts coming from the English encampment, she feared she would have laid her palm open. Her mind clearing, she searched the horizon.

Her sister's name tore from her lips. "Adain!" she yelled. "Run!"

Terrwyn's bow thumped against her thigh as she ran toward her sister. Her heart thundered. Soldiers ran hither and yon, dodging the stones Adain kept pulling from her basket. Their angry curses could be heard over Adain's scream when she must have launched her last rock. Throwing the basket at the men, Adain yanked up the hem of her skirt and ran.

Terrwyn paused. There was no other choice. She had to end this before it went any further. She nocked the arrow against the bow. In rapid succession she let loose her shots until her quiver was empty. Each arrow narrowly missed the soldiers and landed near their feet.

Adain scurried past and peered from behind Terrwyn's skirts. "Ugly Englishmen. She'll curse you where you stand," Adain shouted, punctuating her comment by sticking out her tongue.

Terrwyn pressed her palm over Adain's forehead and shoved her out of sight. "You've done enough, little one."

"What shall you do?" Adain asked from behind. "Go ahead, shoot a few more. Mayhap one will actually hit the big louts."

"Do you not see the quiver is empty? What did they do to you? Are you harmed?"

"Nay, my body is fine."

Terrwyn lifted her eyes from the advancing men and turned just enough to see her sister. "Well?"

Adain's face crumpled. "I could not let it go unchallenged. 'Tis our land! 'Tis my right!"

"'Tis my belief they wish to challenge your Welsh right to pelt them in the head." Terrwyn braced for their outrage. If only her father were there to calm their pride with liquid spirits. Why he had not come when the first cry for help rang out, she could not fathom.

Adain grabbed her hand and held it tight. "Terrwyn," she whispered hotly, "the big oxen didn't mind where they placed their feet. They stomped all over Mam's flowers!"

Although Adain's words were strong, Terrwyn knew her fear was greater. Unfortunately, her little sister had not thought of that before launching rocks and insults at the soldiers' heads.

Terrwyn's worries mounted as a swarm of villagers formed at the base of the hill. They moved as one, pitchforks and hoes gripped in their fists. Their anger buzzed in the air. A voice of calm could not be found. She searched their faces, flush with years of pent-up hatred. The face of their leader was not amongst them. Her father, absent from his flock of sheep.

The soldiers turned. Their advancing progress slowed as their bodies pressed into each other to form a mass of strength. The Welsh villagers did indeed form an army. One made of husbands and wives. Sons and daughters. The soldiers' faces twisted as they swiveled their glances from Terrwyn to the villagers. They waited, determining which flank to strike first.

Terrwyn reached behind her back to hold Adain steady. Her breath caught as she searched for answers. Surely if her vision were a gift, now would be a time she should actually have the ability to avoid this. Nay, the curse brought her nothing. Nothing but ugly black swans. Black swans. A sign of bad tidings.

Adain shivered against her back and Terrwyn's own body began to tremble. It mattered little that she'd set loose all her arrows in quick succession. Now, in this close range, nothing short of hand-to-hand combat would gain them survival. Even with the villagers coming to their rescue, given their match of size, she and her sister had little chance of escape.

"Adain," Terrwyn hissed, "when I tell you, I want you to run as if your life depends upon it."

Adain wrapped her arms around Terrwyn's waist. "I won't leave you to them English dogs! Better to be dead than be their bone to chew on."

"No arguments." She pried Adain's fingers away. "Go!"

She hoped the men would turn from them and confront the villagers. It appeared she was wrong. They did not intend to leave their prey or lose a battle. The soldier some had called Thomas moved quickly for his size. He hooked an arm around Terrwyn's neck and pulled her to his side.

Wide-eyed, Terrwyn turned to look behind her. Adain was gone. Although brief, the small victory warmed her soul.

"Not to worry, boys!" Thomas crowed. "Let the little bird go. This one will serve us fine when we are through with this piss-puddle village."

He drew back as if to strike. His fist froze. His arm dropped to his side and he released her as if discovering she carried disease.

A rock struck her head. The sudden jolt whipped her neck back. The ground shifted under her feet. She heard her name and could not help wondering why she did not hit the ground.

൦൭ജ

Terrwyn awoke to find she sat high upon a destrier's back, cradled in James's arms. She swallowed deeply. Mindful to keep the light from searing her eyes, she squinted to see his face. Concern marred his blue eyes. His lips pressed together, forming a stern line.

"Adain," she whispered through the pain in her head.

"She is fine," James answered gruffly. "Though very afraid."

Terrwyn struggled to sit up. The horizon began to tilt.

"Easy, Zeus is not used to having another on his back."

"Zeus?"

"Aye, you'll never know a better horseflesh than this destrier. 'Tis an honor he allows you to sit upon his back. Normally he tosses women into the nearest thorny bush he finds."

Terrwyn blinked and settled into James's arms. "You sound mystified by that fact."

"That I am." He chuckled softly. "Good to see you've the

sense to keep yourself still." He let his gaze slide over her face. "No need to worry. Young Adain is safe. At this very moment, the captain of our troop is working on your sister's aim. When he is assured she will not harm anyone or anything unless she intends to, then he will bring her home."

"Her aim?"

"Aye. Not counting the lump on your noggin, the little bird hit three of our horses. Which," he said, "then had to be tracked and caught. And as you know she nearly instigated a riot."

Incredulous, Terrwyn pulled away again. "'Tis certain Adain has apologized."

James pressed her shoulder back as easily as if she were a wee babe. "She refuses to apologize to me or to my men. In this she gives no quarter."

Air puffed through her clenched teeth before she spoke. "Where is my father? 'Tis his right to give punishment. Not yours."

"This is not punishment." He shook his head in dismay. "She vows that if she must do it again, she wishes to ensure she hits the men and not the animals."

Terrwyn heard the humor in his voice. She smiled weakly. "That does sound like my little wren."

"Your little wren has the manners of a hawk. If not for her terrible aim, I would almost think she is the archer we have been waiting for."

Terrwyn stiffened, then prayed he did not notice. Of course, she reasoned, it would make perfect sense for her to be incensed that he would even consider taking a young girl into battle. "You may let me down. I am well enough to find my way home."

James shifted his knee and the horse turned toward Terrwyn's family cottage. They rode slowly to her home. She knew full well she would be the talk of the village. Her reputation, what was left of it, would be shredded. Thankfully, her father was still lord and looked to when there was a crisis.

Terrwyn moved to sit up again. "My father..."

"Has been led safely back to your home. By now, he will have slept off most of the spirits." James stopped Zeus in front of her home. "Tell Dafydd ap Hew I carry a message for him."

Terrwyn ignored his hand and slid down from the horse's back. Regret flooded through her body as soon as her feet absorbed the jolt. She craned her neck to look him in the eyes, her head aching abominably. "What might your message be, Sir James?"

Leaning his forearm on the high rim of the saddle, he said, "My men and I leave on the morrow. Will you miss me just a bit?"

"'Tis certain my father will miss your stories."

"And you?"

"I cannot tell you a lie, Sir James. I will be glad to see you and your men on your way. However, that would mean the young men of our village would have to leave their families. Are you aware Erin ap Owen's wife is soon to have their child? Who will ensure the fields are planted so they have food for the winter?"

"They are given wages as good if not better than any English soldier."

"And how does he pay his widow and children when he does not return?"

James flicked the reins. "Their future is not my concern. Tell your father we will return in a fortnight. Have the men prepared to go with England's army. Make certain the archer who attacked my men today is with them."

The earth under her feet began to tilt. She forced the words through the haze inside her head. "And if he is not?"

James's face took on a grim countenance. "I've heard talk that orders will be given to burn the fields, leaving this village as nothing more than a memory."

Chapter Six

That evening Dafydd sat outside their cottage, shut off from his family. Twice now, Catrin had come out to draw him in. And twice he had turned her efforts away.

Terrwyn moved close, Sir James's message echoing in her head. Soon she would have to pass it on to her father. Even now, the villagers whispered of the day's events. It would not bode well for anyone if he heard the tale from lips other than her own. But not tonight. Tonight he needed rest.

She placed her hand upon his shoulder. "'Tis getting cold, Father. Come inside and warm yourself by the hearth."

His haunted eyes met hers. His mouth wobbled as he tipped the mug of strong ale to his lips, emptying the contents in one gulp.

"I won't let you sit here catching your chill," she scolded.

Dafydd wiped his mouth with his knuckles. "I cannot bring these feet of mine to cross this here doorframe." He slapped his knees with a heavy hand. "Appears they've a mind of their own."

"Adain and Glynis worry for you. They need you to tuck them in as you always have."

Dafydd shook his head. "Ah, can you not see, Terrwyn? If I go in there, I'll not see me Gwennie." His chin jerked as he struggled to form his words. "When that happens, what am I to do then, Terrwyn? What am I to do then?"

Impatience began to shift to panic. *How dare he expect me to have an answer for him?* He was the one they trusted to lead them in the right direction.

"You'll remember the goodness Mam brought to your heart.

Then you'll pick yourself up by your bootstraps and make yourself go forward." She smiled to soften her words and held out her hand. "Your son waits for your attention. Would you not care to spell Catrin and hold Padrig for a while?"

"That one took my Gwennie," Dafydd growled.

Terrwyn's anger lit. "For shame! You mock Mam when you deny Padrig your love."

"My only son is Drem. And he is dead."

"You do not know that for certain!"

Dafydd struggled to straighten his legs and stand up. "You will not speak to me with that tone."

She shook her head and opened the door to their cottage. "Open your eyes, Father. Turn them away from yourself and see what you still have."

Terrwyn lifted her heel, then pointed the tip of her toe. Her rocking chair rhythmically tilted back and pushed forward. She held Padrig close and watched the flutter of shadows on his smooth skin. He wriggled and nuzzled while he slept.

Weary from the weight of caring for the younger children, Catrin had eagerly stepped out with Bran, the midwife's son, when he came calling. Father had mumbled something about needing to find a spot at the alehouse. Even the twins had scampered off as soon as their daily chores were finished.

Terrwyn's loneliness deepened. She pushed at it, trying to fill the empty space with good thoughts. Her efforts were in vain. Sir James's absence set her adrift in uncharted waters. She knew not how to reclaim her direction.

The English soldiers had left the village a few days ago, as promised. Their shouts and songs could no longer be heard from the glen. She missed the thrill of catching a glimpse of Sir James as he wielded his sword and shield. More than once, she had sneaked a peek at the play of his brawny back while he practiced with his men.

With their absence, the village shrank in size and lost its beauty. Life returned to mundane routine. Up at daybreak.

Tend to the livestock and fields. Feed their families. Prepare for the start of a new day.

Tension swooped through her veins. She itched to race off to hide in the thicket of brambles like a frightened hare. Time sifted past and would not be slowed. With each day that she did not speak of James's warning, her silence dug the hole a little deeper.

Catrin burst through the doorway, snatching Terrwyn from her worries. Padrig awoke with a start and began to whimper before she teased the rag teat into his mouth.

"Here now, Catrin, take young Padrig," Terrwyn urged. "He must know your smell. He has fussed since the moment you left. Took one of your shawls for him to nuzzle before he quieted."

Anger flushed Catrin's cheeks, mottling her skin with a reddish hue. "How could you? Do you know what you've done?"

"I know 'tis one of your favorites, but I didn't think you would mind."

"Did you stop to think what your actions would do?"

Terrwyn's eyes dropped to the soft woven material wadded next to Padrig's mouth. "I'm sorry, Catrin. I never knew you cared that much for it."

"Not the shawl, goose! I'm not talking about the shawl."

The pit of Terrwyn's stomach began to deepen. "Father?"

Catrin's eyes glittered back at her. "Bran, you idiot! I speak of Bran. Any day now, the English will return for the archer. The archer." She took a shuddering breath. "When they don't find him, they'll take my Bran instead."

Terrwyn pursed her lips and studied Catrin's face. "Oh, well then. Not to worry. He isn't much of a shot. They'll only want those with steady hands and keen eyes."

"And when they don't find who they're searching for," Catrin pressed, "they'll burn us out."

The pit in her belly widened even more. She did not know how her sister knew, but know she did. "Don't worry yourself, Catrin. I won't let them harm the village."

Catrin nearly choked on the air she sucked in through her gaping mouth. "And how do you intend to stop them?"

Terrwyn calmly tapped her heel on the floor. She rocked her foot forward until only her toe touched the hard-packed earth. Slowly, she rolled it back, only to start over again. The soothing motion swirled and floated as the answer settled around her bones. She tried to hide the grin that began to form, and failed. "We shall give Sir James his archer."

Catrin collapsed with an ungraceful thump to the floor. "You cannot do this. I will not let you go on with this crazed plan."

A flash of impatience sparked in Terrwyn's eyes. "I will. And you won't stop me. You gave your word to Mam to protect the children and I vowed to find Drem."

Catrin touched Terrwyn's cheek. "You've had another dream?"

Terrwyn glanced away from the hope glimmering from her face. "Mam stored Drem's clothing for when her next son was born."

"But won't they notice you aren't a lad?"

"Once the soldiers have the archer in tow, their impatience to return to England will outweigh the need to look closely." Terrwyn gripped her sister's fingers. "I have to do this. 'Tis the only way to take care of our promises."

Catrin wiped the tears from her eyes with the corner of her apron. "Do you think your plan will work? Truly?"

Excitement building in her bones, Terrwyn widened her grin. "Of course. Who else do you know in the village whose aim is better than mine? Now go," she said with a flutter of her hands. "Rest while Padrig is content. I've much to think about. But, Catrin—"

Her sister paused at the door.

"Be sure you don't speak of this with anyone. 'Tis our secret to keep."

Though worry gleamed in Catrin's eyes, a weak smile began to form. "Of course not. 'Tis certain anyone would think I'm a madwoman for dreaming up such a scheme."

CR⊗ED

Padrig awoke with a startled cry when the door swung open and wind rushed through the cottage. Bran filled the doorway. Catrin stood behind him, peeking over his bicep.

"Dafydd isn't here. You can find him at the Sheep's Glen. I imagine he's lifting another horn of ale." Terrwyn gripped the edge of the door. "Come, Catrin, shove past him. The big oaf seems to have a hearing problem today. Ouch!"

Bran gripped her arm and hurled her toward the rocking chair. "Have you a bug in your head? You cannot go off by yourself."

Terrwyn glared past Bran's meaty body at Catrin. It took one look and she knew. "You told him. Who else did you tell?"

"Leave her be," Bran said. "She's the only one between you with any sense."

"You broke your promise, Catrin. You lied to me." Terrwyn's nails dug into the rocker's wooden arms. She could not help the pain of betrayal throbbing in her chest, but she would not let the burning tears fall. Her sister was weeping enough for the both of them.

Catrin leaned over Padrig's cradle, soothing him back to sleep. "Terrwyn, I didn't mean you harm," she said through her tears.

"You will not come against your sister." Bran stabbed a thick finger in Terrwyn's face. "She desires only to protect you from your mad notions. You'll stay put until we say you may move."

Seething with indignation, Terrwyn turned and pretended not to notice the looks passing between her sister and Bran.

Catrin's lips trembled. She swayed toward him as if pushed by an unseen hand. He let out a deep breath, wrapped his arms around Catrin and drew her in. He smoothed her head as she wept incoherently into his chest. When the sobs turned into hiccups, he lifted her chin and wiped a tear from her cheek.

Terrwyn shifted in the chair and examined Bran. What new value did Catrin see in him that she did not? He was not as tall as some men. Nor was he fair of face. Why, his straight hair was brown as a bog. Saints above! His eyes were the color of a dense moonless night, dull and dark, without the sparkle of stars.

Even his own mother thought him too dull-witted to learn the skill of healing.

Certain that Isolde's opinion of her son's intelligence was more accurate than her love-struck sister's, Terrwyn moved to make her escape.

She yelped when Bran grabbed and shook her arm. Thoughts of a corgi with a rat skittered into her head. The image dissipated as he marched her into the bedchamber.

"You'll stay here until your father beats some sense into you." At that, he closed the door and braced the latch.

Furious, Terrwyn jiggled the door handle and found it locked. "I hope a dog is gnawing on your bones before nightfall," she yelled.

Her ear pressed to the seams, she listened to Catrin and Bran form their own plans.

"Don't weep so, Catrin. You will take ill." There was a muffled sound, a murmuring, lingering silence. "There now, let me see your lovely smile," Bran urged.

"Adain and Glynis—"

"I will ask one of the women to care for them a short while. Then I will search for your father."

"I don't understand, Bran. He wasn't at the Sheep's Glen. If not there, I don't know where he could be."

"I'll find him. Never you fear."

Terrwyn slumped against the door. There was no getting out of feeling her father's wrath this time. Despite her efforts she would still have to deliver James's message.

CR&SO

Terrwyn paced the bedchamber with determined steps. She had been foolish to think Bran and Catrin were too busy with each other to notice when she tried to slip away.

Her sister's attraction to Bran made little sense. She supposed he would do if one had no other options. But if there ever came a day when she felt inclined to find love in a man's arms, he would be tall and strong, gentle and caring, a fine sense of humor and a will to match. He would be a strong

Welshman, for there were no other kind worthy of her notice. James's name whispered in her head before she pushed the ridiculous thought away.

She rubbed the bruise beginning to form on her arm. And he would know how to handle a lady without leaving a mark upon her person. Aye, she supposed she did have to give Bran credit for coming on a run for Catrin. Although a hound would have served her just as well. Perhaps it would have arrived with fewer fleas.

Guilt nipped at her heels. She supposed the day would soon come when she was expected to accept him into the family.

She flinched when she heard the anger laced through her father's rising voice.

"She's a dreamer. 'Tis a plan for failure!"

Bran and Catrin's voices were low and soft as if they were dealing with a wild boar.

"We will fight them," Dafydd shouted. "We will join Owain again. Hurry, Bran, send a message for his men to regroup. A call to arms. A call to arms against the English!"

Terrwyn scrubbed at her face. Her father still held ties to Owain? After all the times he swore he would never follow the rebel. Swore at the wrongs that befell his family. Swore and pledged his innocence to Mam. He swore an oath that he would never endanger his family and the people of their village. Yet here he was, shouting for all to join his battle. A battle no one wanted. A battle that did not need to be.

Bran and Catrin calmed him, plying his rage with enough ale to make his need for a bed greater than a battle. Terrwyn could see them in her mind's eye, Bran's strong arms around her sister's shoulders, whispering tender words to soothe her heart.

Before long, she heard Catrin move about the cottage and settle into the role that had become as comfortable as her given name. The soothing rhythm of the spinning wheel began to fill the cottage.

Terrwyn waited, thankful the shouting was over. She opened the shutters and tossed out her bag of clothing. Next came Drem's old cloak. Carefully, she dropped her quiver and arrows and pulled herself through the open window.

CRSO

James stopped pacing the tent and picked up the missive delivered with the camp supplies. He read it again, hoping he'd misread it the first, second and even the third time.

He held the paper over the lamp. The edges curled, caught fire, burning until it turned to ash. This he spread across the dirt floor and ground with the sole of his boot. When he was through, there was no sign the king's secret missive ever existed.

Chapter Seven

Cloaked in the safety of a moonless night, Terrwyn's movements around the outskirts of the village went unnoticed. She nearly stumbled over the two large hairy dogs in front of the smithy's barn. Their soft growls rumbled, rising up from their chests.

She hesitated, quieting the urge to run, and turned to face them. Snapping her fingers, she stared in the vicinity of where she hoped were their eyes. "Nimble. Spry. Down."

Dejected groans came from their muzzles as they slowly let their bodies sink to the ground. Rewarded with the soft thump of their tails rhythmically hitting the dirt, she stepped over their paws and worked her way to the grove of trees lining the village. She fixed her eyes on the rise of the hill in the shadowed horizon.

She gave a determined yank to the cord holding up Drem's leggings and walked quickly into the night. Somewhere over the crest was King Henry's army. Their careless trail should be simple enough to follow. She would keep to the trees. Stay out of sight. When the distance was great enough to keep the soldiers away from her village, she would make her presence known and make them believe she was the archer.

Mindful of hidden roots and low-hanging branches, Terrwyn moved through the grove of trees. She walked over the crest and down into another valley. She hurried as if she held the wind in her fist, pulling her farther and farther from the protective circle of her village.

Temptation to return to the warm corner by the hearth and

the sweet smell of Padrig nearly won over her determination. It would be safe and easy enough to find her way home. Certainly it would be safer to face the villagers' wrath than to stumble through the glen in the dark by herself.

Terrwyn felt the urge to turn her back on the lot of them and cast her future somewhere else. Perhaps find her fortune in healing. *Aye,* she thought bitterly, *and mayhap the Queen of Faeries would embrace me as her own. As a foundling in the forest.*

Bits and pieces of every story Mam and Father ever told her about faeries and pixies nibbled at her brain. Her thoughts gathered and pulled at the shifting figures behind every tree and bush. Did they watch her from under the cover of shadows? Their formless shapes hidden until they desired to steal her away to the otherworld? She turned to look at the quivering branch hanging close to her head. They were apt to be just about anywhere. Her heart beat rapidly as sunrise began to peek through the canopy of leaves overhead. Dappled light shifted with the trees' gentle sway.

"Saints protect me," she yelped and nearly fell to the ground when a roe deer jumped out from behind a tree. The stag dashed across her path. Its tawny backside leapt into the air and over the thicket of brambles. In a flash, it was out of sight.

The sound of Nimble and Spry's sorrowful howls could be heard off in the distance.

"Damn and double damn the fates." She had hoped to be farther away from the village when her family noticed her absence. They might have given her another hour or two, at least until the sun hung higher overhead, before the hounds were loosed to find her. She could not imagine who had raised the hue so early in the day. 'Twas not as if she had a beau to worry over her like Catrin's Bran. However, there was a short time, a mere breath in time, where she might have thought someone cared to know her whereabouts.

Without aid of light, she had not realized the slow pace she would be forced to endure. She bit out a curse under her breath. It was a slight miscalculation in her plans. That was all. There was nothing more for her to do but pick up her feet and run.

No longer encumbered with the bulky weight of her skirts, she ran with mindless grace. Drem's leggings covered her legs like loose skin. She leapt over the trunk of a felled tree blocking her path. Her triumph slipped when the mournful howls rose to a high-pitched yelp.

Determined to have her plan succeed, she turned toward the rocky ledges jutting out from the slopes. A small creek wound its way through the woods before ending up at the falls. Beltane, the birth of spring, had been little over a month ago. The water would still be coming down from the mountain. She hoped it would not run too deep.

She slid down the slope of the bank and stumbled toward the creek. Swollen from spring rains and mountain thaw, the water swirled past her feet. She clutched a thin tree trunk and leaned against the smooth bark until her breath came without pain. Gritting her teeth, she stepped into the icy water. Her footing dropped off of what must have been a ledge of rock. The water came up to her waist in an instant. Shock clutched her muscles. The gentle stream of water flowing through the creek had grown into a mighty torrent.

The current pushed against her body. Her boots slid over the moss-covered surface. A dead tree branch lying on the river bed lifted and swung toward her. Its gnarled branches tangled in her cloak, pulling her toward a jutting rock. She unclasped the broach and shrugged off the weighted material. The branch careened in a frenzied swirl. Its hold loosened, freeing her from its trap. Her bundle, which she was trying to hold overhead, dipped low as she tried to right her balance. It caught on the branch and tore from her grasp, bobbing out of reach.

Terrwyn's footing lifted from the creek bed as she leaned after her belongings. Her chin dipped under the chilled water. Her nose and lungs burned.

She stretched once more and her fingers brushed against a corner of Mam's shawl. Mindful to keep her head above the flow, she pushed up and blinked the water from her eyes. She tugged at the shawl and the woven material gaped open. Bit-by-bit, the few belongings she had brought with her spilled out.

The bow and shawl clutched in one hand, she dove toward

her spare linen tunic. The distance misjudged, her effort came up empty. The cloud of fabric escaped, sliding around the bend. She turned to renew her fight against the current. The cold seeping into her limbs, she began the slow angled crawl to the opposite bank.

She collapsed on the land. Triumphant release from the water's hold mixed with her discomfort, leaving her feeling unsure of herself. However, as Mam would say, in for a penny, in for a pound. The price for her decision had been marked when she climbed out the window. Her actions might be thought madness now, but when she found Drem and saved the village, then all would be forgiven.

Determination renewed, she pressed up from the bank. She moved in the direction she hoped—nay, prayed—would intersect with the king's army as they returned to the English border. The vision of celebration lifted her steps.

She shivered. The weight of Drem's waterlogged leather tunic rubbed against her skin. The material of the leggings clung to her legs in a drooping mess. Water squished between her toes and through the seams of her boots as she walked.

Miserable, she could have wept. However, as it would have been a luxury of time poorly spent, she pushed on.

Hours passed. The sun shining overhead began its descent. Surrounded by naught but the sounds of the wooded glen, Terrwyn took little relief in knowing the dogs had given up the chase. Their confused silence came at a hefty price. She had lost almost all she had brought with her.

Hunger gnawed at her belly. She patted her rumbling stomach, speaking to it as if it were an errant child. "Not like you've never been hungry before. I'll feed you soon enough."

With the bread a sodden mess, there was nothing else to do but set off and find the army. A ghost of a smile lifted the corners of her mouth. At least her bow and quiver were no worse for the dunking. She had thought ahead and kept the string dry by tucking it under her cap. Though haunted by fear that her arm would freeze and fall off, she had managed to keep the dwarf elm bow high aloft her head while she bobbed in the stream. There was damage to a few of the arrows, but not enough to lose a tear over. The fletching on some were bent, drying in unmanageable clumps. She would have to keep her eyes open, find a few feathers to replace the ones that were lost.

Terrwyn worried over the delays. She had to find the soldiers' trail before twilight set in. When she found the king's army, she would still have to stay away from them for at least another day. The right timing was imperative.

As the day lengthened, her hunger pressed against her ribs. If she did not eat soon, she would not be able to convince James she was the able-bodied archer.

Thoughts of Catrin's worry-filled eyes reinforced Terrwyn's decision. What she did was right. She might not have been able to save Mam, but her skill with bow and arrow would save her village and bring her closer to finding Drem.

CR80

The stream left behind, Terrwyn soon found signs of where the army had traveled. Marks made from soldiers' hobnailed boots were mashed into the soft earth. Leaves and brush, disturbed by the mass of men and horses, bent in the direction of their destination.

Her hunting skills told her she was not far behind, though far enough to keep from startling the soldiers' mounts. With the sun setting in the western sky, they would have to pull up for the night and make camp. Then she, too, would find a place to rest. If she were careful and kept the fire small, she could dry the damp from her clothes and warm her body without their knowledge. The gnawing of her stomach reminded her again that it needed filling.

She found a rabbits' warren under a small scrubby bush. She settled an arrow, nocking it against the bow. The weight of the weapon felt comfortable in her hands. Her confidence grew. With steady pressure, she began to pull back, stretching the string to full capacity.

Released, the arrow ruffled a wisp of hair escaped from her braid. It shot through the air until it hit the target. A sharp squeal and the rabbit lay where it fell. Terrwyn moved to gather her supper. She would not go hungry this eve. With visions of juicy meat cooking over the fire, she retraced her steps back to the campsite.

Concerned that an English scout might stumble across her path, she chose a spot nestled deep in a ravine. A short wall of stone stood behind her back. A tree hollowed out by time would serve as a hidey spot should she need it. Although she knew it a dangerous decision, she built a meager fire. Readied for a quick toss to douse the flames, a pile of loose dirt laid nearby.

In a short span of time, the campfire was ready and finally so was her meal. Mindful of the heat, she picked up the stick and pulled off the chunk of hindquarters with her teeth. Her stomach clutched and begged for more. Accustomed to having to share her food, she ate as if it had been a fortnight since her last meal.

Terrwyn tore out a strip of cloth from the lining of Drem's leather jerkin and wrapped the remaining bits of meat into it. It would last her until she convinced Sir James she was indeed the archer, one whose skill would assure victory for his King Henry.

The sound of branches snapping cut through the silence.

A man broke through the wall of brambles before Terrwyn had time to dash the flames and take cover in the hollowed-out tree. He stopped, scrubbed at his dirty jaw and sniffed the air. "Look what we have here, Edgar."

Two of them? She brushed her damp palms over her leggings. Then she remembered she must be comfortable with dirt and grease. To allow them to see through her disguise would not bode well for how they treated her. She kept one hand close to the blade tucked in her belt and swiped her cheeks with the other. The smudges of black soot would have to stall them from looking closer.

"I would not know, Simon." Edgar's muffled voice bristled somewhere from behind. "Stuck on them damn thorny bushes. 'Bout to tear clear through my hide."

"Quit your bellyaching, Edgar. I'll remind you to thank me when you ate whatever this fine fellow has cooked up." The man called Simon turned his eyes toward Terrwyn. "Well, here now! Care to share with a hungered man?"

She ducked her head. A deep gnawing filled her belly. The prized packet of roast hare would soon be liberated from her grasp. The knowledge awoke her sated appetite.

"Aye," Edgar piped up, "if it tastes as good as it smells, I'll even pay for it."

Simon sniggered at the apparent jest and slapped Edgar on his back. Edgar's toe caught on one of the stones surrounding the campfire. He staggered forward, his arms wheeling in the air.

Terrwyn quickly dismissed her worries and jumped up. Grabbing Edgar's arm, she spun him away. His thin body landed with a miserable thud against a tree stump.

"G'back!" Simon strode over to Terrwyn and shoved her away from his friend.

She stumbled, then regained her balance. Her fingers itched to test where his meaty fist had struck her shoulder.

Simon's eyes pierced through the shadows of the licking flames. "You'll wish you hadn't attacked one of the king's soldiers, you will."

"I didn't do a thing to your friend but keep him from cooking his arse in the flames."

Edgar lifted his head. His face, reddened with embarrassment, gave way to anger. "No call to sling me against a tree. I coulda broke my nogg'n."

Terrwyn inched her hand toward the hilt of her blade. "You breached my camp without invite. I'll say good eve to you now."

Simon caught her wrist, clamping down with a tight squeeze. "We'll be taking what food you have left."

Indignant fury boiled under Terrwyn's skin. She sized them up. Her head barely came to the middle of their chests. Even the scrawny one would be too much for her. But what right did they have to manhandle her?

Her elbow bent, she pulled forward and kicked at his shin with the heel of her boot. Caught unaware, Simon slackened his grip, and she twisted her wrist out of his grasp and broke free. Before either man responded, she grabbed her bow and pulled an arrow from the quiver. With the arrow nocked and ready to fly, she braced her feet and pointed the weapon at Simon's chest.

"For shame your mam didn't teach you better manners."

She edged the tip of the arrow closer. "Ask me nicely, and I'll think about letting you have a morsel."

"You're a feisty one for your size." Simon squinted at her over the fire. "Welshman, are ya? Doubt you have the strength and know how to set that arrow loose."

Her arrow trained on the men, Terrwyn flipped open the cloth with her toe. Roasted hare, dark and meaty, lay at her feet. She did not stop the snarl that curled her lip when she smiled proudly. "Then I'm guessing I won't share what I downed with me own hand, and thank you to leave me be."

The scent of cooked meat wafted and swirled into the air. The men's wary glances darted between her weapon and the meal before them. Their Adam's apples bobbed as they swallowed in anticipation.

Edgar elbowed Simon in the ribs. "Look what yer mouth talked us out of. Quit being the lout and let me do the talking." Slowly, carefully, Edgar removed his cap. His reddened knuckles crushed the brim to his chest. "Might ye share a bite of yer dinner?"

"Please," Simon added. "We do not mean you harm."

Terrwyn nodded and moved the packet closer with her toe. Still hesitant to let down her guard, she watched as they devoured the meal with lightning speed. The two men sucked out the marrow from the bones and dropped them on the growing pile at their feet. Their lips smacked together, parting only to groan with pleasure and let loose an occasional belch. When there was nothing left, they licked their fingers, one-by-one.

Revolted, Terrwyn tried to hide her building nausea. A leaden weight drew her stomach into a knot when they slowly turned their eyes upon her.

"A feast fit for royalty, that was," Edgar announced.

"Shut your trap. You want to end up in the stocks? Clapped in iron for your pride?"

"No one's here to hear me." Edgar turned to gain Terrwyn's agreement. "Be it so, Welshman?" His eyes narrowed. "There are no others in these woods."

"Course there is." Simon grabbed Terrwyn's elbow. "Look at

this wee muscle. This one does not have the stamina to fell so many varmints."

Incensed, Terrwyn jerked free. "I brought them down. Right as rain, I did!"

Both men stared closely. The reality of her error sank in. She thumbed her chest as she had seen the boys in the village do when they threw down a challenge. "I wager you could do no better. In truth, my spit, flying in a strong wind, has a better chance of hitting the target than the likes of you."

Silence.

A trickle of sweat began to form under her cap.

And then, Edgar and Simon broke up in peals of laughter. Bent double, they slapped their knees and then each other's backs, until air could be pulled back into their lungs.

"Be careful, wee one." Simon gasped between breaths. "One day your challenge will be tested."

Edgar leaned against Simon, nodding in agreement. "Yer luck is with ye for now. If not for having to join our troops, we might have to thump ye for yer own good."

Terrwyn moved over slightly. They would have to look through the bright light of the fire to see her. She let the shadows dance over her face and noticed their discomfort. "If you are soldiers, why are you not with the other men?"

Edgar spoke up, earning himself a fierce look from his companion. "Me and Simon were feeling poorly."

"Aye," Simon added. "Edgar was worse off than me. Had to be nursed back to health before our commander would let us travel with them."

"Didn't help none that our commander is also ye brother," Edgar said. "Sir William treats ye like ye was still wearing nappies and expects me to be yer damn nursemaid.

Scowling, Simon turned his attention toward Terrwyn. "Why do you keep looking at those bushes? Expecting somebody?"

Edgar glanced up. "Thought ye were by yerself?"

Terrwyn shrugged. "My brothers will soon return. All six of them. They will be sorely put out that there is nuth'n to eat."

"Imagine they are the same pint size as you," Simon said.

"Oh, no. I'm the runt of the litter. They are all about your size, Simon. Suppose you could stay put and talk them out of beating me?"

Eyes wary, Simon jumped up. "Six of them, you say?"

Edgar rose slowly as his glance skittered over the bramble bushes. "Sorry as we can be for yer plight—"

"—duty calls us to Henry's army," Simon finished.

Grabbing Simon's sleeve, Edgar pulled him to the edge of the encampment, calling out his thanks. The brambles swallowed up their backsides.

Although grateful they left without doing her great harm, Terrwyn suddenly felt the emptiness of being alone in the woods. She wondered how long she would have to follow the troops before announcing her presence to Sir James.

Dread coiled in her belly, striking fear in her heart. Had she followed the wrong trail? The soldiers spoke of Sir William as their leader and naught of James. Who was this man and where was James?

Chapter Eight

James moved the charcoal across the parchment. The need to see her face once more thrummed through his fingers. Quick, fast strokes scratched over the surface. The shape of his subject slowly emerged under his hand. He softened the lines with his thumb. Half-smiling to himself, he gazed into Terrwyn's face. He had managed to capture the stubborn tilt to her chin. Yet her portrait was incomplete. Some unique quality that was hers alone was missing.

The king trusted his ability to create an image that could not be questioned later. His accuracy brought traitors to the chopping block. Yet this small slip of a girl challenged him in ways he could not fathom. He had attempted to draw her many times. Each time, he could not capture her true essence.

He laid the charcoal down and studied her face once more. Perhaps one day soon he would find the opportunity to return to her village and complete his drawing.

Squinting up from his work, he glanced around the Bloated Goat's dark ale room and thanked the holy saints that the thatched roof allowed some of the smoke to seep out. According to his earlier conversation with Alice uxor Mal, the mistress of this rustic establishment, a certain someone with the intelligence of a billy goat had thought it best to close off the hole in the center of the room. Her recently deceased husband had deemed smoke better for the soul than risking catching their death from the chilly, damp night air.

Alice set the mug beside James's elbow and smoothed back her grizzled hair. She bent low, giving him a view of the additional charms she willingly offered. Jammed in the tight confines, her breasts threatened to burst forth from her bodice. "Sure you won't care for a wee bowl of stew? A fine strapping man such as you needs to take his comfort whenever he can."

"Ah, though it smells of heaven, I shall have to decline." He gave her round cheek a gentle pat. "Perhaps another time, my dear woman."

She giggled as if he offered her a tumble behind the cupboards. Her hip pressed into his shoulder when she stretched to gather the trencher left behind by another patron. The distinct odor of onions and brewed wheat filled the narrow space between them.

"You call out if there is anything else you require. Anything at all."

With his pleasant smile firmly in place, he gave her an understanding wink. "Do not tease me so." He gave her full waist a hug. "Now be a good girl and bring me more ale, if you please."

Another giggle erupted from Alice as she rubbed past him to do his bidding. More travelers entered the establishment and soon her misguided attentions were redirected to more eager patrons. Her laughter mingled with the boisterous activity filling the room.

James sipped the watered-down ale and let it wash the soot from his parched throat. With one eye on the door, he folded the leather packet of drawings and hid them in his boot. He tucked himself into a warm corner near the hearth and tried to merge into the wall. Alone with his thoughts, he nursed the mug of ale he cradled in the crook of his arm. It would not be long now. As soon as the leader of the band of men arrived, their meeting would begin.

Tension in the alehouse mounted as impatience grew. The smell of nervous sweat filled the smoky room. No one spoke of the danger in which they had placed their families by forming this gathering.

The cloud of bravado surrounding the men when they entered the Bloated Goat had slowly evaporated. Their voices dropped as the minutes passed by. The men began to drift away. Sometimes alone, often in small groups, they departed quietly into the night. His presence dismissed, James watched the last of them blend into the dark. Patience learned by the king's side and in his royal court would serve him well tonight. There was vital information to be gathered. Those who kept their eyes and ears open would reap the harvest.

With all but one of her paying clientele gone, Alice laid her weary head on top her folded arms and was soon fast asleep. Ignoring the indelicate snores emanating from her body, James tucked his chin in the folds of his coarse woolen cloak and continued to wait.

The rhythmic pattern of the bar mistress's exhausted sleep pulled to him, reminding him of his own sleepless nights. James grew irritated with the struggle and purposely chose the sharp edge on the rough wall to rest the back of his head. Uncomfortable and wide awake, he listened to the sounds outside. His chest tightened, the telltale sign of his body stirring, alert to the dangers.

The muffled sound of something or someone hitting the ground broke through the woman's snuffle and snorts. James heard it again, although this time it was the quick pounding brought on by a horse ridden fast and hard.

He blew out the candle in the lantern and moved cautiously toward the shuttered window. Slowly, so as not to wake his sleeping companion, he turned the bolt in the shutter and edged open the wooden slats. He peered out in the direction where he thought the noise came from. He was certain he recalled passing a rather rundown shed before he entered the ale room. Its condition had in fact caused him to ponder how it stood upright since most of the building bowed outward and leaned heavily to one side.

A movement.

Shadows, both human and horse, moved and separated. The men trickled out of a side door in the shed. James cursed. Had he been misinformed? Or had someone gotten wind of a stranger asking too many questions?

The night breeze caught the shutter. James could not pull his hand out fast enough. He grimaced as it slammed against his fingers. Sucking back an oath, he pried the slats away. He glanced over his shoulder to make certain Alice had not been awakened from her beauty rest.

Mindful to keep a strong grip on the shutter, he nudged it open for one last look. The wind he recently cursed whipped through the dirt. A tree limb broke from a nearby tree and struck the building. The dilapidated shed vibrated, causing one of the horses to whinny and pull away. The man who had kept mostly to the shadow now stepped out to steady the mount. In his efforts to calm the beast, he did not notice when he moved into the moonlight.

But James did. A tight smile lifted his lips. *Aye, a healthy dose of patience did indeed make this evening profitable after all.*

As the moon dipped low into the pre-dawn shadows, the Bloated Goat's mistress awoke to find her ale room empty, a pile of coins stacked neatly by her head.

CRSO

When Terrwyn first climbed into the hole of the hollow tree, she thought it would suit her needs well. But as the hours stretched throughout the night, her legs and back started to complain. Hours dragged past with the speed of a wintering bear and she began to wonder if the sun would ever rise from its slumber. Finally, with little fanfare, the dark sky began to lighten. The morning air, heavy with dew, cloaked the day with a thick shawl of gray.

Unfolding her limbs, Terrwyn stretched her muscles and yelped when they cramped. Intent on putting food in her belly, she set off for the nearby rabbits' nest she had raided the night before. She would try her luck there again and discover if the warren held a large family of conies. Cautiously, she wound her trail toward a small stream that ran through the dip in the landscape, cutting through the earth and limestone rock of the wooded forest.

Keeping her scent downwind, Terrwyn stood behind the brambles of a wild raspberry bush. Its branches swelled with faded white flowers. The spent blossoms were pregnant with pale green knobs of flesh. Soon there would be fruit. She flicked the hard nubbin and grimaced. For now, they were inedible. She would have to look elsewhere for nourishment.

Well hidden behind the brambles, she sat and watched for

the first signs of movement through the hole of the rabbit's warren. Time slowly passed and she began to worry. Surely if there were hares close by, they would have already poked their heads out of their holes. If she missed them, it would be dusk before having another chance at snaring them with her arrows.

Her stomach growled against her rib cage, reminding her of the night's unwelcome guests. Had the men not eaten every morsel intended for today she would not have to sit here, falling farther behind in her journey.

Aware of time slipping past, she watched the dappled sunlight move over a nearby boulder. She shifted quietly. Her mouth, dry as a fall leaf stripped from its tree branch, begged for a drink. She could wait no more.

After sliding down the bank, she dipped her finger into the shallow stream and shivered. She drank from her cupped hands, licking the remaining drops from her palms. Thoughts of baked trout filled her head. Her tongue poked around her lips as if looking for a remaining taste of fish. Distracted, she nearly missed the soft rustle of leaves. Bushes quivered as the rabbit hopped a zigzag path to safety.

Quickly, she readied her bow. Her aim set, she let the arrow loose and watched it miss as the rabbit changed direction. Cursing under her breath, she peered through the gray mist to see what had frightened the creature.

"Hallo!" Edgar called. "What are ye about?"

"You have eyes," Terrwyn snapped with a hiss.

Edgar shook his head and offered a smile of pity. "There are better ways to snare a conie. Have ye no net?"

Simon followed near Edgar's heel. He ambled over and smacked Terrwyn on her shoulder. "What did you think to do?" he hooted. "Shoot him with yon arrow?"

She jerked her shoulder from his grasp. "Aye, takes brains and a perfect shot. But it can be done."

Edgar's eyes narrowed and scanned the horizon. "Where are yer brothers? Our commander wishes a word with them."

Terrwyn blinked. "They aren't here."

"They up and left ye in the thicket by yourself?"

"And what if they did?"

"Plain to see, you are light in smarts. Dumb as a stump."

"Shows you nothing of the kind. They have only returned to our village to bring back a cart. They know I'll down so many conies they'll need a means to carry 'em home."

Edgar propped his hands on his hips. "Tell us the way to yer village and we'll gladly escort them brothers of yers to our commander."

"My village?"

"Aye," Simon nodded. "Though I do not know how we missed them. Searched all known cottages that held menfolk. The worst was the village near Abergavenny. 'Twas a pitiable show of manhood and skill."

"Commander was fair pissed with the time wasted on their phantom archer. Achk." Edgar spat on the ground. "Shoulda known he was too spineless to show his self and stand on his famed abilities. I told the commander to burn the fields to teach them he means business."

Terrwyn gulped and turned away. "Simon, what shall become of my brothers if they do not return soon?"

Simon clapped her on her back. "Not to fear, boy-o, you may join us. Henry's army is always looking for an extra hand."

"Aye," Edgar cut in with a tooth-gapped hoot. "One hand to carry the shite bucket and 'nother to kill the thieving French bastards."

"And what if I am the archer your commander searches for?"

Simon and Edgar glanced at Terrwyn and then glanced away before snickering under their breaths.

Edgar cuffed the back of her head, nearly unseating the cap that hid her plaited hair. "Enough of your blathering lies, Welshman. I've heard as much as I want to hear. Direct us to yer brothers."

"Take me to your commander instead. I'll prove that I am the one."

"If ye think I am stupid, test me again with yer lies," Edgar groused. "I won't take ye to Sir William and announce ye as the saving archer."

Simon grabbed Edgar's arm and kept him from leaving.

"What's the harm in a little sport? Let him demonstrate his keen abilities."

Edgar rubbed his jaw and stared intently at Terrwyn. "I don't wish to return to our camp without something to show the commander. But I'm no fool. We'll bring back food if nothing else. Show me yer skill by downing another rabbit."

"I thought you said you do not have time?"

"So?"

"They are done foraging for food and won't come out of their warren until the sun sets."

Edgar pulled out his knife, pointing the tip of the blade toward Terrwyn. "Ye trifle with my patience. 'Tis possible yer a French sympathizer and cannot hit a hillside. Mayhap ye used this ruse to lead us away from your brothers. If I showed up with the likes of ye, I might as well slit yer throat and mine. As I intend to breathe for a few more days, ye'll be doing the dying alone."

Terrwyn jammed the point of her elbow into Edgar's stomach. Feeling the impact of bone against soft flesh and hearing his howl, she lunged for her bow and arrow. The weapon aimed at Edgar's chest, she pulled the string taut. "I think, my fair-haired Englishmen, we will have a challenge instead."

"A challenge, Edgar!" Simon crowed as he greedily rubbed his hands together. "By God, I love a challenge."

"Do not get ahead of yourself, Simon," Terrwyn said. "I insist you join us."

"Me?"

"We would not have it any other way. Would we, Edgar?"

Edgar flicked his finger against the sharp edge digging into his chest. "What will it be?"

"Nothing tragic. Target practice. I win, you will be my champion." Terrwyn paused and smiled. "And you'll carry all my shite buckets. Both of you."

"And when ye lose, ye'll lead us to yer brothers and then be gone from our sight." Edgar leaned close and scraped his nail over her cheek. "Forever. A true and final ending for a wench."

Air squeezed Terrwyn's lungs. She tried to pull a breath in.

Her eyes stung as she squashed the urge to flinch. Her hand trembled for a split moment and then was once again steady.

"Here now," Simon grabbed Terrwyn's elbow and felt her arm. "You certain, Edgar?"

"As certain as I am that it will rain again before the day is out. Let's have a bit of sport with this one before we dispatch her from whence she came."

"Enough," she said. "If you are too afraid of defeat, then admit it and be gone."

"Not sure, but I do believe she has a point, Edgar."

Terrwyn stepped back, her weapon still trained on the men. "I should run you through for your disparaging accusations. The challenge stands. Are you man enough?"

"The question is, what are ye willing to give us when ye lose?" Edgar asked.

Terrwyn let her bow drop slightly. She looked him in the eyes. "I believe I'll be enjoying every minute you grovel, instead." She announced the rules. "Fifty paces to start. Increasing each time the mark is hit. You shoot first. I will follow. We'll continue until the best shot is discovered."

Edgar and Simon nodded their agreement. One by one, they shot and hit their mark. Each time, Terrwyn followed, splintering their arrows.

Terrwyn focused on the tree as it was marked off with another ten paces. She waited patiently, alert to Edgar's mounting agitation. Simon trotted back to her side. An excited grin split his face. His eyes beamed with admiration, reminding Terrwyn of a hunting dog her father used to have in the old manor house. When it came to hunting, he was a trustworthy opponent and had a heart made of gold. Loyal as they came. Unless he gripped a bone between his teeth.

"Here now," Edgar grumbled, "I don't have any left."

"That's all right, I'm all shot out." Simon offered him his own. "I missed that last one. Went clear into the bushes. Took me forever to find it."

Edgar snatched the last arrow from Simon's hand. Hitching his shoulder up, he let the arrow loose. It shot out of control and into the trees. "Damn yer hide, Simon, ye messed with my shot." Red-faced, he grabbed Simon's jerkin and twisted. "The fletching was destroyed."

Down to three arrows, Terrwyn held one out to Edgar. "Try again."

He snatched it from her hand and set it loose, only to catch the edge of the tree trunk. Quivering, the shaft wavered in the breeze, threatening to fall out.

Terrwyn ignored his anger and sized up her target. She shifted for a better advantage and let loose the arrow. It arched through the air and cut into Edgar's shaft.

Laughing heartily, Simon caught Terrwyn up in his arms and spun her around with dizzying joy. "We'll champion you!" he crowed. "Won't we, Edgar?"

Standing rigid and angry, Edgar snarled a curse and spat on the ground. Before Terrwyn could think of something to say, he drew out his blade. Simon stepped toward him, his fist raised.

Thankful she still had one arrow left, Terrwyn prepared to place a shot between them. As she braced her legs and began the release, a shout rang out.

Horses barreled through the thicket. Their bodies protected by leather armor, they crashed through the brambles and came to a skidding halt in front of the two men.

Simon and Edgar paused long enough to heed the command to desist their brawling. The man, dressed in leather jerkin and travel armor, sat astride a huge pale stallion. Without helmet, his hair glistened like a wheat field ready for harvest. He caught Terrwyn's attention and pierced her with a pointed stare.

Unaware she took a step back, she stifled the automatic urge to curtsy. Fidgeting, she tugged the cap down, ensuring it was snug upon her head. Worry began to swell inside her chest as she waited to hear Edgar and Simon's explanation for their fight.

CRSO

Satisfied with his work, James rested his elbows on the

small table the innkeeper of the Red Rooster had proudly announced as one of the room's appointments. It had been well worth the coin.

He straightened the contents of the pouch, smoothed the edges of the leather and tucked it inside his jerkin. If there ever came a time that the pouch landed in the enemies' hands, they would think the drawings were no more than a flight of fancy. A weak man's musings and whiling away time while real men of strength wielded broadswords and maces at one another's head. The secrets were embedded in the drawings and only he and Henry had the key.

He had learned all he could. It was time to leave the Red Rooster Inn, wash his hands of the unwanted task and make his way back to his home. First, he would have to come up with some plausible excuse why he needed to leave Sir William so soon after his return.

James pulled out a stick of charcoal and traced the face he could not get out of his mind onto the extra bit of vellum. He sat back and examined the likeness. Admittedly, Terrwyn was a cantankerous sprite, but lord how he would love to strip away that hard edge and find the tender heart he was certain existed. He softened the sharp lines. Perhaps he would find a way to erase the anger in her eyes but keep the fire that burned within.

He paused, then tucked the vellum inside the packet with the other drawings. "I imagine one day I'll have to thank Henry for this damned task after all."

Chapter Nine

The man introduced as Sir John Grey, a captain of the king's army, stood with disbelief written in his eyes. His gaze kept shifting from one face to the next. Relief washed over Terrwyn as the pale stranger pointed his scowl away from her direction.

"You dare report this tale, Edgar Poole? You think me daft?"

Edgar paled visibly. Bits of leaves and twigs flew as he shook his head. "Daft, Sir?" he croaked. "Nay, Captain."

"And you?" Sir John poked his finger into Simon's wide chest. "You expect me to believe this wood elf won a challenge against our best bowman?" His eyes narrowed as if squinting would help him understand. Gripping the bridge of his nose, he threw back his head and let out a bellowing sound of disgust. "Please tell me that at least you gave this imp a run for his money."

Red-faced, Simon shook his head. "I know 'tis hard to believe, but I swear Edgar and I tell the truth of it. You see—"

"Ye see," Edgar cut in, "what with our recent illness, our aim was a trifle off."

"Simon, if you be yet afflicted with dysentery then perhaps you shall return home to Norwich. Despite your brother's orders, I haven't the desire to be your nursemaid."

Simon quickly shook his head. "I'm mending fast as lightning."

Sir John clapped his long fingers over Simon's shoulder. Peering closely, he examined the span of his face. "I am unwilling to lose my commander's young brother before we even set sail."

"Maybe after?" Simon joked.

"'Tis not a time to jest about death," Sir John said. He pinned Terrwyn with a stare. "Demonstrate, wood elf, how you bested Henry's men." Grabbing her jerkin, he added a warning. "No trickery."

Terrwyn nodded. Her legs shook when she bent to pick up her bow. If not for Simon's help, she would have hit the ground in a miserable heap.

Simon pinched the soft underside of her arm before letting go. "Steady, Archer."

"Captain," Simon said. "I'm here to state that this is indeed the archer we have been searching for. Let's be done with this foolery and be on our way."

Sir John's smile held a note of condescension as he lifted a gloved hand. "Allow me to finally witness this archer's skill. 'Tis best I see this miracle with my own eyes before I deliver him to your brother."

Edgar strode from behind and whacked Terrwyn's back. The blow brought stars to her eyes. He gripped her shoulder and nodded with a tight smile. "This one is always ready to perform, aren't ye, lad?"

Though she wondered why they kept the secret of her sex to themselves, she noted the threat laced in Edgar's last word. She allowed herself half a glance at Edgar before turning to nod at the towering figure. Jerking her shoulder away, she kept her head down and tugged the brim of her cap tightly over her ears.

"Course, Sir John."

"Then be done with it. Hit the most recent target with which you trounced my lead archer and you'll find yourself paid handsomely, marching with Henry's army before the day is through."

CRSO

When Terrwyn first heard Simon's announcement that the winning archer should save his strength and ride back to the camp, she was thankful.

Then she saw the beast Sir John expected her to mount.

After allowing her several tries, he lost patience and bellowed at them to hurry it up. Simon grinned like a lack-wit fool and flung himself into the saddle with one swift, effortless movement. He reached down, grabbed Terrwyn and tossed her behind him as if she weighed less than a sack of wheat.

Terrwyn straddled the horse's wide back, her short legs shooting out ungracefully. She gripped Simon's tunic and prayed she would not fall from her awkward perch.

Satisfied they were finally on their way, the captain shouted for them to move out. Laughing heartily, Simon saluted Edgar and the unseated soldier as they began their short trek.

Terrwyn scoured her memory for the skill to master her seat. It had been over six years since her dear pony had been killed by the Englishman's arrow. And from the time she rode upon Zeus's tall back, she did not recall anything but the memory of being in James's arms. Yet, despite her uncertainty, she felt the thrill of strength underneath her legs. The familiar rolling gait warmed her heart.

Lost in her thoughts, she recalled the adventurous young girl she once had been. Now, every step away from the village brought her closer to finding Drem. Closer to rediscovering herself.

The sound of the camp being packed up reverberated over the hillside. Terrwyn tightened her grip. Flinching, she realized that soon she would no longer have the wide expanse of Simon's back to hide her face. It would not be long before they saw through her disguise. Although most of the men were English dolts, she could not count on them to be blind as well.

"Keep your head down," Simon warned. "Beating Edgar's shot thrice does not ensure your safety. When William learns what you are, we'll all have our hides stripped."

"I meant no harm. If not for the other soldiers placing bets, I would have let it go at one shot."

"Watch your step with Edgar. You'll have no friend there, I'll warn you."

"As I am aware," Terrwyn muttered. "'Tis a wonder he has

not exposed me already."

As they came to the edge of the camp, Simon slowed their horse. "His pride won't allow it. Never let it be known that a half-sized woman bested him."

Terrwyn grabbed his forearm as he prepared to dismount. "Wait!"

Frowning, Simon paused.

"What of you?" No matter what Simon thought, he held his tongue in silence and did not turn away when she probed his soul with her eyes. "What do you intend to do, Simon? Why are you willing to help me?"

"I had the stomach ague. The old healer brought to tend me said she was needed elsewhere. The bitter woman did not need to wipe the son of some English lord's arse. Said the fates demand I pay back what is owed." His voice lowered as he added, "Or be cursed by the people that live under the earth."

Terrwyn released his arm and squashed her outrage against fate. Here, standing before her, was the very reason Isolde had not been there to save her mother. If not for the need of his help, she would shoot him and let the devil take the prize. "'Tis why you will champion me?"

Simon nodded. "That and you beat me fair with your skill. Besides, I find your farce amusing."

He hooked his elbow with hers and motioned her to slide off the horse. She dropped to her feet and stepped out of the way.

Simon dismounted and turned to grip her arm. "Soon, Archer, my debt will be paid. Then I'll know why you are out here alone." His hold tightened. "Do not wait too long. Though William is a fair man, he has the disposition of the eldest son. He'll see through you in a day or so and he will not be amused."

Jerking free, Terrwyn took the bundle he held out to her. She could not help noting how pitifully small Mam's wadded shawl looked against his large roll. Her quest to join them in their journey to France seemed insurmountable.

"I'll see that the quartermaster outfits you. Perhaps one of the knights has a squire about your size. Until then, make yourself scarce. Keep that hat pulled low as you can without the danger of tripping over your own feet."

Terrwyn nodded, then, after waiting a moment or two longer, she asked, "Where do I go?"

"Usually you would take a position with the other archers." He scanned the campsite and his jaw muscles tightened. "Though by the looks of it, with or without Sir James in attendance, we're preparing to push on."

Terrwyn could not help voicing her growing concern. "This man you speak of. He will return?"

"Aye, sooner or later. And if you ask me, it won't be soon enough."

"Does it not bother your brother that this Sir James fellow has deserted the camp?"

Simon frown deepened. "I'll ask you not to speak of desertion. 'Tis an ugly word. One we take seriously. Death to those who decide the king's service is no longer for them." He shoved back his hair and chewed on his lip thoughtfully. "Although William has mentioned his suspicions, the difference is Sir James has always returned happy as you please."

"Yet your brother does nothing?"

"What can he do?" Simon said. "Sir James's father may be a Yorkist but his Welsh mother has known Henry since he lived at Monmouth Castle. William has been given orders that James may come and go as needs require."

Curious, Terrwyn blocked his path. "And what do you suppose he does while he is away? Who does he meet with?"

"Take heed, Archer. A man does not ask so many questions. He recognizes when to keep silent. Something you need to work on." He looked over her shoulder as shouts erupted from the line of trees surrounding the encampment. "Yonder comes Sir James's runners."

Terrwyn pivoted on her heels and stood on tiptoe to see around Simon. "Is Sir James with them?"

Simon gave her a penetrating look as he considered her question. "Nay."

"How can you tell?" she prodded.

"Zeus is not with them. I'd recognize that horseflesh anywhere. But with them runners of his here, he won't be far behind. If you still mean to travel with us, you'll need to keep yourself hid from now on. Go off to that clump of shrubs." He pointed with a nod. "Do not move from that spot. I'll find you 'ere we take our leave."

Terrwyn grabbed Simon before he left her side. She held his hand tight as if he were her only line to safety. "You won't forget?"

He looked around to see if anyone watched. Satisfied of his privacy, he squeezed her hand back. "Just do as I say and keep your arse out of sight."

Chapter Ten

The bright sun heated the top of Terrwyn's covered head. She shifted and wished Simon had pointed her to the spot beside the great oak tree. The cool shade beckoned her. Dark green leaves called, waving to her in the soft breeze. Her eyelids grew heavy and she swayed with the rhythm of the trees.

Someone called out to her...his impatient voice comfortably familiar. He pushed at her with the force of his anger. "Fly away home, birdie," he said. "You haven't the stomach for this path where you set your foot."

Drem looked older in her vision, more ferocious than she remembered. His message delivered, he turned on his heel and did not heed her call to wait. He simply left as he arrived. There had been little time for her to respond, to make him understand she could not turn back. Terrwyn blinked and cleared her head from the sight of her brother. "Oh, Drem, do you not understand? I've come for you. I cannot turn back now."

As the dream faded, she realized the time for Simon to return for her had already come and gone. The command of soldiers had finished gathering their belongings. They stood in formation, awaiting their instructions. The cavalrymen sat at the head of the procession. They rose in their stirrups and shouted, "Look alive men! Mount out!"

Sir John moved his stallion back and let the infantry pass. Watchful, he kept his attention on the soldiers, giving stern instruction to some and encouragement to others. The men shouted good-naturedly, happy to be traveling across the border, nearer to their home and closer to their women's welcoming thighs.

"Sir William." Sir John saluted as another man dressed in full armor joined him.

They moved toward Terrwyn's hiding spot, allowing her to overhear a few scattered words. "—Archer—"

"—imperative—"

"—missive—"

Sir John tucked the packet into a satchel hanging from his saddle. He saluted the commander and rode off at full gallop.

Terrwyn moved behind the bush. Her heart beat so hard she feared Sir William would hear it over the sound of the wheels. Certain he spotted her when he turned in her direction, she ducked down, gathering her quiver and bow to her chest. She held the rolled up shawl and weapon close and set off to join the throng of men.

Her eyes cast to the ground, she nearly stumbled into a redheaded boy no older than Glynis and Adain. He gave her a shove and sent her reeling back. Fighting to hold on to her belongings and still keep her cap drawn down, she fell into the path of a heavily laden wagon. The pair of ponies whinnied and sidestepped, pulling on the leads as they danced out of the way.

The wagon's cargo came barreling toward her. The wooden slates belched out various shapes of baggage. What could not be contained within hung from leather loops on the outside. The driver squinted at her. The frown plastered on his face pulled his gray whiskers down, where they hung like a big swooping bow.

"Look alive," the old man shouted. "Get out of the way before you get trampled."

"Me?" she said.

"Course, you! See any other blind fool who doesn't know how to keep out of the way?"

The wagon never stopped moving but swayed as it bounced over a rut in the road. Trotting to keep up, she gripped the plank where the driver propped his boot. "I didn't know where to report." Hearing his grunt of disbelief, she added quickly, "Arrived late."

"The commander won't want to lose an archer. Best hop up in the back of the wagon."

Terrwyn dodged a pothole. "This wagon?"

"Make room. Mind you, don't knock anything off."

Nodding, Terrwyn let go of the running board and allowed the bloated wagon to move past. She tossed her bundle into the bed. As a last-minute thought, her bow and quiver followed. Taking a running leap, she caught hold of the tailgate. Her feet scrabbled for a purchase on the ledge. Balanced on her toes, she teetered back and forth. The wooden wheels caught in a rut and jumped before lurching forward.

Terrwyn flew into the wagon, landing on her stomach with a jolt. She flipped over on her back and willed the dancing stars to disappear. As soon as her lungs were able to fill again, a grin spread across her face. Not since her last challenge with Drem had she known that conqueror's thrill.

"Hey," a muffled voice called out. "Watch where you're sticking that bow. Sir William won't take kindly to you killing off his page."

"Sorry," Terrwyn patted her head, making certain the cap remained secure and her hair had not escaped. Pulling the cap forward, she peeked from under the brim.

A fair-haired boy knelt beside her. He held out the bow and quiver. Before she took it, she turned to scrub her dirty fingers over her face.

"'Sall right! No need to weep."

Terrwyn straightened her shoulders and held her chin high. "Not all slobbered up with tears. Just tired."

"Oh," the little boy responded.

After a long pause, Terrwyn could not stand the quiet hurt any longer. "I'm sorry. I didn't mean to snap."

"'Tis all right. I forgive you."

Where had the young boy learned his manners? If Glynis and Adain were this well spoken, Catrin would proudly serve them berry pies everyday. Terrwyn could not fathom a boy, an English boy at that, speaking so softly. The child had a funny habit of twirling his short curls around his fingers. Much like he was searching for something that was not there. She cringed, praying he did not have lice. She and insects of any kind had an aversion to each other.

"You may call me Gilbert," the little one offered. "That one driving the team goes by Cook. What are you called?"

A vision of patience, the child waited, silently playing with a ringlet that escaped his oversize cap. Unable to tear her eyes from the constant twirling, Terrwyn realized she never thought she might have need of a name once inside the army of men. Her tongue caught on the first name that came to mind. Besides, Simon and the wagon driver had used it without thinking anything of it. Perhaps it would help to keep her in disguise.

"Archer," she stated simply. "I go by Archer."

Gilbert took a bite from an oatcake then offered it to Terrwyn. "Would you like some?"

Terrwyn hesitated, hating to take food out of the small one's mouth. It would be like taking it from her sisters.

Gilbert frowned, the hurt written on his thin, smooth face. "'Tis all right. You needn't worry. Didn't filch it. Cook said to eat as much as my wee body can hold. He vows it won't be a burden on our supplies.

Terrwyn's stomach growled, reminding her how long it had been since she had her last morsel. His eyes sparkling, he handed her the cake. His smile flashed as he fished out another for himself.

"Where are we going?" Terrwyn asked around a mouthful.

"We head east. To England. Then to Southampton. S'posed to have ships big as mountains, waiting to sail for France." His excitement overflowing, Gilbert clapped his hands with glee. Leaning close, he motioned to tell her a secret of utmost importance. "Archer, my mother said to look for Offa's Dike. Once we cross over its border, I am almost home."

"Where is your mam now? Does she not travel with you?"

Gilbert sat back. A frown creased his brow. Terrwyn thought she saw a cloud of pain mar his moss-green eyes. Then, just as quickly, it was gone. Anger thundered back at her. "She's not here."

The boy turned abruptly. He smoothed a spot to rest his head and lay down. Left with only the view of his back, she should be relieved she had a respite from his close scrutiny. Yet she felt the need to draw him into her lap and tell him the same stories she told her sisters.

Familiar with her own close walk with deception, Terrwyn knew it when she smelled it on another. The little one did more than hide his tears. She would make certain she remained close by until he reached his home across the border. She could not understand how a mother might leave her child with strangers. If he were her son, she would fight to stay by his side.

Thoughts of Drem filtered in. He was older than this child, yet she could not help wondering how frightened he must have been on his first days with the English.

CRSO

Her lids heavy, seduced by the rhythmic sway of the wagon, Terrwyn was nearly asleep when they pulled up for the night. She heard the horse as it cantered toward her. It skidded to a stop and snorted softly. Opening her lids a crack, she peered up at Simon. "Did you forget me?"

"You appear well enough, Archer," Simon said.

"'Tis been two days hence the time you abandoned me."

"Best to keep you hidden for a time."

Cramped and dirty, Terrwyn grew impatient. "I am an archer and should be with the archers."

"Walk with me." Simon dismounted and motioned to the driver to hold their position. He waited for Terrwyn to clamber out of the wagon bed.

As their distance from the wagons grew, the permanent frown slid from Simon's visage. "Tell me, Archer, would you have rather been found out early on? Sent packing to your little village by Abergavenny?"

At Terrwyn's little gasp, he smiled. "Aye, we had visitors from your village. Bran and Maffew joined us earlier in the day, spewing threats of bringing Owain and his band of men down on our heads. Swore Dafydd ap Hugh's daughter rode with us. Had William not been beholden to their mother's help for my ailing innards, he might have sent them without their heads, a note pinned to their blankets to come and be bested."

Visions of her family and friends lying in a pool of their own blood nearly brought her to her knees. She gripped Simon's sleeve to keep from hitting the ground.

"Steady, Archer. Their heads are still attached. Your village still stands. William has been calmed. But I know my brother. His travels to Wales have broken open the old wound of a painful memory. He'll not want another Welsh woman sneaking her way into his command."

"Nay! You did swear to champion me."

"That was before all this. I thought he was over her. But when I see his face, I know it pains him when he thinks of the woman who stole his child."

"He lost a child? A little boy?"

"Nay, a girl no bigger than a mite. When the Welsh bitch stole his child, she well as tore William's heart right out. Said she could no longer stomach her life in England." Simon's meaty hand patted her shoulder. "'Tis why I'll only help you get as far as you can from your home, but I will not play my brother false any longer. He deals with lies and deceit from all sides. Sir James has yet to return from his secret affairs. And now—" Simon paused, roughly shoving his fingers through his hair. "Now we're going to have to misplace the archer that Henry has already heard all about."

Terrwyn hated seeing the pain reach his own sad eyes. Yet if she held any chance of finding Drem, she had to reach Southampton before they set sail for France. Unwanted thoughts of James careened around her head. She struggled to focus on what Simon was saying. The worry in his voice brought her back to hear his concern.

"We've a fine mess, you and I. William will be enraged when I cannot bring him his archer. You're going to have to stay hid for a while longer. Least until I figure out what to do with you."

Chapter Eleven

Terrwyn and Simon approached the encampment in silence, each lost in their thoughts. Simon stopped her outside the ring of trees. "'Tis best if we are not seen together."

"If that is what you wish."

"Remember. Do not draw attention to yourself. William is already angry that I cannot seem to locate you." Simon took his leave as soon as she acknowledged his orders.

Her attention was quickly turned from Simon when shouts rang out. Recognizing Gilbert's voice, Terrwyn raced over and skidded to a halt. Simon's words of caution echoed in her ears before she silenced them. Men of various shapes crowded Cook against his wagon.

Edgar Poole led the charge, stirring the soldiers with his slurs against the people of Wales. He swayed on his feet and swung at the crowd with his flagon.

"Weak-bellied women, the whole lot of 'em. Thieves. That's what they are. They'll steal us blind. Take the food from our mouths. The coin from our families."

Their tempers rising, the soldiers pushed and shoved at each other. Indignant from the shouted lies, the Welshmen returned shove for shove against the throng of men. Caught in the chaos, Gilbert yelped when he hit the side of Cook's wagon.

"We might have to follow the commander's orders to herd them up for battle. But I for one do not wish to share my meal with them," Edgar said. "Who is with me?"

"You'll take your hide elsewhere." Cook shook the thick-handled ladle at the men surrounding him. "I won't serve any of you until you cool off and use your heads. You're even bigger fools if you follow this one's lead."

Edgar lunged toward the wagon, wielding his dagger close to the old man's face. "I ought to slice open yer throat for interfering in my business."

Cook twisted to push the young Gilbert out of the way. The tip of the blade cut through the cook's leather jerkin. Grimacing, he fell to his knees.

"Devil take you," Gilbert yelled.

Edgar turned and caught the young boy before he could crawl under the wagon. "No ye don't, ye little bastard. 'Tis time I taught ye some manners."

Terrwyn's breath caught at the sight of the child in Edgar's grasp. The memory of her inability to save her brother rushed back. Frustration bled into rage as she pushed past the men. She climbed to the top of the highest mound of supplies and stood with her legs braced, her bow stretched tight. Remembering her promise to keep herself out of sight, she whispered an apology to Simon and let the arrow loose.

With a yelp of surprise, Edgar turned his glare toward Terrwyn. "Damned fool, I'll kill ye where ye stand."

"You had your warning. Let the child go."

The soldiers nearest to Edgar backed away and left Terrwyn an easy shot. Tempted, she ignored the little voice that urged her to let him have the taste of iron between his teeth. Instead, she let the arrow fly and watched it burrow into the dirt beside his boot.

Edgar spat on the ground in response, earning a half-hearted chuckle from his cohorts.

A second arrow impaled its head between Edgar's feet.

With a startled curse, he pressed the blade into Gilbert's skin until a patch of red began to trickle.

Terrwyn yanked the knife from her belt, threw it and leapt from her high advantage, letting her weight fall on top of Edgar. Gilbert rolled free from his grasp.

Edgar ripped out the dagger from his thigh and tossed Terrwyn off his back. Smelling blood, the men cheered as she struggled to rise.

Edgar advanced, knocking her to the ground again. Gripping her by the nape of her neck, he pulled her to her knees. "I told ye I'd make ye pay," he ground out softly. "Skirts or no skirts, it makes me no never mind."

As she rose, Terrwyn grabbed a handful of loose dirt and threw it into Edgar's eyes. Her fists locked together, she swung her arms with all her might and bashed him against his jaw. He tumbled to the ground.

"Arch-er! Arch-er!" The chant rang through the clearing.

Terrwyn shook the cobwebs from her head. Every bone aching, she bent to retrieve her blade and arrows.

Silence.

Then the thunder of hoofs. A shout, crystal clear.

Zeus and James barreled through the tree line. The destrier charged past as James launched himself from its back. He caught Edgar's arm with the heel of his boot. Stunned once more, the archers and longbowmen stood back as they watched their lead bowman fall by the hand of one of their own.

Terrwyn's knees slowly folded to the ground. The rage began to clear from her head. Keeping the brim of her cap low, she looked up and tried to focus on the one face she had been searching for.

James knelt beside her. "You've much to answer for, soldier. As it is, we are already short of good men. Make peace or you'll find yourself sent packing."

Terrwyn touched his jaw. She could not keep the smile from lighting up her face. There was something about this man that would not allow her hatred to reside. "Yell all you want, English. But please do so after I've had some time to catch my breath."

James leaned in closer. He tipped her chin, his gaze peeling away the dirt. The weight of the heavy braid, hidden underneath her cap, slowly began to work its way out. He paused as Terrwyn stayed his hand with a slight shake of her head. Understanding washed over his face. Without a word, he tucked in the tendrils before they could escape further and yanked the cap in place.

Terrwyn gasped from the sudden movement. Her smile

wobbled before she compressed her lips firmly together.

James pulled back, searching her face. "What have you got yourself into?"

"Give way! The boy needs care." After barking out orders to disperse, James lifted Terrwyn into his arms.

"Wait. My bow and quiver—"

"Be still," he whispered into her ear. "Keep your head down. Your face hidden."

The burden nestled securely in his arms, he turned and found his path blocked.

"He hurt that bad that you need to carry him?" William's young brother said.

"Simon, is it? Be a good lad and move aside." James stepped closer, motioning allowance for passage. Given the way Simon planted his feet, he could only surmise the young fool intended to make himself a barrier. Impatience growing, he shifted his hold. With Terrwyn's face pressed into the crook of his neck, he tamped down the need to shout. "Out of my way, young puppy."

A muffled groan erupted from the baggage in his arms.

"Here," Simon said. "I'll take the ruffian."

James brushed the ham-sized appendage with a glance. "Look to Edgar Poole. See he receives the care he deserves."

Relieved to see Simon's attention cast in the bowman's direction, James moved to shove past and found the path still blocked.

"The men will tend his wound." A fleeting look of concern marred Simon's face while he scratched the back of his neck. "Seeing as Poole injured Cook, the men won't stitch him together none too gently." He paused before adding wistfully, "I'd wager you'd want to question everyone involved."

"Aye," James snapped. "Sir William will want a full report. Start with Edgar Poole."

Simon nodded in hopeful agreement. "Might as well take that one off your hands while I'm at it."

The desire to reach his tent growing, James could not keep the impatience from his voice. "Nay, I shall take this nuisance under my own care." He gave his captive's collar a warning shake, emphasizing his resolve. "I've a desire to keep him in my custody."

"No need to mess yourself with the likes of this one," Simon said. "'Tis certain, the sooner he is out of your sights the better."

James pulled his tired shoulders square. "I intend to question the miscreant myself."

Despite the tightening around his eyes, Simon smiled affably. "Give the bastard a good thrashing. You'll get your answers, sure enough."

James felt Terrwyn flinch, felt the tension building in her body. She was finally frightened. God forgive him, he was damn glad of it. Hell and damnation, did she not understand the predicament she placed herself? Once the men learned from Edgar that she was indeed a female, it would be open season on her virginity.

Hell's bones! The wench had some harebrained notion to wiggle free. James tightened his grip to keep her from escaping. He was sorely tempted to turn her over to Simon. The salivating lummox was eager to get his hands on the bit of baggage. It would serve her well to scare the devil out of her.

As if reading his mind, Simon reached out to pry the small arm that had crept around James's neck. "I'd be proud to lay a hand to his hide, myself."

All thoughts of vindication evaporated as James realized that Simon intended to physically remove Terrwyn from his arms. He took half a step back and growled proprietarily over the top of her head. "I've given you orders, Simon. I would hate to recount your insubordination to Sir William."

A tightening around Simon's mouth was the only telltale sign of his ire. He sidestepped slowly from the path, sweeping his arms wide for James to pass without further delay. "Sir James—"

James turned to see the flash of anger flush Simon's cheeks.

"A full report will be available within the hour," Simon said. "Delivered to you, myself."

James caught Simon's gaze and held it. "I would expect nothing less." Pushing past, he strode down the rough-cut path.

Once certain they were far enough away for their voices not to carry, James asked, "Are your injuries grave?"

Terrwyn snorted a half chuckle. "Nary a scratch."

Relief warred with irritation as James marched silently through the glen. His anger grew with each step.

Terrwyn lift her face from his shoulder and whispered, "Let me down."

"Silence!" James said. "Not a word until I give you leave."

"I cannot breathe!"

"Can you not listen?" he hissed.

"Listen I have, as I heard your threats."

"Then you understand you must obey what I tell you."

"Or you will beat me?" Terrwyn strained against his hand, turning her head so that only a portion of her face remained exposed to his neck. Her lips moved against the strong column of muscle as she spoke. "Nay, I think not. I do not recall asking you to direct my actions."

"Aye, one always wishes a thrashing to gain support." His voice crackled with dry humor.

"I had my position with the men well in hand."

James's hand rested over the crown of her head, dragging the cap down over the escaping tendrils. "Interesting choice of words, Terrwyn. You have no understanding of a man's hunger for a woman when he has been without for so long. For some, any woman will suffice."

"Hmph," she snorted. "Only a baseborn bastard would act on that urge."

"Foolish girl! When need awakens, it matters not on what side of the blanket he's born. A man of royalty or a man of the stews, both are able and willing to tip back the heels of an unsuspecting wench." He lowered his arms until her hip brushed against his own need. "Think you it requires skill to arouse a man? When the merest contact with your body sends me to ache for release?"

"Cur dog! You'll let me down or soon discover your need aching more than you counted on." Terrwyn kicked out her feet.

Arching her back against his arm, she bucked and squirmed until both she and James were left gasping for breath.

James set her down. Her arm held firmly to his side, he dragged her past a felled tree and stopped behind the foliage of a wild bramble. Light flickered through the ragged green leaves of the secluded glen. Ignoring her protests, he pressed his forehead to hers. His mouth remained dangerously close to those pearly white teeth. "What's wrong, little one? Do you worry that I cannot control my need? Or do you feel it as well?"

"Think you that I would throw myself at your feet?"

"If you've a mind to. Although I can think of better places for you than at my feet."

Her eyes widened, then narrowed. Her mouth opened and snapped shut. When she took in a deep breath, he knew she was preparing to rip apart the glen with a scream. He yanked her close to his chest, knocking the air from her lungs. He covered her mouth, his lips pressed to hers. Dodging her teeth, he explored the taste of sweet Terrwyn. Silken strands loosed from her braid wrapped around his wrists, entrapping him. The heat of her breasts ignited his skin.

His hold loosened and she moved closer. Their sudden battle shifted to a sultry dance as she met his steps. Flesh against flesh, hot and moist, matching his until she stole his breath.

James lifted his lips. Her rapid heartbeat, joined to his, began to slow as their heads cleared. Their contact broken, his body shivered from the loss.

"I tell you again. Set me loose, English."

As reality stripped away the fog from his brain, he realized he was standing in the glen, the luscious morsel still in his arms. He had the wild need to shake his head free from her spell. "Heed my warning. You've set yourself on a dangerous path. I'll help you return to your family. But I cannot protect you if you don't let me."

He planted a quick kiss to her lips, silencing her intention to have the final word. Smiling at her upturned face, he noted the flush that swept over her cheeks, the fullness of her mouth. The taste of her, like berries and cream, rested on his tongue. Her scent filled his head until he shook it clear.

The danger of their close proximity to the encampment clarified as the sound of camp dwellers ricocheted through the trees. "Speak your piece when we are out of sight and in the safety of my tent. Until then, you will listen to reason and keep yourself hidden."

"You surely do have a bossy way with you. I'd prefer it if you didn't meddle in my plans."

"That may be, but I won't release you until I have your promise you'll follow my orders."

She stiffened in response to his command and turned her face from him.

"I have never beaten a woman. Do not test me too far."

Terrwyn nodded slowly and pressed her lips to his neck. Her palm rested over his heart. Her fingers moved over his tunic, swirling little circles in the fabric. "Aye, I promise not to burden you with my troubles."

James took in a deep breath, wary of her willingness to give up the fight. He wondered if he was capable of reining in his body's betrayal. His plan to scare her off like a frightened rabbit had failed him. Somehow, she had outmaneuvered him.

He jammed her cap down further, tucking any loose tendrils under its edge. All the while questioning his sanity, he swept her up into his arms and began his march to what he feared would lead to his death. "Right, then," he murmured to the crown of her head, "off we go."

The thicket of bushes and brambles slowed his pace, but he did not stop until he reached the area the officers had claimed as their own. Someone had started a fire for the night. Smoke billowed in dark clouds from a damp piece of wood. The sound of metal ringing against metal punctured the constant murmur of male voices as they prepared for another meal under the stars.

James set Terrwyn down again. Jamming her face into his side, he wrapped his arm around her neck.

He tensed as Sir William stepped out from the doorway of his tent. The flap caught in the breeze, fluttered against the canvas wall. The commander would want to know where he had been, what took him off, away from the camp. As it was, he would be expected at some point to explain his reasoning for dragging a wounded soldier to his personal lodgings. Pretending he did not hear him call out, he strode past both Sir William and Simon's quarters without stopping to consider the curious heads that turned in his direction.

Terrwyn shifted so that she might see where they were. James cupped her head with his long fingers and mashed her face against into his ribcage. Under his breath, he ground out, "Stay where you are."

"Sir James," Sir William shouted. "What are you about? Come. Join me."

James hesitated, tempted by the errant thought of tossing the girl at William's feet and washing his hands of the trouble he could ill-afford. He was already dancing along a dangerous blade of half-truths for Henry. It would not please his king if he failed his mission because of a woman. However, now that he had her, she felt too good to let go.

He kept his distance from the commander and proclaimed as loudly as he dared, "First, I've a few stitches to ply to this soldier's wound. Then I must dole out the punishment to fit his crime."

William stroked his jaw. His eyes narrowed as he searched for meaning under James's words. He motioned James closer as he spoke. "You feel it necessary to carry this out by your hand alone? Certainly there are others more suited to this task."

"'Tis nothing more than trivial bickering among men."

William's silhouette filled the tent doorway. "Yet this trivial matter brings both injury and punishment. Why was I not informed earlier of this trouble?"

"'Twas only a small skirmish with Edgar Poole. A bit of a tussle over their place of rank is all. A few of the younger ones need a closer watch. Nothing more. Meant to speak with you regarding this matter as soon as I had him settled in my tent."

"I see." William eyed James thoughtfully. "Soldier's a bit small. Welsh archer?"

"Aye, so he says. However, I've seen his skill. If you wish to keep your carcass whole, keep him away from our weaponry. Best make him a knight's squire instead."

"Never heard tell of a Welshman who could not hit a target solid and true." William took in Terrwyn's dust-covered jerkin. "Not much there for even a squire. Think you he can manage army life? Has he the sense to obey an order or two?"

"He understands 'tis my duty to beat him if he does not."

"Ah, I see." William continued to frown. "You wish to take on the training of an injured squire? I do not see the need to have one. Not when a simple page will do."

"You and I both deserve some comfort. And 'tis fitting of our station to have either page or squire. Would it not be a joy to have your boots polished and waiting for you when you arise? In truth, as the king's chosen commander of this army, you should require both."

William's chin rose as if he sniffed the air searching for truth. Rocking back on his heels, he folded his arms and finally nodded. "Well then, so be it done. However, I shall refrain from drawing the extra weight of an unruly Welshman and let you deal with your own choice of squire."

James ignored the pinch he felt at his waist. Tilting his head just slightly, he could hear Terrwyn's muffled words. He responded to her appeal by giving her a none-too-gentle squeeze, ramming her nose further into his armpit. Barely able to contain his curiosity of her strange request, he kept his attention on William. "Though you say you have not the need, I must also report that there's another young whelp who already fancies himself as your page. I imagine his enthusiasm would serve you or your brother well. Goes by the name of Gilbert. Of course, if you feel your brother is incapable of training a page—"

The commander's stance stiffened, alert to the news of more trouble from his brother. "Where is Simon now?"

"Conducting the interview with Edgar Poole." James noticed William's demeanor relax as soon as he learned his young brother was not at fault. "A thorough soldier, indeed. 'Tis certain to be several hours before he has our answers."

"Then I will not detain you from your—meting out of punishment and care. I will send a runner as soon as we hear from young Simon. I assume you will want to attend the report as well." William paused a heartbeat and then added, "Perhaps at that time you will share with me the results of your latest absence."

"'Tis nothing more than documenting another wildflower for Henry." James let his gaze warm with enthusiasm and moved in closer. "I vow, I never entertained a thought that you would be interested in my findings of flora and fauna. As soon as I rid my person of this baggage, I shall regale you with my notes and drawings."

"Flora and fauna?" William smothered the pain that dashed across his visage. "Perhaps, if time allows. Please." He motioned James on. "Proceed with your task at hand."

Chapter Twelve

James smiled and waved good-naturedly at William. He marched on as if nothing were amiss. He kept his smile firmly in place until he reached the safety of the tent. Stepping into the darkness, he paused long enough to guard his face from his emotions.

His task was difficult. King Henry required crucial information to protect his throne. If William were determined to dog his every step, it would slow down what little progress he made. He could not fault the man. If he were in that position, he, too, would challenge his own trustworthiness. Indeed, he must ensure he did not attract more undue attention.

Once safe inside the gloomy darkness of his tent, he slowly released the disturbing young woman from his side. The tension in her muscles leapt under his touch. The ruse of her sweet nature had turned to vinegar with the closing of the tent.

He clasped her shoulders and held her in place. "Well? Never tell me you have nothing to say."

Terrwyn lifted her stormy gaze. Her anger filled the small tent. "Oh, aye, 'tis much to be said. But I'll not waste words on a lying hound."

"Lying hound?" James asked. "And what cause have you to name me thus when I just saved your hide from Sir William's ire? Do you think to placate him with your pretty ways and make him forget you're a woman? Though his need for archers is great, do you think he will believe your greatest wish is to march on France and kill the enemy? You, the daughter of a fallen Welsh lord?"

Terrwyn jerked her shoulders out from under his grasp and glowered in silent response.

"My little dove, I admire your skill and misplaced bravery. I do."

"You'll do well to remember that I am not your dove." Her hand strayed to the little dagger she kept at her waist.

How he managed to miss it while he carried her, he did not know. Thoughts of smooth skin and the fullness of her breasts had overshadowed the possibility that his little dove had talons for claws. He tamped down his growing irritation. "Terrwyn, you are no match against a man like Sir William. There would be no end to danger if you remain with the king's army. It would break my heart to see you harmed."

"You expect me to believe you hold a tender place in your heart for me? Didn't the promise of burning my village come from your own mouth?" Resentment dripped off her voice. "You cannot expect me to trust you when all about me is proof that you are a stranger to speaking the truth."

James found his position oddly uncomfortable and strangely unfamiliar. Never had his honesty been boldly discounted. At least not to his face. Nor in close proximity. Anyone else and he would have run his blade through the knave's gullet at first opportunity.

Stepping forward, he narrowed the space Terrwyn had placed between them. "Have you considered what will happen if you are discovered?"

"Simon treats me with respect."

James shook his head. "Young Simon serves one master. Forced to choose, he will choose Sir William." He tentatively touched her hair, much like he would a wary mare. "I dare not describe their ill-treatment. You've had but a brief taste of it from Edgar." His satisfaction welling, James noted Terrwyn did not move from his hand. "I offer you my protection. Stay here, where I will keep you safe from those who do not have your best interest in mind."

The back of her head cradled in his palm, he drew her close. He could not help noticing the way her eyes glittered in the shadows. Senses heightened, he smelled her delightfully female scent, her essence more striking than he recalled. Never had she been more beautiful. Passion for life flowed through her. The memory of her grace had called to him in his dreams, and here she stood.

Despite all the warnings in his head, this time he could not let her turn away. He wished to taste the crest of her ear, the nape of her neck, the smoothness of her skin. He needed to run his hands over every portion of her body, memorizing for the days and nights when he had no one, nothing but his sketchpad and his thoughts.

Pulling her to his chest, he brushed his lips over her own. He pressed the small of her rigid back, nudging her closer to his need. His teeth slid against her throat, the scorched path soothed by the trail of his tongue. She tasted of salt and sweet nectar.

Her mouth remained sealed and once more he urged her to open under his touch. Hearing her breath catch, he swore he felt her quiver as he played her as carefully as he would a fine instrument. Emboldened, he found her hand and pressed her fingers around his burgeoning flesh.

James smiled against her lips. Soon he would weave his way into her deep valley and find release from this woman's unwelcome distractions. "Spread your wings, little bird. Soar with me," he whispered into the satiny flesh of her nape.

Groaning softly, Terrwyn shuddered and hastily pulled away.

The warnings in his head ignored, he stalled her efforts with a gentle caress. His attention lost on all but the coaxing of yet another sweet response from Terrwyn, James drew her back into his arms. He left a well-placed kiss upon her lips. Encouraged by the awakening of her body, he delved deeply yet again.

James jerked. Incredulous, he held her at arms length and wiped the nick on the edge of his mouth. "You bit me! Hell's bones, woman, what manner of threat is this?"

Her smile flashed in the darkness. "Dare press me further, Sir James, and you'll find my teeth in you again."

He slid his gaze over her elfin face, the defiant set to her chin. His lips twitched slightly. Drawing her to his chest, he felt the beat of her heart racing to the same rhythm as his own.

"Tread carefully or I will mete out your punishment as I told Sir William."

"I have no fear of your threats."

"I would have never thought you dense, little one. Why would you think my words are empty?"

"You won't set a hand of violence against a woman. You stated so yourself."

James shook his head despite the faint hint of guilt nipping at his conscience. "Nay, you miss my warning. I have no intention of harming you." Seeing the look of triumph warm her cheeks, he quickly forestalled her with, "Yet, if I must, I shall apply whatever means your cooperation requires."

Terrwyn's heated stare scraped over his face before the small hint of a smile lifted the corners of her mouth. "You shall surely be taken to the faeries to live for eternity for the lies you tell."

James growled, yanking her close. "I warn you. I shall not be alone in the land of the faeries."

"Nay?"

James shook his head and flicked the tip of Terrwyn's nose, enjoying the glare that quickly followed. "For you, my dear, will be there by my side."

"Hmph!" Terrwyn snorted, pulling her arm free from his grasp. "I told you before. I do not consort with those who know not the difference between truth and a lie. You would not recognize it, even if it jumped up, sat atop your head and crowed."

His attention drawn to the commotion outside, he held his hand up in response. "Silence, imp. There are certain bits of knowledge that are better left known only to a handful."

"Such as?"

James sighed as if humoring a petulant child. "Such as, it would be best if we agree to keep your identity secret for as long as we are able."

"Obviously."

"This is why you are my newly obtained squire of the body."

Terrwyn looked like she was about choke on the words before she spat them out. "Your squire." She rolled her eyes heavenward before pinning him with a snarl. "Leave it to the English knight to ferret out a servant for his every whim. I won't wash your lily white backside."

The world outside their tent forgotten, James eyed Terrwyn from head to toe. He let his gaze caress the curves he knew remained hidden under the travel-stained jerkin. He watched until a flush pinked her cheeks and tiny rosebuds formed where her chest rose and fell. Satisfied he held her attention, he said, "Although I see a few advantages to this situation, I will remind you that this is temporary. In truth, an untrained squire in my service hangs on my being like a mace ball. The hazard will most assuredly outweigh any benefit."

Terrwyn shook with indignation. "Liar! You say you cannot abide my presence, yet your lips tell a different tale."

"Then we both fabricate the untruth. As your lips lie as well as my own. You do not leave the safety of your home to fight for the English. A wise man such as I asks why you are here." He ran the ridge of his thumb over her mouth. "Ah, such lovely, beautiful lips."

Drawing her in, he gently, carefully, slid his arm around her back. Folding her close, he lightly trailed kisses from the tip of her chin to the lobe of her ear. He scraped his teeth across the tender flesh.

He felt Terrwyn's outrage wane as she entwined her hands in his hair. She shivered when cool air touched where his lips had been. Her breasts pebbled. A soft moan bubbled. Lost to his ministrations, she loosened her hold on the shield of anger.

James was caught up in a storm of his own making. Lightning moved swiftly through his veins, striking the center of his being. He lifted his head. His attention caught on the exquisite expression on her face. Her lips upturned, her eyes glistening, she shimmered with a light he had never seen before. A dash of wonder caught at his heart. If not for the fact that both English father and Welsh mother had raised him, he would have surely thought they had been transported to the other world where time stood still. There, under the earth with the faeries, they would stay until their lovemaking brought them to their grave. *Oh, but to die with ecstasy resting on your lips, like dew on the morn.*

Terrwyn's chuckle reverberated under his lips.

"What brings you laughter, little bird?" He swallowed, surprised at the gruffness in his voice. He brought his mouth near the hard pebble of her breast.

Terrwyn boldly gripped his head, gasping when his teeth made contact. "You have a smooth way with your tales. Tell me, Sir Knight. What shall you say when Sir William asks to see those lovely drawings of flora and fauna? Will you produce a packet of lines scratched out on parchment or have you another line to feed the commander?"

"Ah," he breathed against her flesh. "Your lack of belief in my skill pains me to the quick. I'll have you know 'tis said that I have a gift handed down from God."

Terrwyn shivered as his fingers moved over her body. A waterfall of sensation filled every nerve ending. Searching to satisfy a need she never knew she hungered for, she reached out and pulled him closer. "I won't argue you have a gift, but I do not think it is the kind that Sir William will want to examine too close."

"Trust me," he whispered over the crest of her breast.

Aching to gain access, James nuzzled the neckline of her jerkin. Entranced with the feel of her fingers as she slid them along the band of his leggings, he could not immediately answer her question. Focused on breaching her portal, he did not hear the soft rustle of tent flap. Nor did he hear the clump of feet behind him.

"I brought this for the archer." Simon held out Terrwyn's bow and quiver. "If all goes well, he'll pin you back with an arrow or two."

James slowly extracted Terrwyn's arms from around his waist, moving effortlessly until she was ensconced behind his back. "I'll take it."

Simon ignored his hand and set the weapons down. He drew a dagger from its scabbard. "You'll find 'tis best that you unhand the archer."

"I fear you have it wrong, 'tis not an archer but my squire I embrace." He turned to Terrwyn and shook his head with a warning. "Nay, squire, say not a word."

With ire flushing his face, Simon moved forward. "When my brother hears how you handle the king's archers and your intimate servants, he will have a say against the matter."

James paused. The affable smile slid into place, belying the coldness in his tone and the edge in his eyes. "Oh, 'tis certain Sir William will not be pleased, but why bother him with trivial matters when he already has so much on his plate? What say you?" He clapped a hand on Simon's forearm. "Shall we leave sleeping dogs to lie where they may?"

His frown deepening, Simon shook free. "Sir William requests your presence." Apparently feeling the need to enforce this request, he pointed the tip of his blade at James's chest. "Now!"

James slowly extricated himself from Terrwyn and bowed stiffly. "Squire, it appears our large friend has lost patience with us." Mindful to keep his movements slow, he motioned toward the corner of the tent. "Hand me that journal and oilcloth packet lying on the bench."

Terrwyn scurried over to do James's bidding and held out the packet.

Noting the worry that marked her eyes, James slid his thumb over the ridge along her jawline. "Not to fear. I'll return before you notice I'm gone."

"I wouldn't waste your worries on him, Archer," Simon warned. "Nor would I trust him with my life. Once England's good soldiers do their duty, he'll spill what he knows. Like he was a stuck boar."

"Do not fret, little one. William has no need to cause me harm." James winked at Simon. "Nor, despite what your champion believes, will I reveal you to save my hide."

A rosy hue darkened Simon's high cheekbones as he shook his head. "Think, Archer, if he means you no ill will, then why make you his squire? You were holding your own. I would have made sure of it." He poked James with the tip of his blade, directing him out of the tent. "And if he's a traitor to the king, you won't want your name attached to his."

Terrwyn's eyes narrowed. Glancing at Simon, she stepped cautiously around the tip of his blade. She reached out, flipped back the oilcloth and revealed bits of charcoal. Reverently, she took the journal from his hands and opened it. Her breath caught and she paled. Pulling out the second and third sheet, she held them so that Simon could see the shape of bluebells and a field of wildflowers.

Her hands trembled as she folded everything back up. Her dark lashes flicked rapidly over her nut-brown eyes. Drawn to the pulse beating along the smooth column of her neck, James nearly forgot to take the drawings from her hand.

Terrwyn turned to Simon and, giving him a generous smile, she nodded toward James. "I believe I'll bide my time here for a while longer."

Simon shifted his attention from Terrwyn. His face reddening, he took his time as he struggled with the rest of his message. "'Fraid that won't do. You're to come along too."

"Me?" Terrwyn exclaimed.

James quietly slid the oilcloth packet inside the fold of his tunic. He turned with a pleasant smile and shook his head. "I'm certain Simon misheard. Sir William has no pressing reason to see you in his chambers."

Terrwyn glanced up to read the truth on Simon's face. "What has taken place to put me in William's notice?" she asked softly.

"He heard things. About the fight."

Terrwyn's eyes widened with clarity. "You vowed you were my champion, you would not reveal me."

"Aye, I am still. And I have not."

James's palm slammed against Simon's chest. "Yet you deliver her to your brother when the least wind blows."

Simon stepped back, righting his balance before he fell. "Nay!" He turned to grab Terrwyn, catching only air as she moved lithely out of his reach. He held his hand still, fingers spread in supplication. "'Tis not what it looks."

She shook her head in dismay. "It does not look well, though, does it?"

James pressed forward. "We'll tell your brother I was overtaken, the soldier ran off before I could apply punishment. That his hide is nowhere to be found."

Although Simon outweighed James, he shrank from the

deception. "It won't do. William heard of the competition in the forest."

"The famed archer?" James turned to Terrwyn. "You?"

Terrwyn smiled helplessly as Simon explained the events. She cast a furtive glance at James and caught his pointed glare.

"You knew she was a maiden? Did the dysentery touch your brain as well as your innards?"

"Leave him be, James. 'Twas an honest challenge. If not for Edgar's wounded pride, no one would have taken notice."

"Aye, perhaps. But now William has." James stroked his knuckle down Terrwyn's cheek. "Well, then, if he asks, I will say I found you lacking and sent you away."

Simon returned his blade into the scabbard and folded his arms. "Nay. William would wonder why you would jeopardize his relationship with the king."

"I jeopardize no one."

"Aye. Nevertheless, word of our archer will reach King Henry and he will await his delivery. Should the archer disappear—"

"—the king will exact payment on all our heads," James finished.

"And retaliation against my village would be deadly." Resolved in her decision, Terrwyn smoothed the leather tunic over her hips. "There is no choice but to play out this role I have begun."

James leaned over, smoothing the hair from her face. He carefully tucked the strands behind her ear. "And when Sir William discovers that you are a woman?"

She smiled up into James's worried eyes and could not help thinking, if only fleetingly, that they were the exact shade of the sky right after a storm. Finding comfort in his gaze, she found her courage. "Then he will accept me as I am, or our deception is over."

"And there will be hell to pay for all of us," Simon said.

"'Tis sorry, that I am, Simon, for making trouble between you and your brother."

Simon shrugged good-naturedly. "He will forgive me in time."

"Let us pray it will not come to that," James said. "If we play our roles well, we will find a way to remove Terrwyn from this mess and keep both the king and your brother content."

Terrwyn grabbed James's hand, tugging as she spoke. "Do you have something in mind?"

James winked up at Simon.

The big man grunted his own response. "Would say your agreement to not stand so close to one another might be the first order of the day."

"Of course," Terrwyn muttered hotly under her breath. "Makes perfect sense."

Simon moved to duck under the flap, sticking his head through the opening before he left. "Well, Archer, you had best equip yourself well. 'Tis certain my brother grows restless." He added as if an afterthought, "Sir James, whatever games you play, do no harm to king or country, for it would be my pleasure to run you through."

James smiled and nodded. "Aye, just you remember to honor your own vows."

Terrwyn held her palm up. "Stop, there is no need. I won't come between brothers. When you feel you cannot hide my secret any longer and must reveal me, know that I will release you from your vow."

Simon's face flushed red. "I pray it does not come to that."

"So do I," Terrwyn said.

James wrapped her fingers around his and pressed his lips to the inside of her wrist. "We dare not tarry." He plied another kiss to the back of her hand and drew her near. "Frightened?"

Biting her lip, she gently drew her hand away. "Terrified."

James kissed the corner of her mouth. "Good."

Chapter Thirteen

"You're to come with me." Thin of body and stern of face, the young soldier standing at the tent entrance motioned for James and Terrwyn to follow.

James turned to Terrwyn and, giving her a steady smile, pulled the small blade from her belt. "I think we had best put this away."

"But I've already agreed to leave my bow behind."

"A lowly squire cannot come armed to the hilt. 'Twould certainly raise Sir William's brow."

Terrwyn glanced at the soldier. His impatience became evident in the increase of his frown.

"Come, squire," James said loudly. "I have the surprising desire to have my back scrubbed yet this eve. Let us meet with Sir William and be done with it."

They stepped out of the tent and were immediately flanked by guards. Terrwyn stood close behind James, noting the slight pause in his step. It took everything in her power to keep from striking out when pikestaffs halted their pace. Her feet danced over the dust as she scrambled to keep from running into James.

"Get that damned thing out of my face," he said.

"You will stay with us." The guard grabbed the back of Terrwyn's neck, causing her to yelp in surprise.

"Hands off," James barked, breaking the soldier's grasp. He drew Terrwyn close, and smoothed the jerkin over her shoulder. The tension in his body belied his pleasant tone as he added, "Though I admire your enthusiasm, soldier, I am under King

Henry's protection. I advise you to use wisdom before I deliver
my report to my protector."

Two bright spots rose over the whey-faced lad. "Orders is
orders. Commander says to bring you and bring you now."

"Well enough, soldier. But you will do so with respect for
rank." James walked forward, purposefully ignoring the men
flanking his sides.

ca⁊ɔ

Terrwyn tucked her chin into the folds of her tunic and sat
quietly in the corner of the tent. Feeling the absence of her bow
and quiver, she cursed the need to leave them behind.
Unarmed, she felt as helpless as a babe in swaddling. Should
her situation deteriorate, she would be forced to rely on the
shiftless Englishman. As far as she was concerned, James may
have warmed her heart a time or two, but an Englishman he
remained.

Her stomach clenched. The shadows of the two soldiers
guarding their meeting could be seen through the thick canvas
material.

Ducking her head as if to inspect crusted dirt on her
leggings, she looked up through her lashes at the men seated at
the small camp table. James and Sir William had taken great
pains to angle their chairs so that neither back was to the
opening in the tent, nor pressed against the outer wall. James
had slyly worked his seat so that he might catch her attention
now and then.

With the slightest hint of a smile, James lightened the
grave expression on his face before turning to William. "You'll
excuse me if I feel a trifle irritated with your treatment at my
expense." He motioned toward the corner with the flip of his
hand. "As you have already made mention of the presence of my
newly acquired squire, I find it necessary to beg your
forgiveness and a little latitude in normalcy."

"I did not ask to see a squire. I ordered you to bring the
archer."

"But I haven't a notion where the famed archer has hidden
himself. 'Tis certain you can see that this boy is smaller than a

turd. He cannot possibly be the archer. No muscle at all."

William swiveled to eye Terrwyn from head to toe. His impatience soured his expression, heating his eyes to dark coals, drawing his mouth into a thin, firm line. "I've heard from Simon that you've meted out the boy's punishment already." Having assured himself the contentious lad had all his limbs intact, William returned his gaze back to James. "In a rush to punish, aren't you?"

"Is this truly what this inconvenience is about? Your concern for the boy? Perhaps you want him for your own? But I warn you, 'tis like being saddled with a mongrel puppy. 'Fraid I cannot let the wretch out of my sight until 'tis fit for those of us of refined taste." James sighed deeply, pausing to let the effects dig into William's tight control. "One never knows when the Welsh puppy will relieve itself."

Terrwyn's fury bubbled. If not for the slight wink, that infinitesimal movement of the corner of his dark lashes, she might have launched herself at his throat.

"I care not of your damnable puppy!" William's shoulders flexed irritably. "While you find it necessary to cast your attention to the infractions you believe your squire has committed, an archer of great import cannot be found! What will you report to King Henry when he asks the whereabouts of the famed archer?" William's control began to slip and his voice rose in agitation. "Shall you entertain him with your drawings of flora and fauna as we mount an attack on France?"

"I should say not." Amusement laced his next words. "Imagine Henry standing up in his stirrups, giving one of his rousing speeches to the men, and I shove a piece of vellum under his nose. I fear 'tis certain he'd lose sight of the details I worked so hard to give him."

William rose and braced his palms on the narrow table. "What spell have you cast on our king for him to think you bring more than embarrassment to his throne?"

The silence that followed crackled with tension.

James lifted a single brow in disdain. "You'd do well to remember my conversations with the king are of little concern to you. My orders come from Henry. I move as his schedule demands. Not yours." He slowly released his hold on the hilt of his sword. He leaned forward and motioned the commander toward the abandoned chair. Icy steel coated his voice. "Sit, William. Anger solves nothing. We will talk only of things which I have been granted ease by our king."

Terrwyn noticed the tension, though still present, became less pronounced in William's body. He listened with rapt attention to the words James spoke so softly. Only after William acquiesced to a bargain did James bring out his drawings. One by one the drawings were exposed until the final sheet of vellum lay upon the table.

William's hand trembled as he ran it through his blond hair. "Wha—where... How did you come by this image of the woman?"

"Tavern meeting."

"The people with her?"

"There are some who cannot live between Welsh and English worlds. Some accept change and others choose to fight. I believe this one simply chose to run away."

Tempted to forget James's warning, Terrwyn shifted her seat, cursing her inability to hear and understand all of their discussion.

William turned abruptly and tossed her a key. "You there, boy, fetch us the wine from the trunk."

Pulling down the brim of her cap, Terrwyn nodded obediently and walked to where he pointed. The lock snicked open with ease but when she attempted to lift the trunk's lid she found it to be extremely heavy. It took her three tries to gain access to the contents.

"God's bones," Sir William said. "The brat is weak as a kitten. You can keep him without argument from me."

Terrwyn swallowed a curse and refused to listen to James's response. She braced the lid to keep it from crashing down and turned her body to block the men's view as she examined the trunk's contents. The jug of wine nested among his possessions. A leather-bound journal lay atop a neatly folded woolen blanket. A small iron-studded box angled crookedly in the corner of the chest. Quietly nudging it aside, she spied iron arrowhead tips rolled in a strip of soft leather. Their willow shafts gleamed in the candlelight. Although tempted to touch the smooth wood, she realized she had stared at the contents for far too long.

Hurriedly pulling the wine from the chest, she slowly let the lid fall into place and slipped the lock over the latch. She cast a prayer to the heavens and hoped no one noticed she did not close the lock completely.

Grasping the jug of wine, she picked up two cups and set them on the table. Mindful to keep her face hidden, she moved so that whenever William moved, so did she. She felt James's questioning glance slide over her, which she dutifully ignored.

After filling the cups, she placed them by their hands and set the jug in the center of the table. Waiting for permission to sit, she took a half step back and stood near James's left elbow. She could not help noticing that when she drew too close to the drawings, his hands moved protectively over them. Her curiosity piqued, she set about devising a plan to look at those drawings more closely.

Sighing wistfully, William saluted James with his cup. "Looks like your puppy's a quick study."

James tilted his head. One eyebrow arched as he let his gaze move over Terrwyn's flushed face. "So it seems. Though his wound is slight, it will not do to overtax him so soon." He motioned to the corner stool. "You, boy, may take your seat until my say."

As James began to gather up his leather pouch, William gripped his wrist and motioned toward the drawing. "Must you put it away already?"

James hesitated. One corner of the leather square remained unfolded. His fingers flexed and curled before pulling the parchment out. "Protect it well."

William's surprise welled in the shadows of his eyes. With a tentative fingertip, he dragged the parchment closer. "Many thanks."

Terrwyn stepped up to the table to replenish their mugs. The edge of a lady's slender neck and bare shoulder peeked out from under Sir William's sleeve. Although the maiden was quite pretty, she saw no other reason for the fuss.

Sir William's weight shifted as he held out his mug for more wine, allowing Terrwyn a thorough look at the pretty maiden's ringlets and soft cheekbones. The maiden was strikingly familiar. Terrwyn stepped back and sat on the three-legged stool. She could not shake the feeling she knew this woman and began to sort through the faces of all whom she ever met.

The men's brief camaraderie was lost the moment the tent flap rustled. William folded the parchment and placed it inside his tunic as Simon pushed his way through the entrance. James sat quietly, his good-natured smile plastered in place.

Simon shoved the hair from his eyes. He cast a fleeting look around the tent, purposefully looking past the little corner where Terrwyn sat.

"Come." William motioned to the empty wooden bench beside the table. "What news have you to share?"

Eyeing the spot, Simon shook his head and took off his hat. "I'll not stay long."

Terrwyn half-listened to Simon drone on with his report until he finally got around to the telling of the disappearance of Edgar Poole.

William's voice rose. "How is it you misplaced the best longbowman in this army? Poole was your friend, was he not?"

"His pride was wounded," Simon said.

"God's Mercy! He attacked Cook and some of the others. He should be in irons."

"He cannot be far," James said. "The man sustained an injury."

"By the archer, who, I might add," William said, "is missing as well."

James wearily kneaded the back of his neck. "Reluctant as I am to admit it, perhaps 'tis for the best to lose the both of them before we land on France's soil."

"Aye." William nodded. "Their mettle has been tested and is found wanting. Yet I cannot allow Poole's absence to go without retribution. He signed on as one of Henry's men and his absence can only be reported as desertion. As for the archer, well, we'll see how much his freedom means to him when he has no village to return to." He pointed at James. "The archer is

115

yours to find again. Best see to it before we travel much farther."

"Not to worry, William. I'll replace him with two equally skilled archers if I have to."

"And you, Simon, must find Poole," William said. "Help him reconsider before he puts his bow and arrow for ill gain."

"Takes a big man to have your skill tested and found lacking in front of your friends and foes alike," James observed. "Use caution when you confront your friend, Simon. I'll wager he'll be as angry as a wild boar."

"Worse," Simon muttered morosely. "He was heard threatening to kill the archer and any who got in his way."

With her thoughts deep in making a plan to retreat to her village and prepare them for an attack from the English army, she did not hear the growing commotion outside Sir William's tent until little Gilbert pushed his way under the soldier's arms.

Another man popped his head in, one hand filled with a horse's reins, the other with his sword. "Here now," he yelped as the horse attached to the reins jerked his arm, nearly dragging him back outside. "I do not have the skill to handle them two horses by myself."

The impatient boy marched up to William, stopping at his feet. "Do you be Commander of King Henry's army?"

William nodded warily. "I am."

A smile flickered in James's eyes as he lifted a finger to his lips and motioned for Terrwyn to remain silent. "Sir William. This is young Gilbert." He placed a gentle hand on the slim shoulder. "I spoke to you regarding his filling the position of page."

"Aye," Gilbert said, "but only if I can care for your horse, too."

William looked Gilbert up and down, doubt filling his gaze. "I see."

"Begging your pardon, Sir William, but you'll have no regrets. I'm the best horseman in Wales, is what I am."

"Aye? Let's see how well you acquit yourself with the duties of a page before I trust you with my horseflesh."

Gilbert nodded and, tilting his head, he motioned to James.

"You shouldn't treat Zeus like you have. The stallion deserves to be fed and brushed down when you're through with him."

Stunned, James removed his hand as if Gilbert had poisonous fangs. "Zeus?" Dark guilt flashed over his face. "You handled Zeus? Alone?"

"Aye," Gilbert said. "Given the proper consideration, he'd be a happier stallion."

William chuckled. "And how do you come by your great knowledge of horseflesh?"

"My mother comes from horse people. She taught me what I know. That way I'd be of use to my English father when I find him."

"And where are your mother and father now?"

Gilbert's frown deepened. "My mother passed during the cold months. Don't know about my father. Last she spoke of him, she had cursed herself for taking me away."

William's gaze pored over the child's fair face as if searching for something he lost long ago.

Gilbert asked irritably, "Do you not want to know the troubles that are in your camp?"

"Hm? And what bits of information do you suppose you will provide that my brother Simon did not?"

Gilbert eyed the other people in the little tent as if noticing them for the first time. "Cook is surgeon, see. And since Cook needs stitching where Poole cut him, someone else has got to do it. 'Sides, he needs help with feeding the men." Long pale lashes blinked away the tears. "His pain's real bad and his head is blistering hot."

"I'll do it." Terrwyn rose from the stool and left her corner. "I've the skill with needle."

James moved to block her path. "That won't do, squire. You're needed elsewhere."

Sir William's frown deepened. "I believe my orders outrank yours. And I say your squire must attend Cook's wounds."

Worry faded from Gilbert's face. "Aye! If Archer's sewing skill is as fine as his aim, Cook will be good as new in no time at all."

With the men struck confounded and speechless, Terrwyn

grabbed Gilbert and dashed out of the tent. Half-expecting an arrow in her back, she cringed as angry voices trailed after her.

Saints' bones, 'tis certain we're in the shite bucket now. There would be little time before Sir William of Norwich cast her out of the camp and sent her home. Her stomach clenched. She dared not think what they would have to say when they discovered she refused to go anywhere unless it brought her closer to her brother.

A shiver ran over her arms. The last time she depended upon her healing skill had ended with the loss of Mam.

Chapter Fourteen

"The archer?" William's face reddened. "You knew it was him and you let him run out?" He shouted for his men to come to aid. A few of the soldiers standing nearby rushed to the entrance of the tent.

"Hold!" James lunged and caught the sleeve of Sir William's heavy leather jerkin. In the uproar, Simon swung at James. James dodged Simon's blow, pulling William in line with Simon's fist.

The commander hit the floor.

The stunned silence that followed gave James time to catch his breath. He turned, striking an order for the men to return to their regular duties.

"Sir—" one of the men began.

William looked up from where he sat. The slight stain of blood trickled from his nose. "Go."

"God's blessed bones, William," Simon said. "You walked into it."

"Silence, brother."

James bent over and held out his hand. Their grasp firm, James pulled William up and led him to the up-righted bench.

William settled gently on the wooden seat. He tested his nose again with his fingers.

Simon cleared his throat. His Adam's apple jumped in a nervous tick. "William—"

James glanced up at Simon and smiled. "'Tis certain your brother holds no grudge. Do you, William?" He drew up a stool and sat across from him. "An innocent mistake. Your eyes told you one thing and your body found another. We all know the blow was meant for me. I should be insulted but will hold my temper in check."

William grunted.

Encouraged that he had William's ear, James continued, "'Tis painfully clear that young Gilbert's eyesight is lacking. That is not the famed archer. I say, let my squire work on Cook while you give it consideration."

"Simon." William's voice was nasal and muffled from the hand he cupped over the bridge of his nose. He glared over his knuckles. "I trust you know if this is the same archer that bested you in a target match."

Simon shifted uncomfortably. "I'd have to look at him again. To be certain." His flushed cheeks deepened to a rosy hue. "I find the Welsh tend to look a great deal alike."

"Then I shall be about finding my squire," James said. "I swear, he best be at Cook's tent. Or I shall beat him soundly."

"Aye." William nodded. "Best look closely at him. And when you question Gilbert you'll not use force. He's but a child."

James snorted as if the idea was too coddling for his own good.

Lost in thought, William leaned over his folded arms resting on the table. He touched his chest where earlier he had hidden James's drawing inside the folds of his jerkin. He dismissed the two men with an absent-minded wave but stopped James at the doorway. "Simon will go with you and have another look."

08⊱0

James and Simon paused outside Cook's tent and squared off. James lifted his chin as if daring Simon one more time. He waited, then, nodding at him, quietly lifted the doorway flap. The stench of sweat assaulted him as he stepped inside. Well-traveled and coated with years of dust and dirt, the oiled canvas held against the evening chill and kept the heat within.

He paused a moment before making his presence known to the three in Cook's small tent. Terrwyn and the child moved as one. Trust warmed the space between them.

The need to see his own family bloomed in his heart. How long had it been since he had seen his mother's lovely face? Memories of her laughter filled him with longing. Perhaps, when he was through with this latest task for Henry, he might send word home. It would be good to see them before he sailed for France.

"Saints above and devils below." Terrwyn bent over Cook and hissed a warning. "Hold your body still. I promise not to hurt you."

"Well, how's a man to trust the likes of you?" Cook said. "I don't know one blitherin' Welshman from another."

"As far as I can see, old man, I'm the only one standing here with needle and thread. And the only one offering to pull your wrinkled hide together." She waited patiently before adding, "Though my sewing skill is a mite rusty, I believe I'm up to the task."

Concern for the care of his own hide continued to mar his face.

She patted his uninjured shoulder as she bent low to speak softly in his ear. "Not to fear. I've enough skill to put you right."

She returned to his wound. The needle trembled in her hand as she began her work. It took several stitches to seal the edges of his flesh. With studied care, she made the final jab, pulled the thread taut and cut it at the knot. Ignoring his renewed complaints, she placed a steaming poultice across his shoulder and rose from the bench.

Gilbert stood at Cook's head. Worry darkened his cherubic face. His fingers found the coil of hair and twirled it absently. "Think you he'll be all right?"

Terrwyn smoothed Gilbert's tawny head. "Aye. He'll be right as rain. Back to ordering everyone within sight to do his bidding."

"'Twas said the same of my mother," Gilbert said. "Though the surgeons tried, they couldn't fix her up."

"Not to worry, young Gilbert," James said. "Once Archer sets his mind to it, fate bends its knee to his will."

"'Tis true?" Gilbert whispered in awe.

Terrwyn glanced up. Her smile, warm and welcoming,

broke through the heaviness that had settled on James's heart. Her eyebrows arched as her smile fell into a worried frown. Nodding in Gilbert's direction, she gathered the bandages and thread, wrapped the bone needle in the leather pouch and placed it on the table. Murmuring a word in Cook's ear, she punctuated the message with a pat to his balding pate.

For the first time, James noticed the tension in his muscles. Only after she moved in his direction did he let loose the breath caught in his chest. Holding out his hand, he felt the jolt of lightning when she touched his skin. He heard her tiny gasp of surprise and knew she felt it too. He drew her out of Cook's sight and into the darkened corner.

"Gilbert meant no harm and feels mightily sore of heart for it," Terrwyn whispered.

"I'm surprised you haven't been exposed before this." He trapped her hand with his. "'Tis time you turned from this farce." Before she could pull away, he tightened his grip. Resolved to make her understand the danger of their situation, he entwined his fingers around hers.

Terrwyn eyed him with a weary look. "Why do you refuse to understand that it is impossible for me to do so?"

"Help me understand."

"You won't change my mind." She drew back her shoulders and lifted her chin in defiance. Wispy tendrils of hair fluttered against her cheek. She tucked them back as she continued as if her plans had not altered, "The poultice will need changing every few hours for the next couple of days. You'll find that Cook will survive Edgar's attack."

"Your skill with needle and thread will not prove strong enough to withstand Edgar, should he decide to return and finish the task."

"Aye, but surely they will set a guard by Cook until he can defend himself."

"Nay. Their focus will be on finding the archer. As will Edgar's."

"William believed Gilbert? I held hope that he thought it no more than a child's silly imagination."

"Perhaps I should have added that I've persuaded William

in believing there is no possible way for you to have the skill." He tightened his grip as he added, "Yet, that will not be easy to support unless you cooperate." Seeing the question in her eye, he answered. "There'll be no more competitions for you, nor will you draw attention to your stay here."

"I didn't draw attention to myself on purpose. Events happen whether I give my leave or not. What would you have me do? Hide under your cloak until we reach England's port?"

"If necessary."

"What is necessary is seeing that Cook's work is tended until he is able to handle the weight of it."

"The king's men are a hardy lot. Even now, Simon is enlisting the help of few able-bodied men and one of the women who follow our camp. Since the commander is interested in having him as his personal page, Gilbert can practice his bathing techniques on Cook."

Terrwyn glanced at Cook, caught his eye and quickly shook her head no. She returned her attention to James. "I've had a change of mind. The boy cannot possibly tend to Sir William's personal needs."

"Why ever not?"

"I—I've discovered certain qualities that wouldn't make it fitting for—the lad." Terrwyn grabbed James's arm, clutching his sleeve. "Please. Mayhap my care will ease Sir William's ire and he won't be so quick to toss me out."

"Enough. The boy is bound to find a more comfortable pallet if he is serving under Sir William."

"Some things are more important than where to rest your head."

"Ah, but see, there you are wrong. By the time I return you to your home, you'll be wishing for a soft bed."

"I'd rather be chained to a post with the sea up to my earlobes than listen to you tell me one more time that you're taking me home."

James skimmed the crest of her cheek with the pad of his thumb. Thoughts of her lying on his pallet, awaiting his return, assailed his mind. Would it really be so hard to keep her by his side for a little while longer? Holy Saints, how he would love to sketch her form. His fingers itched to engrave her image upon a canvas.

"Then it is agreed," Terrwyn continued.

James blinked, dragging his thoughts from the treasures hidden under her tunic. "Agreed?"

Terrwyn spun out of reach and ducked under the tent flap. "Aye, I'll see to the commander's needs and then return within the hour to change Cook's dressing."

"Wait!" So confused were his thoughts, he wondered if she'd spun a spell of magic over him. "You're not to leave without escort."

She turned, shushing him with a finger to her lips, and mouthed the words he had used earlier. "Do not draw attention to yourself."

James scrubbed his face with his hands. It was only after he shook free from her spell that he realized that Gilbert, too, had managed to slip out while he tangled with Terrwyn.

Dropping to the stool beside the old man's cot, James flinched when Cook grabbed his wrist.

The old soldier bore into him with one watery eye, the gray bushy eyebrow amplifying his glare. "Don't see it, do ya?"

"See what?"

"Let Archer do what she can."

James looked over at Cook. "The commander won't like it when he learns Archer is indeed a maiden."

"Aye, but would it not increase Sir William's discomfort to learn he has *two* females smuggled into his command?"

CRART

Sir William had galloped out on his white stallion just as Terrwyn arrived at the edge of the officers' compound. Several of his mounted soldiers trailed after him. Had they found Edgar? Or did they search for the archer?

She wondered why James had not been called to ride along with them. Yet, the longer she stayed in the camp, the better she understood that James was a man unto his own self. He answered only to King Henry. And this, she began to see, ate at

Sir William as if he were the bone to a hungry hound.

A thunder of hooves raced toward the camp. Wooden stirrups beat against the beast's sides as the rider-less horse blindly tore past surprised onlookers. A few brave souls made a half-hearted grab for the loose reins. The gray stallion reared, its deadly hooves cutting through the air.

Terrwyn ducked as the tall gray spun in her direction. She was too slow. Surging forward, its broad chest knocked her down as easily as if she were an old rag doll. Pain shot through her body when she struck a rock half-buried in the ground. Curled protectively in a tight ball, she rolled off to the side and out of danger.

She worked to clear her head and push the fear back into the shadows. It took only seconds, yet the terror felt like it had been there for an eternity. Perhaps it had. Or at least for six years. Despite her vow of never knowing defeat again, it still plagued her, trailing after her like a hound after a fox.

Her dismay plummeted further as Sir William came charging up. Terrwyn flinched as his mount skidded to a stop in front of her. Several soldiers rode behind him. They pulled up, their faces grim. She choked as dirt filled her nostrils, assailing her with more memories.

"You, traitor, will stay where you are. Think to move from that spot and the next thing you feel will be the weight of English iron around your ankles."

"What is the meaning of this? Someone grab that horse." James strode to where Terrwyn lay. "Are you harmed?" He knelt down beside her. Running his fingers over her limbs, he poked and prodded her flesh. His examination stopped when he heard her gasp as he pressed on the bruise forming on her hip.

Terrwyn pulled her thoughts together. Her focus was clearer now, clearer than it had been for several weeks. Though concern marked James's face, she saw him as he once was. A bit younger, less sure of himself.

Her heart hardened. There had been times when she desired his touch, entranced by the graceful beauty in his strong hands, the tenderness in his words. Now, the thought of him anywhere near her flesh was almost too much.

He had been there the last time she saw her brother.

Accompanied by the creaking sound of leather, Sir William swung out of his saddle. Mounted soldiers drew their blades and moved in. Flanked by his men, Sir William motioned for several lengths of rope.

Terrwyn started to rise, scrambling for a purchase with her feet. She stopped when an English soldier pressed his boot into the small of her back.

"Halt," James ordered the men. "You will cease this at once."

Sir William held the rope out to James. "Tie it around her wrists."

James's eyes widened and then narrowed as if he could not seem to comprehend the audacity. "I see no reason for this."

"Perhaps a little persuasion will change your mind." Sir William tilted his head at the man beside him.

With one swift motion, the soldier struck James from behind. The cudgel made a hollow thud as it made contact. James grunted and toppled like a felled tree, his body landing near Terrwyn. His face. So near, she could see each curved lash lining his closed lids. Blood trickled from somewhere on the back of his head. It slid down the smooth skin of his neck and pooled at his jaw. His lids trembled as he tried to force them open.

Terrwyn winced as the soldiers pulled her arms behind her back, tying her wrists together. She moved to sit up and found the weight of someone's knee pressing her down.

Terrwyn focused on James, on the fullness of his lips. Although she could not hear what he said, she knew anyway. His words, "I'm sorry," blew softly against her skin.

Before she could respond or ponder her confused feelings, strong hands picked her up and tossed her unceremoniously into Sir William's quarters. She had never been treated so harshly. Fear washed over her in waves, taking her breath with it. All reason left her head. Once the air returned to her lungs, the shadowy fuzz of confusion began to fade.

Her uncomfortable position became all too clear.

Tied to a post, my ankles and wrists bound—she bitterly recalled her rash words to James as she'd left Cook's tent. She had foreseen this earlier but thought by using it as a threat herself, she had removed the danger.

The soldiers brought James in and dumped him beside her. True to his word, Sir William carried in iron manacles. "This will slow you down. Owain Glyndwr will not be so willing to wait for you to show yourselves."

Terrwyn struggled against the ropes as they brought the irons close. "Please, 'tis a terrible mistake."

Sir William paused long enough to give hope to Terrwyn's heart. "That it is, my dear Archer," he snapped. "Though it did not go easy with Edgar Poole when we captured him, he explained how you conspired to create havoc in the king's army. You should have reconsidered your plans when you chose to deceive me and join with the Welsh sympathizer." He patted her head. "Mind you, there was a time when I admired a sweet Welsh maiden. Once, I might have even found you a delight. But now, I've a vow to my king to uphold and with it comes my pleasure in administering your punishment."

"Nay. You have it wrong."

"You've made your bed," said Sir William. "Now deal with the fleas."

"Pray, listen to me."

"You have nothing of interest to say."

"I know where to find your child."

Surprise flashed across his stern eyes. They were soon shuttered behind uncaring lids. Without another word, he rose and strode from the tent.

Terrwyn rolled over where James lay. Although tears blurred her vision, she could see that he sank deeper into oblivion. The voice of caution dissipated with each new wave of fear. "Wake up, James," Terrwyn screamed. "Wake up!"

Her head snapped back. The soldier who struck her began to bind her to the man she had vowed to hate. "Nay—"

Chapter Fifteen

Pain erupted, forcing Terrwyn to quickly regret the decision to shift positions. After testing her bonds, it did not take long to discover her movements were limited by rope and iron. Her wrists were bound together. Her arms burned from the constant stretch behind her back. She rested her head against the tent pole, concentrating on relaxing the cramp wedged between her shoulder blades.

She no longer wore the cap she had used to conceal her braid. Her ruse exposed, it mattered little that she did not have a cap to hide under. Still, she felt naked without that scrap of material sitting on her head. And she did not care for that feeling at all.

A length of iron chain attached her ankle to James's dead weight. With the tips of her fingers, she inched the iron links closer until she dragged enough of it into her hands. She gave the short length of chain a swift yank.

James's foot shot out to the side. Awaking with a start, he groaned when he tried to rub the back of his head. His body stiffened as if suddenly aware his arms were bound and wrapped behind him.

"'Tis good to see you yet live." Terrwyn jerked the chain again. From the growl emanating from behind her back, she may well have taunted an injured bear.

It took great effort to yank the heavy chain and she did not feel so sparkly herself. Her head felt as if it were twice its normal size. The fact she was bound to an idiot did not improve her mood. Based on the state of James's injuries, Sir William's ire was mostly directed toward him. At least she prayed that was true.

Until recently, she had not realized her father and some of the villagers still held ties to Owain Glyndwr. She always thought the warnings from her mam were silly twaddle, worry based on myths and stories told by the hearth. And, sure as she was bound to this post, she never thought James a Welsh sympathizer.

The memory of a young man's youthful face, awash with embarrassment and concern, flashed in her head. She was certain James—the bastard!—had been there by the prince's side when the English took young Drem away.

Hope sparked.

When she had peeked at James's drawings, she'd been taken aback by the image of a man who resembled an older Drem. She needed a better look at those drawings. Although it had been a considerable span of time since she last saw her brother, their father's craggy nose and high cheekbones were easy to recognize. It looked as though they had also found a home on her brother's face. Never had there been two more alike.

Terrwyn's heart grew heavy with a bit of guilt. She would have to convince Sir William that she and James, that stump-headed man, held no sympathy for Owain Glyndwr. Telling a story of the Welshman's betrayal would not be so hard. Had she not heard at her own mam's knee how Father's involvement with the uprising had cost their family everything? This tale she could do with a tear in her eye. Yet, to persuade Sir William of her love for England would be a difficult task indeed. If she were to gain even half a chance, James must believe her story as well. She prayed he would not make a mess of it.

It was her poor luck to think adding him to her list of champions might make her task easier. She had thought to attach herself to James's side until she found her brother, though being tied to a post with this man was not at all her intention. She hated to admit it, but no matter how much of a bother he became, if she removed herself from his side, she would lose the opportunity to fulfill her vow.

James shifted his seat. The heat from his body radiated

through the sleeves of their leather jerkins. The sound of the iron scratching across the ground taunted her with her inability to move as she wished.

The weight of the chains grew heavier. The coarse rope around her wrist became as scratchy as a pinecone.

Freedom. Right now, she would not care if the villagers poked their noses into her business. She had not seen the amount of freedom she had until she lost it. The need to regain her freedom grew. Her heart began to leap. Her thoughts raced from rational to insane possibility. Goodness knows, whatever trouble James had been in up 'til now had somehow included her. She found herself in the same pot of danger. She did not have the faintest idea how she would get them out of camp, but get them out she would.

Wait! Them? Terrwyn's breath caught in her throat. Her mounting anxiety crested. Her heart began to slow. She felt as if she were a boat settling itself after a storm.

Fearless of James's ire, she gave the chain another jerk and smiled when she heard his groaned response.

"What in Satan's retreat do you want?"

"Do you mind telling me what you did to bring Sir William and his soldiers crashing down upon our head?"

James cleared his throat before answering. "Edgar's tale reached Sir William's ear sooner than mine."

"Should think 'tis simple enough to refute his tale."

"Aye, but I have no proof and Edgar has enough men to say they saw me at a well-known den of Welsh traitors."

"He weaves a fine web of lies. There must be just as many willing to refute his word against you."

"One small problem. I did frequent the Bloated Goat."

"As I'm sure a countless number of men do."

"On a night where several disreputable subjects gathered."

"Never figured you for a Welsh sympathizer. You're a cur hound to turn on your friend and king."

"Enough, Terrwyn! Cease speaking of things you don't understand."

"Wait!" Terrwyn said. "If Poole saw you there, then that means he was there too. Did you not point that out and demand Sir William to ponder that fact a moment or two?"

"My only satisfaction is in knowing Poole is under guard and unable to deliver his messages to the sympathizers."

"If only you had something to show you are innocent of Edgar Poole's charges."

"'Tis not just Poole's story that I plot with the Welshmen that has stirred his temper. Your duplicity revealed in front of his men must have struck a nerve and fanned his ire. He won't be willing to think straight until he has had time to cool. When he is ready to be reasonable I will speak to him again."

Terrwyn tensed. She had nearly managed to forget the disdain dripping from Sir William when he spoke of Welsh women. If not for James's interruption, she might have worked out a plan to gain the commander's good graces. It would have taken a few sweet words. Words so sweet, they melt on your tongue before you said them. If pressed, she might have even offered a promise of a maiden's greatest gift.

Course she did not intend to keep that promise. That gift would remain intact until she determined it was time—preferably with the man of her heart on her wedding night. That love match did not exist, but one could tempt the fates to bring it about with a wish.

She sighed and attempted to ignore the imp's voice inside her head. To no avail—she could hear its devilish taunts. *What need do I have for keeping my maiden's gift intact? Without dowry, land or family position, there will be no wedding night. No love match, either. Why wait for the unattainable?*

Terrwyn leaned her head against the post and let her shoulders press into James. His warmth flooded her back. Fluid heat flowed through her body, pooling in the center of her core. The image of their limbs tangled in a mass of passion blurred. Terrwyn shook free of the vision and shuddered. Certainly the act between a man and a woman caused nothing but trouble for a woman. Sometimes even death. She would do well to remember that instead of wandering where she should not.

She jerked her foot. The chain between them stretched taut.

"Cease your infantile tantrums," James said. "You'll have a soldier on top of us before you take another breath."

"Infantile?" Terrwyn gripped the rope, working the knot around her wrist.

James lifted his leg and held it. The chain between them stretched tight. Gathering momentum, he swung his foot out and let it drop.

Terrwyn tilted nearly on her side, one leg close to his. The other she was busily scooting closer to keep from splitting herself in two. "One day you'll regret the day we met," she warned through gritted teeth.

Satisfaction wove through his voice. "I already do, infant. I already do."

Terrwyn felt the burn from her hatred begin to grow. How could she have thought she felt something for this man? She sniffed, hurt by how easily he agreed with her. "Do not bother yourself with worry for me. I'll leave you to yourself, just as soon as I relieve myself of these chains."

James shifted. "I do not know if you've noticed, but we are both in a bit of trouble. Give me half a moment to think of something."

"No doubt when I speak with one of the brothers from Norwich, I'll be able to extract myself from this situation."

"Terrwyn, Sir William ignores my relationship with the king and has me bound to a damn pole. How do you purport we convince Sir William of our usefulness?"

"I don't. I do not know of *your* innocence, therefore I cannot swear by it." Hearing the exasperated sputter behind her, she continued, "I plan to manage on my own. Convince him of my loyalty."

James grunted. "William has no reason to believe anything you say. Even if you wag your fine bottom in front of him, you'll not win out."

"You forget they still need me." Terrwyn leaned her head back. "Though Sir William may not care for me, King Henry needs archers for his war. 'Tis certain, Simon will offer his appreciation of my talent."

"Do not be foolish. Even though Henry needs archers, he won't want a maiden in his ranks. Not unless she's providing comfort."

"I think I can persuade William otherwise."

"Your pride misleads you, Terrwyn. I've spent enough time with Sir William to know that he doesn't change his mind often. Where we are concerned, it will take a great deal to move his decision about us."

"'Tis why we must separate ways," she said. "I will be about my business and you shall move about yours."

"You get ahead of yourself and the small problem that stands between us."

Terrwyn's heart caught. Did he recognize her from so long ago? Six years was a long time. She scooted to sit straighter so that she might move her ear closer to catch his words. "What stands between us, James?"

"Should think it obvious." He twitched the chain, causing the metal links to jingle. "This. Until one of us finds a way to remove it, we must move as one."

Hope for a word about Drem evaporated. James was right. As much as she wished to rid him from her life, she needed him. Perhaps sweet fate had played a cruel game. As their pasts linked them together, so were they tied together by iron links. In her mind, both sets of chains were equally heavy. Once she figured out a way to get them out of the encampment, she would work on gaining information regarding her brother.

Terrwyn let her shoulder blades meld into his warmth. "James?"

"Aye?"

"Think on your tent. Do you recall where everything is placed?"

"It matters little if I do or do not. They've probably packed everything up."

"What makes you think that? Why would they be so quick to do so?"

"The camp sounds. There's a change about to take place."

Terrwyn listened to the rushed clatter. The horses stomped their hooves, whinnying to each other. "How soon?"

"Probably not until morning. Get a good fresh start on the day."

"What are we to do, James?"

The sound of footsteps arrived at the tent before he could respond. The tent flap was raised and Simon entered. He cleared his throat and held out a jug.

James turned his head to look over his shoulder. "Come on, man, she cannot take a drink unless you untie her hands." Hearing Simon's grunt, James added, "Not to worry." He lifted his leg that was bound to Terrwyn's. "We're stuck at the hip, so to speak."

Terrwyn let her smile slide to Simon. "'Tis all right if you do not feel comfortable untying me. You could bring the vessel to me, press it to my lips. 'Twould be as if I sipped from your hand." She ignored the disgusted snort that came from behind her back. Her smile grew. She closed her eyes and tilted her chin up. Her throat bared to the enemy, she parted her lips and waited.

Simon stepped forward and pressed the vessel to her mouth. He tilted it so that she might drink a small sip. As they learned each other's silent signals, he allowed her to drink deeply. A trickle of watered wine slid from Terrwyn's lips. It ran down her throat and under the leather jerkin. The coolness left her lips as he drew the jug away.

Emboldened by the liquid fire, she licked the remaining drops from her mouth. Under a veil of lashes, she peered at Simon's hands. There was a slight tremor where he gripped the wine jug. Her head still tilted back, she smiled languidly. "Many thanks."

At a loss for words, he simply nodded.

Terrwyn pulled the pretty pout she had seen some of the women from her village use. "Oh, dear."

Simon dropped down, kneeling beside her. "What is it, Archer?"

"Saints' bloody bones," James said, "our being chained together would be a good place to start."

"Not much I can do about that," Simon said.

Tears slid down Terrwyn's cheek. She sniffed loudly to cover up anything James might say. Once again drawing Simon's attention, she let a little sob escape. "Not to fear. I've trusted you since you gave your vow as my protector. I know if there were something you could do, you would have already done it. I was only thinking of the time in the woods, when you and I first met. How you gave me your word and how well you've kept it." She sighed deeply, a hiccup of a remaining sob followed. "I had so wanted to serve in our king's army. 'Twould do a body good to teach the shiftless French a lesson."

The sound of Simon scuffing his feet like an errant child filled the quiet of the tent. "I can speak with William. Let him know your intentions are pure."

"Oh, would you?" she simpered.

He turned to leave, the jug of wine forgotten beside James and Terrwyn.

"Simon?"

He stopped at the tent flap when Terrwyn called out to him once more.

"Oh dear. How do I ask this of you?"

"For the love of all that is holy," James snapped. "The woman needs to use the bushes. To make water."

Simon rubbed the back of his hand across his mouth. "I suppose—"

"You suppose nothing. She'll have to relieve herself some time. It might as well be now. Besides, I could use a bit of a stretch myself."

"Really, Sir James," Terrwyn said over her shoulder, "you could give me a moment of privacy."

Simon returned and bent down to unlock the chain around Terrwyn's ankle. With the first task completed, he pulled out a dagger from his belt. He hesitated as if questioning his decision. Seeing a look of concern cross his face, Terrwyn smiled and did not move. Her breath caught in her chest as she watched the blade cut through the rope tied around her wrist. The freedom to move her legs and arms at will sent a thrill across her flesh.

"Hold your hands together," Simon ordered.

Terrwyn was swift to do as he bid. Her hopes dipped as he tightened the knot around one of her wrists. He bunched the tail end of the rope in his hand and motioned for her to stand.

"Wait," James yelled. "You cannot leave me. I demand a word with Sir William."

Chapter Sixteen

Terrwyn swallowed the surprised yelp when her cramped legs took their first step outside Sir William's tent. Refusing to show any signs of weakness, she flexed her shoulders, straightened her back and stood as tall as her small frame would allow. With a flick of her free hand, she dusted off her leggings and tugged on the hem of her leather jerkin.

"Many thanks, Simon." She flipped her braid over her shoulder.

She cringed at James's next curse aimed at their backs. She stopped, nearly forgetting the task she had given herself. Thoughts of retribution, thumbscrews and flames hurled through her mind.

Simon cast a tense look around before drawing her away from the tent. "Best get moving."

After a few failed attempts to keep up with Simon's long legs, she soon realized she could never match his strides. Her boots scuffed the dirt as she simply trotted along.

Before she knew it, her legs and shoulders began to loosen up. Despite her concerns for James, each step brought a renewed joy of freedom. Even the rope swinging between her wrist and Simon's fist failed to dampen her spirits. Catrin always said it was a poor soul that did not see the blessings in front of their nose. Intent on following her sister's advice, Terrwyn filled her lungs with the cool evening air. Her nose twitched from the smell of pine and smoldering wood. The air was so thick with the scent that it rested on her tongue.

Aware no man enjoyed being manipulated, she held her

pleasure from view and ducked her head. Simon could have ignored her pleas and turned his back on her.

The army was indeed in a state of transformation. Soldiers moved about, their attention on the activities needed before leaving a campsite. Terrwyn saw the glances cast toward her, the down-turned corners of their mouths. Apparently her presence did not sit well with the men.

Simon skirted one of the campfires lit for the evening meal. Smoke swirled into the magenta sky. The scent of meat cooking over the flames permeated the air. This was yet another sign that Sir William intended to move his men. The soldiers traveled quicker on well-fed stomachs.

"Here." Simon pointed sourly down a path leading away from the campsite, just outside the camp perimeter. Vines wound up tree trunks, draped over their limbs. A canopy of shade trees swayed as one. Their green leaves, empowered by the setting sun, gave the illusion that the forest floor undulated in waves. Nature's chorus, birds and insects, stilled when they heard Simon's deep voice. Though the men's voices were muffled, it would not take much for someone to hear a warning shout.

Terrwyn looked down at her wrist and then up at Simon. Silence grew between them. Simon's face began to blossom into a rosy hue. His mouth remained set in a firm, hard line.

Terrwyn jiggled her wrist. She waited, determined to win this war of wills. Now that the opportunity to relieve her bladder was available, her body rebelled. She could not do this with Simon in easy sight. Her need grew with each passing minute.

She shivered as she listened to the camp sounds and searched for James's angry voice. Relief, bitten with a trace of guilt, flooded her thoughts. Though thankful he had finally quieted, she hated to think on what means it had taken to silence his demands to see Sir William.

She nearly jumped out of her boots when Simon touched her elbow and motioned her to the little patch behind a scraggly-leafed bush. Terrwyn eyed the lack of privacy afforded her. When the day came that she forgot her position as a Welsh lord's daughter, she would then know her end had come. Today was not that day.

Lifting her chin, she let her nose drift into the air, her lip curled in disdain. "If you think to stand and sneak a peek while I'm about my private business, you best think again, Simon of Norwich."

"You know I cannot cut you loose. William would have my hide sent home to our mother."

"I did not ask you to cut the rope. Just loosen your hold so that I might scurry behind the bush. Besides, it will make my task go much quicker if I have the free use of both my hands."

Simon let go of the rope leading to her wrist. "Make haste," he grumbled. "I've spent too much time away from camp as it is."

She walked sedately past the bush Simon had indicated, squashing the desire to scamper away. Although her impulse was to run as fast as she could, she knew the truth of it and could not fool her heart. She could not leave James behind. And she needed to find those sketches.

Finished, she returned to where Simon stood, a hard glint in his eyes, a tightness around his mouth. His patience taxed, she hoped he held a bit in reserve to deal with her next request. She held out the end of the rope. "How does Cook fare?"

The length of rope swung between them as they moved away from the clearing. "He lives."

"Has the poultice been changed?"

He answered with a shrug.

"'Tis imperative a new one is placed every hour or two. Or all manner of troubles will befall him and the members of the king's army." Since Simon did not speak, she decided to press her point. "Stink of putrid flesh."

Simon grunted and turned his head away slightly.

"I cannot think what your brother would say if we lose another man. Someone else will have to take his place. I've spent but a few days traveling with the army and see they need to eat. Aye, they value their cook, they do."

The encampment loomed closer. Simon brought their steps toward Sir William's tent, closer to where James awaited her return. Terrwyn's heart beat heavily against her ribcage. Her steps slowed.

Simon turned to cast an impatient look her way. The lines around his mouth deepened. The shadows grew as the sun began its descent for the evening.

"You'll need to know how to mix the herbs," she continued as if oblivious to his impatience. Her thoughts drifted at the sound of hooves pounding against the ground. They came in a rush, skidding to a stop at the other edge of the camp.

Terrwyn gasped as Simon grabbed her arm and drew her out of sight. Keeping to the widening shadows, they made their way to Cook's tent.

"What worries you, Simon?" Her rush of questions was silenced when he shoved her head through the tent flap and hustled her inside.

Terrwyn stumbled in the gloomy dark. A meager candle flickered on the table beside Cook's cot.

"Who's there?" Cook called out.

Simon strode up and placed the rope in the old soldier's hand. "You need to return to your duties. I brought someone to help you get there."

Cook's watery eyes flashed in the gloomy tent. "So you bring me Archer? Where's young Gilbert? He serves me just fine."

Simon moved to leave. "Most of the camp leaves at dawn. I would have you strong enough to go with the men."

"You think I cannot fend for myself?" Cook asked.

Simon smiled. The shadows danced around his high cheekbones and candlelight caressed the waves of his pale hair. "The Archer informs me that you need your wound tended. I'm told you will heal quicker if it is." He motioned Terrwyn to move closer. "There's plenty of rope to play out if you need it. Don't think to move past this tent. I'll come for you when 'tis time."

Terrwyn nodded. Her mouth set in a placid line, she kept her thoughts hidden from Simon's examination. She found it a relatively easy task as she could see his attention drift to the commotion outside. Was it her imagination? Did his skin pale considerably?

"You will not stray from here," he ordered as he turned to leave.

The tent flap swung open. Little Gilbert stuck his head in. Flaxen-haired ringlets bounced in excitement. "Sir William is in a fit. Says I best find you yesterday."

"He does, does he?" Simon ran his fingers through his hair. "Well, I best not let him stew himself into another boil."

Gilbert hung back, an uneasy look about his face.

Simon clapped a wide hand on the child's thin shoulder. "Remain here. Archer will teach you the fine art of poultice making. I hear an army runs as much on a fine poultice as on a slab of meat."

Terrwyn watched Simon's back retreat from the tent, then turned to question young Gilbert about Sir William's latest reason for shouting. She hated not knowing how her village fared. Although James had threatened to raze it, he had yet to show the temper to do so. Saints' dry bones, had Sir William discovered she was not tied up next to his other prisoner?

Before Terrwyn could ask her questions, Cook had put the first question to the child. "What stirs the young commander?"

"Don't know. He's unhappy." Gilbert's tears glittered under the flickering candlelight. "He doesn't want me to draw his bath or lend a hand with anything."

"Well," Cook said gently, "'tis a good thing for me that you have some extra time on your hands. I'll need your muscle to help me with the horses when the commander says time to mount up."

Gilbert nodded and stood back to watch Terrwyn mix the herbs. He absently twirled the coil of pale hair around his small finger. His full lips were a smaller version of Sir William's wider, larger mouth.

Terrwyn paused from uncoiling the binding from Cook's ribcage. *Has Sir William noticed the resemblance as well?* Her thoughts gathered, rushing, forcing her worries to the forefront. She nearly forgot to apply the herbal poultice before wrapping a clean bandage over Cook's wound. Her task completed, she sat back and stared blankly at the mess as she sorted through her predicament.

A smile slowly began to drift over her mouth. She would see to it that things were set aright. Simon would explain her absence. Cook needed her care. That would buy her time to find what she needed in James's tent. If luck were her friend, she would be back at Cook's side before anyone knew she left.

Terrwyn wadded up the bandage she'd removed from Cook's side. "If 'tis to be used again, I must wash it out. Might you loosen your hold so that I may do this for you?"

Cook eyed her cautiously. "Simon's orders were for you to stay where he left you."

Terrwyn dipped her cleaning cloth into a bowl of tepid water. "True. Yet he knows not of the difference between clean water and putrid water." She shrugged, gesturing as if it was a simple fact of life. "His station wouldn't understand these things. There are others to do for him. You and I, we are aware and value the difference."

Cook nodded and patted Terrwyn's hand. He placed the end of the rope into her palm. "Fetch it quick. I imagine 'tis not so far that anyone will notice you wandering about."

"Are you certain 'tis wise?"

"Perhaps young Gilbert—"

"Nay," Terrwyn interrupted. "He should stay here. Keep you company while you instruct him on the tasks ahead."

Draped in one of Cook's old woolen cloaks, Terrwyn slipped out and threaded her way through the encampment. She skirted past the area where most of the soldiers milled around awaiting their next meal. Although their cook lay abed, the soldiers' need for food could not be ignored. Every Welshman who ever came in contact with the army understood their need for sustenance. They left behind a clear path as they marched across the Welsh countryside.

In her village, many a field once full of sheep now stood nearly empty. In fact, the night before she left home, she dreamt of the fields. She could still hear the cold wind whipping through the tall grass. The meadow, barren of the life it supported, warned her of their future.

Hearing a familiar laugh, Terrwyn stumbled over her own feet. Maffew, one of Isolde's sons, stood amidst the throng of men. His shock of hair bristled around his ears. She could barely see his compact body because of the men crowded around him.

"Aye," he said, "you've helped me see reason. 'Tis my duty to take my rightful place as one of King Henry's finest archers."

Terrwyn heard his nervous bray again. It was one that few could forget—laughter blending with his rasping breath made it sound like he choked on a wad of mutton. Lord knows there had been many a meal stopped to ensure he remained alive.

Worry gripped her stomach. Edgar Poole's threats echoed in her head. The king's army had returned to her village. If they did not gather the number of able-bodied men required for a long battle, they would return again.

James's tent loomed before her. She moved swiftly and slipped inside. She blinked, working to adjust her eyes to the gloomy shadows. Her ears pounded, echoing her rapid pulse. Drawing in a shaky breath, she braced her legs as the makeshift room tilted.

She blinked again. She had hoped everything would remain as they'd left it. Finding James's drawings depended on it. Her eyes focused on the shadows as she listened to the camp sounds. Not only had James's contents been tampered with, the camp atmosphere had changed as well. She could almost feel the tension building with the change outside.

Hunkered down, Terrwyn dropped to her hands and knees. She ran her hands over the canvas floor and along the corner of the woolen rug placed in the center of the tent. A chest stood in her path, its contents spilled out. Chausses, jerkins, undertunics littered the floor. Using broad sweeps of her hand, she moved the clothing out of the way. A small part of her mind, the whimsical side, searched for a way to gather up a few extra pieces for their trip. Her practical side won out. They would make do with what they had on their backs.

With little natural light left from the day, the shadows deepened as evening poured over the sky. She was spending too much time searching and very little finding what she needed. Simon would have a fit if Cook did not produce her. Lord, she would hate to be the cause for his discomfort.

Terrwyn scrambled to search the last heavy chest in the corner. Relieved to find it unlocked, she lifted the lid and peered inside. Empty. All its contents were removed. Her hopes deflated, she sank to the floor. Even her bow was missing.

The scraping of boots drew near. The sound pulled her from her dejection. She shook herself free. Her thoughts skittered to James. He would be furious when he heard she went out without telling him her plans. They needed those sketches as a bargaining tool. Now the proof of his innocence was lost to those who wished him harm. Fate resisted her desires, blocking her path from all sides.

Pushing herself up on her hands and knees, she paused. The edge of the rug bunched as if it had been kicked. A lump similar to the size of the journal formed under the woolen material.

Her hand stilled.

Angry voices carried into the tent. "Edgar Poole—"

The men paused outside. Their conversation dropped as they spoke in hushed urgency.

"How is this possible?"

"—broke through the guards—"

"—spies plot against the crown."

Her heart thumped against her ribcage. She flipped over the edge of the rug, slid the packet out and shoved the leather-bound drawings inside the folds of her jerkin.

As she moved, the tip of a small knife caught her attention.

The tent flap snapped open. "Hold," Sir William ordered. "One move and I will cleave your head from your shoulders."

Chapter Seventeen

Terrwyn kept the small blade cupped in her palm as she followed Sir William in silence. Aided by the additional length of the tunic sleeves, she had kept the knife's existence hidden while he glared at her. His initial surprise at finding her in the tent quickly shifted to irritation. Try as she might, she could not blame him. Why would he expect to find her standing somewhere other than where he left her? He, himself, had secured the manacle around her ankle. She prayed his anger would not storm against James.

The leather journal rubbed against her flesh as she half-skipped to keep up with Sir William's long strides. Luckily, she had tucked it in the band of her leggings, barely discernable under the folds of her loose tunic.

When she quickened her pace to a trot, she felt the journal shift. Her breath caught as she searched for a way to keep if from sliding any further. The journal simply could not fall into sight. Its presence would be hard to explain.

If she had the use of both hands it would have been an easy thing to fold her arms over her middle, propping James's drawings while they walked. However, that was not the case. As soon as Sir William gathered his wits, he had that damn rope back in hand, jerking her to follow.

There was no reason to fight him. Where would she go? Two steps out of camp and one of the soldiers would have her strung up like a suckling pig at Michaelmas. Instead she waited until the commander reeled in the rope, pulling her to him. It took but one look to know she had best take care while his ire was up. Unfortunately, meekness was not her strong trait.

Terrwyn stumbled over a tree root hidden by the evening shadows. Her palm now itched where the metal blade bit into her skin. Perspiration made it slippery, hard to keep out of sight. Her fingers ached as she kept her hand cupped. She thanked the fates for the small consolation that she held it in the hand farthest from Sir William. 'Twas certain he would have noticed. Her thoughts raced as she searched for a tale that would sway him from his own determined course.

Stumbling once again, she dropped to one knee. "A moment, if you please."

Sir William turned. Even under the cover of night, she saw his impatience glinting from his eyes. She must make haste. Pressing up from the ground, she began to rise. Her free hand stole near the neck of her boot. With the slightest movement, she slipped her fingers inside and prayed he did not notice.

She looked up, her gaze softened in hopes of diminishing his ire with her entreaty. "I didn't intend for my absence to cause concern. I meant to be gone for only a wee moment or two."

"Did you not?" Sir William grunted. His glare bore into her very soul. "Pray tell. What am I to think, finding you where you should not be?"

A twitch began to build under her skin. No one but Mam in a temper could make her nerves jump like a river trout. To make matters worse, the leather-bound journal felt like it was inching its way down again. A corner dug into the crease between her hip and abdomen.

Hugging her stomach with one arm, Terrwyn moved quickly to Sir William's side. She hesitated, her hand suspended near his sleeve. The heat from his body filled the space between them. She licked her lips. Caution rang in her ears.

Ignoring the bell of caution's peal, she lightly pressed his sleeve. A tick, a slight jerk, drew one corner of his mouth down. She ignored the need to shut her eyes and quieted the brush of faerie wings against the walls inside her stomach.

Sir William trapped her hand and held it a moment too long. One by one, he pried her fingers off his arm. Terrwyn felt her cheeks flush with fire.

He stepped back, putting space between them. "You know

not what you are about, Archer. I forswore your ilk long ago."

Turning on his heels, he jerked the rope tethered between them and did not question whether she would keep up with his steps. The pace he set to reach the tent gave her no time to voice her discomfort.

Breathless and aided by Sir William's impatient shove, Terrwyn stumbled into the tent.

James lifted his head. The bruise on his cheekbone stood out against the pallor of his skin. The corner of his mouth, swollen and split, created a crooked smile. His head dropped, his chin resting on his chest as if its weight were too great to bear.

Her heart lurched at the sight. "James," Terrwyn whispered.

She flinched when Sir William whipped the end of the rope around the tent pole. She ached to reach out and trace James's face, the tendons running down his neck. Her chest tightened, fighting the draw of air. If only he would turn his anger on her, let her know he had not given up. If only she could catch his eye and let her thoughts feed into his. She would remind him they would find a way out as they had promised each other.

"Look what I've brought back to you, James Frost." He kicked at James's outstretched legs.

"Stop it." Her anger fed on fear. It rose, driving through her blood. "You cannot do this! He is Henry's man."

"Henry's man?" The rope tightened, singing as it spun around the post. Sir William pulled it tighter. "Kneel," he ordered.

She dropped to her knees and bent forward, trying to keep the journal from showing. It dug into her stomach. The idea of producing it to save James jabbed into her thoughts. She quickly squashed it. What if Sir William destroyed the drawings out of spite? She could not release them. Not until she had the opportunity to look at the sketches. James would understand her decision. Someday.

Sir William yanked her arms behind her back. "Many a king has had a confidant turn on him. Commit acts of treason. Spy for the enemy," he said as he tied her wrists together.

"Though there are some who are charged unjustly," Terrwyn said through gritted teeth.

He lifted her arms and looped the rope under the binding. With a grunt of satisfaction, he finished by tying it around the peg above her head. He flicked the taut piece of hemp with his finger, testing the area where it pressed against the tender side of her wrists.

He stepped back to admire he work. "Unfortunately for James, his accuser Edgar Poole has disappeared. And you he hid from me. Let you infiltrate my command. And now I see 'tis obvious that you have corrupted my brother against me."

Terrwyn kept her mind off the slow ache in her arms. James's journal threatened to slide further down her chausses. She flexed her fingers, willing the pins and needles away. "James would never turn from his king. He loves King Henry over Wales. He chooses devotion for his king over family. He's been with him since he was a young man."

Sir William bent forward. "And you know this, how?

"He—he was with Henry when they rode through Wales, stealing Welshmen to serve as archers for England's army."

"And he stole you to shoot pretty arrows into the air for the king's entertainment? I think not."

"My pretty arrows will hit their mark every time. Will yours?"

"You still maintain your pride?" A sudden jolt of surprise struck his face.

It gave her some small bit of satisfaction. Yet she would have given it all away to know she had won a few more moments for James to gather his strength.

Sir William pressed her shoulder against the post. His weight bore down, grinding into her skin. "I think you lie."

"You are right," she conceded hotly. "I fight because I must. You Englishmen care not for my country—my village—my family. But I do! When those lives I care for are threatened I cannot turn away. I must do all within my power to protect them."

"Anything?"

"If it returns my brother and brings peace to my family,

aye."

"That comes near to an admission of guilt. I wonder if you speak only for yourself."

Sir William pulled a chair close. Sitting down, he leaned forward and grabbed a handful of James's hair. He pulled back, lifting James's head. "Have you nothing to say?"

James groaned from the movement.

"You and your fauna," Sir William said. "You would rather let a woman speak for you instead of find your tongue? Though if I were you, I'd sleep with one eye open. She'd flay you as easy as she would the rest of England's men.

"See here, Archer, I am in a quandary. His journal is gone. This king's man has no proof he draws something more than flowers and the beasts of the forest. I didn't even see a simple map."

"The woman—"

"By his own admission he saw her when he frequented a popular meeting place for traitors." He held up his hand for silence. "He has been accused by someone in whom I entrusted the care of my young brother. What am I to do?"

"If Edgar Poole is a fine example of good character, then 'tis your opinion that should be in question. That swine is not fit to lick James's boots."

She felt a slight poke on her hip. Then another. Saints' lovely bones, James would recover. She prayed he did so quickly.

Sir William rose to tower over her. "Mind your tongue. 'Tis within my power to judge James Frost. Give him a traitor's death. His friendship with the king is what keeps him alive. Until we reach Southampton. If I find the charges are accurate, he will indeed die. Otherwise, if he survives the trip, he will be set free. You," he added, "I have yet to decide. I hear your father sympathized with Owain Glyndwr for Wales's throne. He backs a toothless mongrel."

"Better an old mongrel than a braying donkey." Terrwyn bit down her next words when James renewed his incessant poking.

"Fool woman. I should turn you out, let you fend for

yourself. Stripped naked. Bound, blindfolded and alone. That will silence that serpent's tongue of yours."

"Nay," James said.

"Ah," Sir William said. "At last he responds."

"She'd never survive. Nor would you," James said.

"Don't tax yourself, James," Terrwyn entreated. "Rest."

"Your burden, Sir William, would be in the knowing that you lent a hand in an innocent's death. It would weigh you down, adding to the memory of the woman you loved and lost. Nay," James pushed. "You cannot turn her out into her death. For that would be your death as well."

Sir William held his face rigid, revealing no expression of his thoughts. He bent to leave the tent. Without another word he was gone, their fate undecided.

Exhausted, Terrwyn closed her eyes. She tried to lean the back of her head against the post. The simple action drew her arms taut. Her shoulders burned. She flexed her fingers again, nearly crying out with the movement.

The guilt of keeping his drawings a secret ate at her insides. But how would telling him now serve her needs? Once she had a good look at Drem and his surroundings, she would return them. Until then, she would have to hope James's joy in recovering them would overshadow her deception. Still, it did not stop the gnawing in her stomach.

"Well," Terrwyn said. "That went well."

"Aye." James sighed deeply, a groan mixing with his breath. "I missed you, little one."

"Aye?" she asked, before conceding, "From time to time, I found myself missing you too."

James's words were slow and stiff. "From. Time. To. Time."

"Perhaps a bit more." Terrwyn tried moving to a more comfortable position and found it made little difference. She turned her concerns to James. "Did you happen to figure out a way to free ourselves from this spot of trouble?"

He did not speak for some time. He drew his breath in short shallow pulls before answering. "'Fraid not. Busy regaling our hosts with tales from Henry's court."

Terrwyn shut her eyes, trying not to see the vision of his

assault as the soldiers entertained themselves. Nor did she need the night visions to come over her, foretelling what would happen if they did not find a way to free themselves.

"Never meant to cause you or your family harm," he said.

"Aye, well, we cannot always know what our actions will bring. Wicked Lady Fate sometimes steps in and leads us on a merry jig or two. Or shoves us down a well of pity and condemnation."

"Do you hate all with English blood flowing through their veins? Or only me?"

Did she hate him as much as when she first realized he'd ridden with the men who abducted Drem? She had vowed to bring each and every one of them down, but how far had that brought her? She remembered how he had argued with the Prince of Wales. Flashes of memory danced before her. His kindness after Mam's death. He had offered his protection, even when he knew it was unwanted. Indeed, at times, unwarranted.

"I despise the power that constantly wields its hammer over our heads," she finally said.

"Ah, then, there's still hope for me."

Terrwyn heard the gentle plea in his jest. "Very little."

"Better a little hope than no hope at all."

Terrwyn shook her head and smothered the smile that began to form. She would not allow the ember to grow. "'Tis not the time to make foolish vows."

He leaned his head back, turning so that his breath brushed against her neck. "Later, when we are free, I'll turn all that is in my power to finding ways to gain your affections."

"James, I need you to listen well." Very carefully, Terrwyn slid her knees to one side. The shift in weight pulled on her shoulders, stretching her arms tight overhead. She swallowed a gasp as the rope bit into her flesh and sinew, burning where it creased her skin. Gritting her teeth, she made one last move. The heel of her boot scraped across the worn dirt and settled close to James's hands. The chain links rattled, the metal loops hitting together as he dragged it out of her way with his fingertips.

She blew out soft breaths to ease the pain and wiggled her

boots closer. "Try to reach my leg. Can you feel it?" She listened for the soft stir of cloth, his sleeve moving against his body. Warmth shot through the woolen leggings where he touched her calf.

"Aye," he said.

She ignored the coarse sound of his voice as he choked out the single word. It would do them little good to cry over his injuries. "Good then. You'll need to reach a bit more. Tell me what you feel."

"Do you wish to torture me? What good would my feeling your leg bring?"

"'Tis to a wee knife I'm directing you. In the boot."

She listened to him breathe in and exhale. His fingers moved over her calf again. They inched up to the crease of her knee, in between her legs.

"Not that one," she said. "The one on top."

"My apologies." The movement of his touch stilled, pausing over the curve of her knee.

"Please hurry, James." She winced, the need to shift and ease the throbbing in her arms growing with each breath. "Oh," she cried out, "'tis madness. How am I to direct you if I cannot see where your hand is?"

"Close your eyes. Pretend you are blindfolded. We'll feel together."

The heat of his hand left her leg. The weight of their troubles bore down on her shoulders. It caught her fears, swirling her thoughts until she could hardly breathe. "Please James," she whispered.

"Hush, Terrwyn. Listen to my voice. Take a steady breath. Like when you prepare to shoot your arrow." The sound of air drawn in and blown out whispered between them. "When I touch you again, I want you to feel me."

The tips of his fingers graced the folds of her chausses. The woolen material brushed against her flesh. He pressed his fingers to her knee. Warmth flowed over her, soothing her soul. The grace of his movements slid over her leg. He paused where the boot cuffed her calf. His fingers dipped inside, testing the area between leather and wool.

"See me. Think of the blade as our prey. Where is my hand? Where do I go from here? Am I close?"

"No good. The little blade has slipped. 'Tis too far for you to reach."

She knew the moment he withdrew his hand. She felt his absence again and wished for another try, if only to feel the comfort of his touch for a while longer. Her thoughts scattered, searching for an answer to their freedom.

"Can you scoot your foot closer?" he asked.

"James, 'tis no use. You cannot reach it."

"Steady, little one. Let's try again. But this time, I'm going to remove your boot."

When he finished giving his instructions, she nodded, though more to assure herself since he could not see anyway. Her teeth clamped tight, she gripped the rope overhead with both hands and pulled with all her might. The weight of her body lifted. She could hear James as he strained against his ropes. Her arms trembled as she held her body as still as she could. The tug of her boot jerked against the rope, against her wrists. She kept the cry trapped inside and focused on dragging a breath. Just when she thought she could bear no more, she felt the leather slip from her foot.

"I have it."

Her grip lost, she slid down to the ground. The burning returned to her arms. Her wrists stung where the rope had rubbed the skin raw.

Slowly, the sharp blade scraped against the bindings and the strands began to fray.

James groaned from the release. Still bound by the manacle around their ankles, he moved with measured steps. The rope above Terrwyn's head shuddered.

She gasped as James gently drew her arms down and blood rushed to her fingertips. He squatted in front of her and cradled her unbound wrists.

Terrwyn scanned his cuts and bruises and cringed with empathy. "Your poor face." She leaned forward to kiss his pain away and James met her.

He covered her mouth with his, draining her anguish. He

hovered over her lips, letting her taste his tears. A crooked smile lifted the corner of his bruised mouth. Her hands still in his, he turned them over, exposing the reddened flesh. Streaks of blue and purple formed over the swollen skin. He brushed a kiss ever so gently beside the wound. Placing a finger to his lips, he motioned for her to rise.

Terrwyn caught his hand and accepted his help. Her legs, deadened by their position, took a moment or two for the feeling to return.

James pulled her to his chest, folding his arms about her. "Well played, little one," he whispered into her ear. He flicked her nose, adding, "Have you an idea up your sleeve for our next move?"

Weary, she leaned into his arms. She nearly forgot that the chain between them would hamper their escape. "The chest, over there, holds a bow and arrows. We can start there."

"We'll need more than a bow and a few arrows to hold Sir William's soldiers at bay."

"Aye, but we cannot stay here like a rabbit trapped in its warren."

Picking up the slack of chain links between them, James led her to the trunk. Terrwyn pulled open the lid. Nestled within the folds of cloth lay the bow and a quiver of arrows. She balanced the smooth wooden bow in her hand, feeling its weight. She found comfort in being armed with a weapon she understood.

James turned, forgetting to warn her of his decision so that she stumbled against him. "Will take me a while to get used to this."

"Thank the saints, we won't have to grow accustomed to being linked to each other for long. Simon will release us."

"Your Simon will do nothing of the kind."

"He vowed to protect me."

"Maybe so," James said. "But a vow to his brother will stand stronger than one he made to you. Besides, Sir William relieved Simon of the key when he discovered you went on a little walk. We'll have to take our chances and find help outside the camp."

Terrwyn grabbed James's sleeve. Since her strength had weakened, he slipped out with ease. "We cannot go about the camp. 'Tis certain they'll notice us."

"We'll get my horse. Zeus is the fastest mount amongst the soldiers' nags." He lifted the tent flap and peered out through the slit in the canvas. "Nearly dark. They'll think to feed us soon."

"Then we best move on."

James let the flap drop. "Go back! Go back," he ordered in a harsh whisper.

Chapter Eighteen

Terrwyn shivered beside the tent pole. She gripped James's hands, interlocking their fingers. Her breathing slowed as she matched every intake and release of breath with his. Their quiet rhythm allowed her to hear footsteps draw near the tent.

She felt his muscles tighten, his back become hard and rigid. His tension was like that of a wolf ready to attack at any moment. He released her hand. Panic began to bubble up her throat. They had come so close to escaping. She could not let him risk his life to save hers.

"Stay," she whispered.

"If we are separated, promise me you will return to your home," he said.

"James, I cannot—"

"Promise me."

Terrwyn thought about the vision she had seen so long ago. Drem was out there, somewhere, waiting for her to find him. How could she make another promise when she had yet to fulfill the one she made to her mother? She thought of her father, his ability to smooth a ruffled feather without really promising a thing. A vow could be made without any intention of following it through to the letter. Smiling despite the heartache, she agreed, "Aye, I will find my way home."

James grunted something akin to satisfaction. Terrwyn hoped he did not notice her failure to promise she would head directly home the first chance she had. Not a lie, really, merely an omission. She pushed away the small voice of caution. Nothing would keep her from finding her brother. Not James and certainly not the fates. Not this time.

Sir William and his brother stood outside, arguing about what to do with Archer. Simon's voice began to rise. "She should be sent home."

"If we cut her loose, will you accept the blame if it is discovered she's a Welsh collaborator?"

"C'mon, brother, 'tis plain to see she's not a traitor."

"She's Welsh, isn't she? I've heard her father still seeks Owain Glyndwr's return to Wales's throne. The threat of murdering the king was mentioned."

"Ack," Simon said. "Who did you hear this from? Edgar Poole?"

Terrwyn tensed. James sat behind her. His fingers once again entwined with hers, keeping her from rising up in furor.

The tent wall wavered. Shadows grew. The inside bulged, an imprint of a man's arm pressed into the canvas.

"How did Edgar Poole come by this information? 'Tis a wonder you did not question him of his whereabouts the night Sir James went missing," Simon said. "Frost may be involved, but Poole is just as guilty."

"Any word of Poole's whereabouts?" William asked.

"The new man called Maffew can take her place in the archers' line." Simon continued to press. "He says he's from her village. Her family's beside themselves with worry. Allow me to return the woman to them."

"I'll give the matter some thought, Simon. 'Tis all I can promise."

Terrwyn fought to hold back tears of frustration and rage. She had come too far to let the English return her like an errant lamb. When the tent flap moved, she tilted her chin and readied to fight Simon in his presumptions.

Small, delicate hands bore a tray laden with a pitcher and a loaf of bread. Careful not to spill a drop, Gilbert entered through the opening. His face a structure of concentration, he nodded to them and put the tray on the ground.

Terrwyn bit her tongue, stopping the harsh words before they poured out on the child. She blinked. "Saints above," she whispered under her breath.

This was no time to have a vision fall on her.

A woman's hand, pale and delicate, encircled in dainty ruffles at the wrist. A bracelet with a silver star dangled from the edge of the sleeve. She carried a tray covered with linen. Her tinkling laughter filled the room then faded away. She turned and left, leaving a trail of sadness in her wake. The heaviness stole Terrwyn's breath.

She blinked again.

Gilbert stood in front of her. Her eyes drifted to his hands. A smaller version of what she'd seen moments earlier. An odd look crossed between them.

"You have to eat it." His thin shoulders lifted in a shrug. "Thought you might be hungry." The child moved past her and stood out of her line of vision. She heard him tear off a chunk of bread. The scent of warm butter sailed into the confines of the tent.

James moved against her as he shook his head. "Wonderful though it smells, young Gilbert, I'm unable to take it from your hand. You'll have to come closer and feed it to me."

The boy's heels scraped the ground as he edged near. James struck out, catching the child's jerkin in his fist. A surprised yelp slipped from Gilbert's little mouth.

"When you take Zeus for his nightly exercise, bring him to the clearing behind the tent."

His eyes wide, Gilbert nodded in affirmation of James's request.

"James, you cannot put the child in danger."

They turned, mild irritation registering in their eyes.

"He won't be in danger. He'll say I escaped and fought him for the horse. Everyone knows that no one but I can truly handle Zeus."

"Serves them right if I let Zeus go." Gilbert flashed with outrage. "I won't stand by and watch the soldiers mistreat him."

"Gilbert will have to come with us," Terrwyn said.

"Zeus can take two, but three on his back will slow our travel. Even if the third is small."

"We cannot leave him here," she said.

"I won't go with you," Gilbert muttered. The tears he reined in with purposeful control glittered back. "It will be as Sir James says. They won't think to harm me. Besides I have Cook to care for and I won't leave him behind."

Terrwyn slid over and held Gilbert's hand. Its older form flashed again in her head. Aware she gripped too hard, she gentled her clasp, cupping her palms over his. "Gilbert, are you certain you won't join us?" She peered into his eyes, lost in the awareness of how similar they were in shape and color to both Simon's and William's.

Gilbert shook his head and smiled. "Nay, my mother once told me I must stay with the commander if I'm to find my way home." He lifted his hand from hers and slid a soft fingertip over her cheek. "'Tis all right," he whispered. "Sir William and I have matching stars. I saw his today. Once we cross Offa's Dyke, I'll show him mine."

"Perhaps Terrwyn is right. We can load you on Zeus's back. He's a warhorse, he won't mind a little mite like you."

They all flinched as angry shouts outside carried through the tent. Gilbert rose, dusting the dirt from his leggings. He picked up his tray and made for the opening in the tent wall.

Simon stuck his head through the doorway. "Make haste, young Gilbert, you've more duties to perform before the night is out."

"Aye." With an agreeable nod, Gilbert slid past him.

Simon followed the child's movements before pivoting to look at Terrwyn and James. He squinted into the fading light and then, apparently deciding all was well, left without a word.

Terrwyn released her hold on James's wrist. The small blade between them rolled out of his hand. "We have to find a way to protect Gilbert. I won't ever sleep another decent night if we don't."

"The child is determined."

"Aye, as am I."

James lifted her hand, brushing her knuckles with his lips. "So I've come to know."

Mystified, Terrwyn found it odd that his touch both soothed her and set her yearning for something more. She wondered if he felt her pulse jump and skip under his fingertips. Her eyes closed, she pressed into his embrace, resting, pulling in strength.

As she relaxed, pieces of the vision returned. There was familiarity in the hands. A young girl's. A woman's. A mother, perhaps. A child. The star. A bracelet. Stars. Eyes. The eyes so similar. Moss-green eyes. Lost in the pieces, she drifted, weaving in and out, searching for the answers. She cursed the fickle gift. It gave her nothing when she needed it.

Ringlets of blonde curls. Much like the sketch James gave to Sir William. "The portrait of the woman. Who was she?"

"You ask me now?" He looked at her as if she had finally lost her senses. "Do you really believe this is the best time for jealous feelings?"

"Hush! I cannot concentrate when you are being ridiculous. Of course I'm not jealous. All I am saying is that she looks familiar."

James kissed the nape of her neck. "I don't know how. The last I saw her, she was preparing to follow Owain Glyndwr."

"And why did Sir William covet it so?"

James paused to weigh his answer. "I believe she was the mother of his child."

Before she could question him further, shouts rose up. Riders charged into the camp. The thunder of horses' hooves filled the night. Two whistles, one short, then one long, came through the tent walls.

James grabbed the remains of the loaf of bread. He slid the small knife inside the band of his leggings. "Make haste while their attention is drawn elsewhere."

Her questions forgotten, Terrwyn crawled toward the large chest. The heavy lid groaned when she lifted it. The bow and arrows lay where she had found them earlier.

A lacquered wooden box sat atop a folded leather jerkin. She traced a finger around the crest. The familiar pieces began to fall into place. Peace settled. Her indecision dissipated.

She pivoted on her heels and joined James. The arrow-filled quiver hung from her shoulder. She held out one of Sir William's linen washing cloths, which she had pulled from the chest. James placed the chunk of bread in the center and tied the corners together, then tucked the ends under his belt.

They wrapped a soft woolen blanket around the chain to muffle the rattle of the metal links and, moving with care, they slipped out of the tent.

James pointed to the wooded glen behind the tent. The shadows were darker, the vegetation grew deeper there. Each step moved them farther from the camp. A large shadow wavered restlessly.

A low whistle, two shorts, one long, and then the slight snap of fingers brought the shadow closer.

Zeus stood, regal and impatient. Trained to keep silent, he did not bother the bit with his tongue. He bent his neck and nuzzled the leaves on the ground. His ears twitched, listening for instructions.

James strode up and stroked his palm firmly over the lean muscles in the horse's neck. He led the horse to stand near a boulder. Cupping his hands, he made a stirrup for Terrwyn to step into and lifted her to balance on Zeus's back. The destrier quivered under the unfamiliar seat.

James mounted behind her. He adjusted the chain, keeping enough slack between them to make their ride easier. Nudging the horse's sides with his knees, he moved them from the encampment, away from Sir William's tent.

Terrwyn shivered. It was a dangerous plan. They would travel throughout the night, stopping only to water their horse. She searched her thoughts, testing, waiting for the vision to show her if they were on the right path.

Dejected, she let go a soft sigh. Her gift was as dark as the wooded glen. Instead of relying on what she could not trust, she decided to rely on her eyes. The shadows danced as James turned them to the left.

Wait. Terrwyn jerked her thoughts from her dismal curse. They were returning to the camp where his tent once stood. "What are you thinking, James?"

"We cannot leave things as they are."

Terrwyn turned, nearly upsetting her seat. The journal she'd kept hidden all this time poked into her ribs. It was an uncomfortable reminder that she had not been quite as forthcoming as she should have. "'Tis no cause to go back to your tent. Everything is tossed and scattered. You'll not find what you're looking for."

"How do you know what I'm looking for?" James said. "You think I jeopardize our lives for a trinket?"

"Nay," she soothed. "I would rather we rid ourselves of this place. Be gone."

"You were in agreement with me a few moments ago. I intend to find Gilbert and make him come with us."

Terrwyn did not know how to explain she knew it, but she had to try. "The child will be happy here."

"I cannot take that chance. As you said, we need to be able to sleep at night." He pulled on the reins and slowed their mount. "I cannot very well do this alone. I need your help. We'll slip over to Cook's tent and find Gilbert. If 'tis safe, we'll search my tent for anything to help us on our way."

"'Tis a poor plan," she hissed.

"I know you're afraid. If not for this chain, I'd go by myself." James stopped and made a shushing sound.

Zeus's ears twitched forward, backward and then forward. His muscles rippled under their legs. A dry twig snapped. The crunch of leaves crushed underfoot drew near.

"Don't move, either of you." Simon stepped out of the shadows of a scraggly bush, his broadsword drawn. Gilbert stood by his side, the back of his neck clutched in Simon's ham-sized fist.

"Please. Don't harm the child." Before James could stop her, Terrwyn slid from Zeus and took a cautious step toward them. Caught by the same chain linked to their ankles, he was dragged off, falling in an undignified manner. He scrambled up from the ground. Barefoot, he stood as tall as he could make himself.

Terrwyn felt his rage but could not focus on it. This time, standing side-by-side, Simon and Gilbert showed her the answer to her vision. James grumbled a curse and she made a point to ignore that as well.

"Simon, I cannot believe you intend to dismiss your vow to me."

Simon narrowed his eyes and grunted. His grip showed no signs of loosening from Gilbert's neck.

"Simon, what did you say was your niece's name?"

He jerked as if she had struck him in the stomach. "What?"

"Her name. Before her mam took her away? What did they call her?"

"Gilly. William called her his Gilly-flower."

Terrwyn took another step toward them. The chain between her and James grew taut. "'Tis all right now, Gilly. Deep down, your uncle's a good man. He keeps his vows."

"Gilly?" Simon whispered. "Gilly-flower?"

He swept the oversized cap off Gilbert's head. Waves of pale wheat unfurled. Transformed in front of their eyes, Gilbert became Gilly.

Hesitant, Gilly nodded. She stepped away, rubbing the back of her neck. Her fearful eyes flicked between Terrwyn and Simon.

"Wait," Simon said. "How do I know this is not Welsh trickery?"

Terrwyn knelt down beside the young girl. She held Gilly's small hands and gave her a gentle squeeze. "Show him the star, Gilly. 'Tis time to show him the star. Your uncle will make an easy path to your father. To your home."

Gilly pulled out a bracelet from a pouch hidden in her leggings. A silver star dangled from the links. It matched the one Terrwyn saw in her vision. The design was similar to the one hidden in the crest on the small decorative box in Sir William's chest.

Simon lowered to one knee. His hands shook when he lifted the star to look close. "How—how do you know of this?" he stuttered.

Terrwyn smiled and shrugged. How could she explain something she did not understand? "You and your brother will need to get yourself another page."

Simon stood up. He rested his hand on his niece's shoulder, as if to make sure she did not disappear from his sight. "You best be leaving now. Though my brother will be forever grateful, he has his duty to uphold. He will need to detain you and James until he has his answers."

"But I—we—found his daughter."

"Reuniting with his Gilly-flower may slow him down. I will do what I can to see he does not slight her return. His attention will be turned to his little one for a time, but he will renew his search for you. I'll say what I can to redirect my brother from returning to your village."

"I thank you, Simon of Norwich," Terrwyn said. "I know I ask a great favor, but can you hold to your promise for a little while longer? Please. For the children. They're as innocent as young Gilly."

"Said I'd do what I can," Simon snapped. "Then my vow as your protector is fulfilled."

James stepped up and wrapped his fingers around her waist. He whispered into her hair as he drew her to where Zeus still stood. "Come. He is letting us go tonight. We can ask no more."

Once again on Zeus's back, James pointed them away from the camp. When they were out of the clearing, he brought the horse to a halt and glanced over his shoulder.

William's young brother stood with Gilly and watched them take their leave. A shout rang over the treetops. Simon saluted and turned to walk toward the tents, his arm wrapped protectively around his niece's slender shoulders. He bellowed orders at the men riding toward them and sent them in the opposite direction that Terrwyn and Zeus rode.

James leaned in, embracing her tight to his chest. They rode in silence, sliding in and out of the shadows. The half-moon followed them until it was neatly overhead. A wide span of meadow opened out before them. The moonlight gave them rest from the shifting shadows but took away their protection.

Chapter Nineteen

Night moved in. The dark shadows stretched and blended until they pooled into one. The mountains and valley dipped behind them.

Terrwyn rode in front of James, nestled in his arms, her weight pressed against his chest. The urge to hug her closer began to bloom. He knew she slept when her body went lax and her breathing changed. A delicate snore interrupted the silence of their ride. A soft breeze whispered over them. Her hair grazed his lips. He smiled and inhaled her scent.

James took a circuitous path that he hoped would cause the soldiers to scratch their heads. While the hours passed, he had come to a decision without discussing it with Terrwyn.

He could not leave Wales without sketches of those who plotted against Henry. He had to return to the Bloated Goat's ale room one more time. Perhaps the tavern's mistress would give him aid. It would mean Terrwyn would need to keep to her men's leggings and tunic, and replace the cap she lost. Most of all, they would need to remove the manacles from their ankles. He was thankful the soldiers had wrapped the metal around Terrwyn's slim boot. The leather would shield her from the constant rubbing that had begun to plague his skin. He added the procurement of a pair of boots for himself to their growing list of needs.

Taking in a deep breath, he leaned forward to cradle Terrwyn tighter. He slid his hand around to the flat of her stomach.

He paused.

The air he drew in abruptly expelled. He felt along the familiar shape hidden under her tunic. He withdrew his hand and let it rest on the crest of her hip.

He worked to control the erupting dark thoughts. How had he been drawn in? He knew deception—he sat by its side every day of his life. How did he not recognize it? Why had she not presented it to Sir William if only to save her own skin?

No matter how long he rode, James could not shake the inexplicable hurt that this Welsh woman had betrayed him. Why it mattered, he could not fathom. The simple fact that she had lied to him hurt more than the concern that she might work to protect her father.

As his memory flashed to those he saw earlier, the faces hidden under the shadows at the Bloated Goat became clearer. He recognized the craggy nose and high cheekbones. He would imbed another face in his latest drawing. He was certain it was Edgar Poole and Dafydd ap Hew who were in deep conversation as they left the meeting that night. James marveled at Dafydd's temerity. He placed his daughter's life in jeopardy while he plotted against the king. James ached for Terrwyn, knowing the pain she would endure when she learned her love and loyalty were misplaced.

CরৡঠO

A few hours before daylight James and Terrwyn entered a dense grove of trees. They rode over the rise of the hill and dipped into a low ravine. James searched for a protected spot for them to rest. They would wait in the cool hours of morning and watch the trail behind them. If someone followed, they would know soon enough.

Anger over Terrwyn's betrayal simmered in his head. He did not want to be in as close proximity, stuck on horseback, when he pressed her for answers. After giving it great thought, he had decided to let her keep her secret. He would find a way to use it to his advantage.

A small measure of pride in her ability to scoop it up under watchful eyes swept over him. It was her betrayal that kept him wary. The knowledge that she had his drawings and did not tell him began to burrow into his skin.

Under the waning moonlight, he paused to examine Terrwyn as she slept in his arms. Despite his care, the weight of the chains rubbed her leg. If they did not stop to rest now, the decision would be taken out of his hands. He would not allow her to become crippled because of his urgent need to push on.

He twitched the reins and Zeus came to a halt beside a low-growing branch. The horse sighed, nickering softly when James shifted his weight. He listened to the quiet of the woods. The lapping, gurgling rhythm of a stream worked its way into their surroundings.

"Time to open your eyes, love," he said.

Terrwyn stirred. Before she could ask, he gave his directions on how he figured they would dismount. Bound by the chain between them they maneuvered until they slid off as one.

"Where are we?"

"Safe, for now."

"'Tis good to hear." Her eyes soft with exhaustion, she smiled up at him and placed her hands on his cheeks.

James bit back the curse he laid at Sir William's feet. A deep purpling line encircled each of her wrists. He knew she would object if he asked if it pained her. Careful to keep his concern hidden behind an amiable smile, he placed a kiss beside the tender skin.

A soft gasp brushed the air around them.

He found her mouth before he realized he intended to do so. She tasted sweet, like honey. Nay, more than honey. She tasted like a honeycomb dripping with honey, fresh from the beehive, waiting for the taking. A heady mixture of earth and life. The desire to taste the rest of her, testing for more of the same, pulsed through his veins.

He released his hold and searched her face for uncertainty. She trembled beside him but she did not pull away. She stood, swaying slightly, leaning into his hands. Her pulse raced under his fingertips. The center of her brown eyes enlarged until he thought he might fall into them. Her lips, swollen from his abuse, looked bee-stung.

The realization he stepped where he dared not go without caution bit at him until he drew back. "There," he said, giving her a chaste peck on the cheek. "Something to help you remember me."

Terrwyn looked at him with wonder and confusion darkening her eyes. "You think me addled? How am I to forget you when you are strapped to my ankle?"

"Ah. We won't always be so joined, will we?" The need to taste her, just a nip, flooded his senses. He gathered her into his arms, pulling her to his chest, and stormed her mouth once again.

He pressed his forehead to hers and slowed his racing breaths. He stroked her flushed cheek, stopping when he caught a teardrop on his fingertip. The moment he released her from his embrace he felt it. Loneliness filled the empty space she once filled.

He turned, pointing toward the sound of the stream. "If we are careful, we should make it down there without mishap."

"But—" Terrwyn's tongue lost its usefulness for language. Her lips buzzed from his onslaught. Words she'd used since she toddled at her mam's knee evaporated with his kiss. As she tried to put sense to her reaction, she realized James had shuttered his face. He was moving down the ravine before she had time to form her questions.

"Place your feet where I've placed mine."

Terrwyn carried a portion of the chain and limped behind him. Mindful of hidden ruts and stones, they moved slowly down the bank. Zeus followed, his great body brushing against the low-hanging branches.

James moved in exact, thought-out movements. One misstep and either she or he would be tripping over the cursed metal between them.

They stopped by the stream. Given his head, Zeus drank deeply. James clasped his hands behind his back.

Puzzled by his behavior, Terrwyn sat on a nearby rock. A deep sigh radiated from her chest. She could not help wincing when she shifted her weight on the hard stone. She was relieved the moon hid her face, or James would have spent his time hovering over her as he did Zeus. Although to her eyes, the horse seemed none the worse for wear. She tamped down her irritation. The man stirred her blood until she could not think and then his ardor vanished like an early frost.

When the horse had its fill of water, he led it to a nearby tree. Terrwyn hobbled close beside him. His movements were fluid, efficient and effortless. She swayed from fatigue and watched him caress Zeus's sleek coat. She wondered what it would be like to have his gentle hands on her back, rubbing the crest of her hips. He might even glide those long fingers over her neck, stretching the aching muscles. The dull aches she had managed to ignore awoke and demanded his attention. Instead of pleading, she kept her silence.

James patted the satchel behind the saddle. His wide smile smoothed the deep furrows that had begun to form around his mouth. "Look here, Zeus." He held out a handful of grain. "Young Gilly ensured your needs come before mere humans'."

The horse bent to nuzzle the palm of his flattened hand and ate as if he had not been fed for days. James pulled the saddle off, bringing the woolen blanket with it.

Terrwyn fussed with the quiver of arrows she had taken from Sir William's chest. She huddled over the bundle she brought with her and pulled out the loaf of bread Gilly gave them. When she held out a portion to James, she could not help noting the exhaustion marring his eyes, even though he tried to hide it when he turned his attention on her.

"Come, James, rest a while beside me." She motioned toward the stone seat. "You cannot go on without a bit of sleep."

"Sleep will come when the king's safety is secured."

"And if you collapse?"

"Don't worry your head, Terrwyn. I've gone without sleep longer than this."

She folded her arms and looked at him in disbelief. "I'll not have you falling down while you're bound to me. You're too large a man to make me drag your arse out of the way."

James pulled her close. "Is that all that worries you?" His fingers laced gently around her waist. His hand paused over the flat plane, noting the journal's absence. He leaned in and let his lips play across her cheek, along the angle of her jaw, the length of her slender neck and back up to her full mouth. She tasted so sweet. He dipped in, memorizing each crest, each valley. With each intentional action he removed another layer of loneliness. He built memories for the days when he sat alone and drew her portrait. Somehow, he would place it into his memory and save himself from his solitary existence.

He bunched her braid in his hand. The silken strands wrapped around his wrists, as if to bind him to her.

"I recall you have a smithy in your village."

"Aye."

"Then don't fret. Soon, you'll be free of me and I will retrieve my drawings from Sir William." He watched for signs of guilt, nearly missing the slight flutter of lashes. She did not like what she heard. He waited, hoping she would reveal where she hid his packet. And, Saints' bloody bones, why she continued to keep them hidden.

Terrwyn shivered. The metal links whispered when she shifted to draw close. "No need to rush off. When you pick up your sword instead of the charcoal pieces, you won't be such a heavy burden to have in my way."

"You want me to give up my drawings?"

"'Tis what got you into trouble, was it not? Sir William needed you to serve as a soldier, not as a pale-handed man who draws flora and fauna." She kneaded his shoulder. "There now, I didn't mean to hurt your wee feelings. I've seen your drawings and they are lovely. Why, even the portrait I spied was uncanny, but what can the king be thinking? Sending you along with the army slowed them down and vexed the commander to no end. I've given it considerable thought and now understand why Sir William was so willing to believe the worst of you. Perhaps if we spend time together after we remove the shackles, I can teach you some weaponry skills."

James tried to see if she'd sustained a head injury without his knowledge. How else could she come up with her outlandish ideas that he could not handle a weapon? She continued to gaze at him, her brown eyes full of concern. Her hand slid over his arm, stroking him as if he were a pet. He drew in a breath and had to force it out when her breasts brushed his chest. Her closeness almost wiped away the anger he had been carrying ever since he discovered she had his damn drawings.

He dragged his thoughts from useless yearnings. He could not ignore his vow. It was not just a vow to a king. This was a promise to his friend. He would see Henry live to be a ripe, wrinkled old man. Though Henry would indeed understand the lure of a maiden's charms, James knew he could not follow the distraction. The king's safety sat heavily in his hands.

"We will ride for your village," James said. "I give you my word, I will make certain you arrive without harm."

Terrwyn shivered again. It was as if an early winter freeze fell over her. Guilt nipped at her heels. It took but one kiss from James's lips to push the worry for her family away. "Nay! We cannot return. It won't be safe." Her protests were silenced by the finger resting on her lips.

She searched her memories. There had been dark dreams threaded with fear, laced with anger. Flames danced from torches. Only recently those dreams had shifted. Now she heard the sounds of children laughing as they danced in a field of clover. Their laughter turned to shrieks of terror. Her efforts were never enough to save them.

However, she was coming to understand what she saw was not always what would come to pass. If she remained strong in her decisions, it was possible for her to step in and change the outcome. She had seen Drem taken away, yet she did not heed the warning. This she regretted with every breath. With regret comes learning. She had seen the joy of Padrig's birth and the sorrow for Mam that soon followed. She had misunderstood what she saw. It was not the truth. The truth came with the living of the moment. Until that moment occurred, she still had the opportunity to change the fates.

She gently lifted his finger from her lips. She did not shove him away, but held him. "I cannot return to my village." She gripped James's hands. The need to make him understand her fears was overpowering. "We must stay away from my village. What other direction can we head? 'Tis certain you are under the king's edict, placed on you before we met. Where did you intend to travel before the fates tangled us together?"

James shook free from her grasp and shoved his hands into his hair. His nostrils flared and narrowed as if he fought to control his breathing. He spun on his heels, dragging Terrwyn along beside him. "We've rested long enough. Mount Zeus now."

Chapter Twenty

They kept to the trees and off the dirt trail that some liked to call a road. Although the terrain was rough, traveling by horseback reduced the days Terrwyn had walked through the forest into hours.

The time to talk easily about the drawings of Drem had long passed. Guilt danced over her shoulders. What if James had drawn that picture of her brother while he waited at the Bloated Goat? His imagination would carry him away on some ridiculous notion that Drem played a role in the plot against the English king. That could not be. If Drem were free from the English, he would have returned home as soon as his feet hit the Welsh shore. Of that she was certain. Of course, if Drem were there she'd protect him this time.

Whether James knew it or not, he would not rid himself of her presence. Not until she saw her task clear through to the end.

She glanced at James when she felt a vibration through her back. He was humming a ditty about a young wench who wore posies in her hair. His deep voice danced over her in waves. By the time he came to its end, she decided he must have made it up as he went. The lyrics made no sense. It began with the wench who lived with haughtiness in her heart and the poor besotted soul loved her until he died. She beat him stoutly every day, yet he was the death of her. The song ended with the young lovers wrapped in their love as they sailed off to sea.

To Terrwyn's frustration, the senseless song remained in her head. Or rather, it was the beauty of his voice she could not release. No longer distracted, she noticed the path they rode over was not one she remembered ever traveling.

Aye, the man was a treacherous distraction. It would serve her well to walk cautiously. James was still King Henry's man.

"Why does Edgar Poole's hatred flow so deep?" she asked.

"He plays to both parties."

"And you know this how?"

"Saw him come out of a meeting. He stepped out of the shadows and there he was, the moon shining brightly on his narrow face." James chose not to mention Edgar's companion. The night had been too dark, the shadows too deep for him to be certain of the person's face, but he had his suspicions. Perhaps, given another opportunity, he would know it well enough to add it to his drawings.

James searched the horizon for signs of riders coming their way. "Edgar must have seen me as well."

"Then we won't return to my family," she said. "I won't play any part in reminding the king's soldiers where my village lies." The tone of her voice brooked no arguments.

James thought it best to ignore her threats. Like as not, she was more frightened of her father's ire than that of Sir William.

Dear God, she must have brought her family to their knees when they discovered she had run off in the middle of the night on some addle-brained scheme. Of one thing he was certain, if she belonged to him, he would find a way to keep her under lock and key for a good stretch of time. The idea of her out on her own in the wild squeezed his chest until it felt like it might explode. Life in the village may have been a trial of patience, her capabilities questioned at every opportunity. However, he could not fathom the hurt that had led her to jeopardize her safety.

She was right. They could not go to her village. By now, Sir William's men would be headed in that direction. It would better serve her family if there were no signs of them having been there.

"There is an inn not far from where we are," James said. "If you can last a half-day's ride we will continue on."

"Connected as we are, I don't think it likely they'll want to help us."

"Then we will borrow the smithy's tools and break free on our own."

Terrwyn glanced over her shoulder. James's face was set in a study of perfect calm. That was one thing she could count on. He was steady.

Except for the times when he looked at her like he wanted to eat her. Then he near made her want to jump out of her clothes and head for a cool stream.

"Then, if you are a very good girl," James continued, "we'll see about renting a place for us to bathe and rest properly."

"What?" Terrwyn restrained the need to smooth the dirt from her jerkin. She'd worn it for so long it had begun to stick to her skin. Instead, she tucked the random stray hair behind her ear. She was surprised to find numbness in her fingers. It matched the same feeling in her head. Exasperated with her body's frailty, she startled when James smiled down at her. "Why are you looking at me like that?"

"What way is that, sweeting?"

Although his response carried the tone of complete innocence, Terrwyn wished she could see his eyes. Perhaps her edginess was nothing more than an overreaction to exhaustion. Her back wedged against his chest, she took a deep breath and tried to relax.

James's voice dropped an octave lower than normal as he began to hum a new tune. This one was a fighting song, one of powerful thrusts and parries.

"There now," Terrwyn said. "You'll learn fine if you keep those words in your head when I'm helping you find your skill with a knife and sword." Feeling the need for honesty, she patted his thigh to soften her words. "I cannot promise I can keep you alive, but I can promise to teach you how to live a while longer."

James shouted his laughter until his shoulders quaked. At her vehement rebuke to keep quiet, he squeezed her tight. He shook his head in wonder at the woman who sat before him. She was actually planning his first lesson in the art of hand-to-hand combat. He looked forward to letting her win. The first few times.

She launched into a discourse on the art of wrestling, and he nearly dropped the reins. Visions of their limbs locked together made him shift uncomfortably. Entertained and aroused, he listened intently to the seductive timbre of her instructions. When the Inn at the Crossroads came into sight he was annoyed to have their ride end so soon.

He would have to ensure she continued her instructions in detail. He particularly enjoyed hearing that when in wrestling mode he should lock his thighs around her waist. He considered whether he would request she demonstrate the move.

James drew up on the reins and stopped Zeus in a grove of trees. They dismounted still as one. Only this time he came off a few seconds before Terrwyn. He caught her and held her close. They wavered, teetering, trying to sort out the balance of their weight.

Zeus jerked his head to reach a fresh growth of grass. His motion ended their battle. They fell into the bushes, the air knocked out of their lungs.

A startled shriek erupted. Then Terrwyn began to laugh. Her laughter was muffled instantly when James pressed the back of her head, bringing her lips to his.

Still lying across his body, their legs entwined, she pushed up from the leaves. "Your injuries—"

"Are improving with your every touch."

Her eyes wide, she stared at his mouth. She blinked before lowering her head to drink from his lips.

James allowed her full access. His body hummed from her onslaught as she pressed her hips into his belly, stirring his loins. His body bucked instantaneously.

Flipping Terrwyn on her back, he covered her mouth, quieting the surprised squeal. She lay beneath him. His hips opened her thighs, spreading her legs. He grabbed her wrists and pushed them over her head. When he glanced up, he saw the bruises that spread into a wide ring. Although he ached to press his body into hers, have her drain him senseless, he released her and pushed up. He was staggered to find his hand was trembling when he swiped his hair from his eyes.

Still lying where he left her, Terrwyn watched him. His quick reflexes stunned her. She would have never believed an artist could move quickly. Without warning, he had her flipped under him, swift and easy. A proud smile tugged at her mouth as it wove its way over her face. He would be wonderful in close-quarter combat. Aye, there was hope for them yet.

Being kissed into submission was a tactic she was willing to learn. Always an eager student, she decided she must convince him to kiss her again. This time, it would be she who turned away first.

"Stop that," he said.

Torn from her plans to tutor him as soon as they were free from the damn chains, she took a moment to register he was angry. A storm had formed over his sky blue eyes. His anger stemmed from something she had done. "Stop what?"

"Woman, don't pretend you are unaware of what you are doing."

Terrwyn licked her lips and stared hard at him. His breathing came in short bursts. Wary of his mood, she moved slowly as if he were an injured creature. She studied the pulse beating along the thick cording of neck muscles. He seemed to squirm under her observation.

"Bless the saints' ugly bones! You cannot look at me like you are and expect me to keep my hands off of you." He turned, tugging on the front of his jerkin, a glare in his eyes. "And unless you want me to take you here in the bushes, contain your tongue."

Terrwyn clamped her lips together. Mystified by his anger, she reached out and stroked a soothing hand over his back. His reaction was to roll on top of her, knocking the air out of her lungs in a whoosh. His hand slid over her mouth. His lips were close to her ear. Puffs of air pushed her hair, caressed her skin.

Her heart slammed against her ribcage. It beat out a fast tempo as she struggled to draw in a breath. While she contemplated biting his hand, he whispered, "Riders."

They lay still, hidden in the brush. Their harsh breaths came and went until each breath gentled and worked with the other. "Zeus," Terrwyn said against his hand.

Moving as one, they turned their heads to look at the horse. The stallion continued to eat at the grass, moving down the sloped ditch. He paused and lifted his head as if he sensed other horses drawing near.

James made a clicking sound. Zeus moved farther down the hill and went back to munching on the greenery.

The horses whinnied when their riders brought them to stop in front of the inn. Why Zeus never responded, Terrwyn would never understand. Perhaps James had another secret to share with her. Whether he was surprising her with his ability to silence the stallion's nature to another horse's call or drawing pictures of flora and fauna, the man had magic in his hands. When she shivered under his touch, she wondered what it would be like when he finally decided to use his magic on her.

CЯ୫୨

Terrwyn sat on the ground. Her legs were bunched up close to her bottom, her heels close together.

James sat out of reach, the chain stretched between them. The saddle lay upside down. A small knife in hand, he pried off a panel underneath the arch of the pommel. A linen cloth pouch sat in the well. He pulled it out, balancing it in his palm. "There's enough gold here to procure the smithy's help. Maybe a night's stay at the inn."

She shook her head. "Nay, once they lay their eyes on these English-made manacles, there won't be enough coin to be had. And if there is, they will reveal us as sure as you need to take another breath."

"Are you certain you want to do this?"

"Aye, we have little choice in the matter, now do we. We cannot walk up to the man and say, 'Hand over your tools like a good boy'. Those tools are his livelihood. You may as well tell him to hand over his wife and children."

James ran his fingers through his hair, tugging on the ends. He glanced over at her. "And you remain determined the tools come back after we are through?"

"Even if he was as fair and good as they come and we had all coin in England, he won't want to help us. It would put his family in danger."

"All right then. Soon as the light is dimmed and they appear to head for bed, we will make our way to the stables."

Terrwyn knelt over the saddle and kissed his cheek. "'Tis a grand plan."

James caught the back of her neck before she could withdraw. He held her suspended over the saddle. She swayed as he drew her closer. He pulled her in, caught her bottom and yanked her into his lap. Enticed by the taste offered before them, they ignored the clank of the chain.

His breathing erratic, James lifted Terrwyn from his lap. When she thought he would push her away as he had before, he surprised her once again. "Come." He held his arm out, his side ready for her to slip beside.

Reluctant, she scooted over to sit next to him. His back resting against a rough boulder, he cushioned the hard surface, allowing her a place to relax.

They sat, hip to hip. Terrwyn tucked her head into the crook of his arm. James smoothed her hair and kissed the top of her crown. He released a deep sigh and gave her a one-armed hug. "It won't be much longer. Then we will be free of the chains."

Terrwyn nodded. Aye, soon the chain that kept them together would be broken. She did not know why, but the thought was not as appealing as she once believed it would be.

CRID

A single lantern hung in the window of the smithy's shed. The dim light spread into the moonless sky. Terrwyn and James watched the innkeeper close the doors behind him after the last post of the day rode in. His shadow wavered against the outside wall of the establishment as he rounded the building and entered the Inn at the Crossroads.

The noise of muffled evening talk carried on the wind and into the glen. The innkeeper and his staff moved about, preparing for another day of toil. The slap of the door announced their presence each time they came and went. They brought in firewood. They carried out slop buckets. Refuse was tossed to the pigs in the pen near the barn. If the wind was right, their existence would not be known until the slab of salted pork hit the trencher on the trestle table.

Angry shouts broke through the quiet of isolation as the innkeeper and another man stumbled out the door.

James laid a hand on Terrwyn's shoulder. "Steady."

The innkeeper's punch whiffed past the man's jaw. "Guest or not, you look at my wife like that again and I'll pummel you into the ground."

A young woman stood in the doorway. Her wide hips and full bust blocked the light seeping through the open door. The kerchief on her head worked to contain her frizzing hair. "Here now, Hywel, there's no call to act a fool." She held up two jugs and tapped them together. "Who's goin' to help a lovely lady like meself drink this fine ale?"

The men paused, swaying, their chests puffing from exertion. Hywel wiped his mouth with the back of his hand.

"Come, husband. 'Tis no way to treat a paying guest. Let the man go. He meant no harm."

Their guest slipped quickly back inside, past the innkeeper's wife. "Here," she said, thrusting the jugs into his hands. "Have Magda pour us a large portion and play us a song or two."

"Will you dance me a jig, Tilda, my love?" Hywel called out as he waddled to the door.

Tilda gave him a punch to his arm, softening it with a teasing laugh. "Aye, you play your cards right and you won't tear your mind from me."

He grabbed her waist, pulled her to his large belly. "You dance only for me, you hear?"

"Oh, go on with yourself." She slapped his chest and shoved him inside.

As Terrwyn rose from behind the shrub, Tilda paused in the doorway. The woman held the door half-open and looked out into the night, across the dirt lane that marked the crossroads. Satisfied she saw nothing that should not be, she turned and closed the door.

James jerked Terrwyn to the ground. "Have patience."

Chapter Twenty-One

The moon moved out from behind the clouds. Though it offered them light to see, it encumbered them with the knowledge they would have to wait until the inhabitants of the Inn at the Crossroads were deep into their cups.

James counted six people. The innkeeper and his wife. The char woman. The one they called Magda. And two riders who had arrived at sunset. Any one of them might step outside to use the privy and notice them.

Terrwyn and James sat side by side, their backs resting against a log. James's movements were slow as he propped his foot on his knee.

"This might be the first time I'm grateful for my wee stature," Terrwyn said. "'Tis glad, that I am, that they didn't take my boots too."

Too tired to speak, James smiled wearily, acknowledging his own relief.

She leaned in for a closer look. "Your wound is weeping."

"Aye, my feet are worse for wear, too." He chuckled at his own misery.

"Now why didn't you say something before? I would have found some herbs to hold the redness at bay."

"I had other matters on my mind," he said.

"Well, there's no need to be an irritable bear about it." Terrwyn stretched to reach the small blanket they were using to muffle the noise of the chain. "Hand me your little knife."

James complied without a word.

She made short work of cutting narrow strips. Then she

lifted his foot onto her lap. "'Tis a good thing Sir William was stingy with his comforts. This blanket is so thin I can nearly see right through it. It will do well."

She tucked the pieces of fabric under the metal ring around his ankle. The padding lifted the manacle off of James's wound. When she was done, she looked up to see the pain fading from his face. It warmed her heart to know she eased his hurting. Isolde, the healer and midwife from her village, would have been amused at her efforts, but it would hold until the irons were broken.

She trapped his leg when he began to draw his foot from her lap. She caught his gaze. There was something about him that showed in his eyes. When he was calm, the color of his eyes reminded her of a clear blue sky. Then there were the gray shades of winter. But this blue was rich and deep, like the color right before dawn.

When James jerked at her touch, she made the same soothing sounds she used to calm one of the lambs. Only this seemed to have no effect. She trapped his foot under her palm. Her fingers trembled as she smoothed the dirt from the arch. She held him until his foot was wrapped in a layer of blanket strips. When she motioned for his other one, his hesitation held for only a few seconds, long enough for her to hear his quick intake of breath.

The air heated when they made contact. She did her best to ignore what looked like faerie dust sparking between them. Either her imagination was getting the best of her or the faeries had cast a spell. She decided exhaustion was the culprit. She methodically wrapped and padded the other foot. Her task completed, she released him as if she held a hot coal.

While she brushed her hands over her leggings, she used the time to settle her own reaction to the warmth of his skin against her palm. It made her mouth water. Saints' bones, it made her want another taste of his lips. Faerie dust, indeed.

"I don't believe anyone has cared for my wounds as finely as you." His voice was low and thick. He paused, then turned to lift her hands. He cradled them as if he held precious jewels. "I wish to thank you properly."

Terrwyn felt her face flush hot. Never had her healing

efforts been so appreciated. A part of her wondered how he aimed to thank her more than he had. Instead of letting her imagination get the better of her, she struck out for neutral ground. "Hush. You rest while we can."

James nodded, then after placing a gentle kiss on each knuckle, he released her hands.

The warmth where he had touched her began to recede. Emptiness took its place. Guilt nipped at her, reminding her that she had not told him she had the journal. Filled with good intentions, she opened her mouth. It snapped shut on its own accord. Now was not the time.

Something inside pushed at her, wanting to see what lay ahead. Fearing her night visions would reawaken and lead her down the wrong path, she closed her mind.

CR&O

They waited until the music began to rise. The fiddle player set into a rambunctious rhythm. Laughter spilled into the night.

James crawled onto all fours. Then he stood and held out his hand for Terrwyn. They would move as one creature. Traveling over the uneven ground slowed their pace. Their breaths came and went as they ventured out of the shadows and into the moonlight.

They paused beside a storage shed and James listened at the door. No one stirred from inside. He lifted the wedge of wood that held the stable doors shut. Restless, one of the horses nickered. Soon as they were inside, Terrwyn found a bag of grain standing next to a stall. She grabbed a handful and held it out for the horse.

The blacksmith's tongs and hammers hung on the wall. Various sizes of horseshoes littered a nearby bench. The tall worktable held the smaller versions of hammers and hooks. Rods of iron waited for turning into nails and the sundry iron needs.

James locked arms with her and pointed to the anvil. He swept up a handful of already-formed hooks and a few nails, then grabbed a medium-sized hammer from the table. Terrwyn took the chisel lying beside a pile of tools.

Their arms still locked together, they headed for the door. James looked out. The sounds coming from the inn were beginning to wind down. He motioned that they would stay against the shadowed side of the building. They skirted the small privy house and slipped into the wooded glen.

James gripped the hammer and eyed Terrwyn's leg. She sat on the ground, her leg propped on a stone. Moments earlier, she had stuffed the thin blanket inside the boot to act as padding. He feared it would not be enough protection if his aim was wrong.

Sweat dripped down his forehead and slid down his cheek. The hammer's wooden handle was smooth and worn. Perspiration lubricated his hands until he worried the hammer would fly out when he took the first swing.

Terrwyn looked up at him, her eyes alight with impatience. She placed the chisel on the lock. The blunt end created a target for him to hit. She took a deep breath and offered him an encouraging smile.

James put the hammer down. It was a relief to have its weight out of his hand. He squatted next to Terrwyn and wiped the sweat off his upper lip.

"I will be fine," she said, as she grasped his wrist.

"You trust me to do this? What if it doesn't work?"

"Then we think of something else." Her thumb ran over his pulse, soothing him with her touch. "We discussed this. The manacle comes off me first. If the din we make brings unwanted company, then we run. I would slow us down if I had to run with the weight of the chain. You are a strong brawny man and can handle it by yourself.

"What if my aim is wrong and I maim you?"

"Then you'd have to carry me on your big broad back." She cupped his hand in hers. "Now cease your fretting. Time is passing. We need to return the smithy's tools before he knows they're gone."

"You remain stubborn on that notion?"

Terrwyn frowned. "I am. I will borrow but I will not steal.

'Twould be like taking the bread out of his mouth."

James brushed a kiss over her forehead and then her mouth. He rose. She was right. Precious time was slipping past them.

After handing a strip of blanket to Terrwyn to wrap around the chisel, he picked up the hammer. He ordered her to hold still, took a breath and made the first swing.

The sound of metal striking metal echoed through the glen. The air shivered with the impact.

They did not move. Their eyes locked. Moonlight glistened on the tears on Terrwyn's cheek. She drew the blanket away from the chisel to examine the lock. The iron held.

"'Tis as you said. We will find another way."

Swearing under his breath, James threw the hammer down. He turned and began to gather what he could reach. The bundle slipped from his fingers. The nails and iron fishhooks flew in the air and rained out over the leaves.

He knelt down. "Stay." He pulled her foot into his lap.

Holding up the nails, he began trying each one, prying, twisting and turning in the lock. After several tries, he used one that entered the lock with ease.

Terrwyn cut through the silence between them when he withdrew the iron from the lock. "What are you doing?"

"Patience."

"Perhaps the soldiers have left my village. We could enlist the smithy's help."

James held out a nail. "Its shape is similar to some of the keys I've seen on a set of jailer's rings. I need to make a few adjustments. Then it should do the trick."

He rubbed the sharp end until it was squared off. The sparks from metal dragging against stone twinkled in the dark. It took several attempts until, satisfied with his work, he inserted the key.

The lock snicked open. He pried apart the manacle and it fell from Terrwyn's ankle.

"'Tis a brilliant man who sits before me," she whispered in awe.

Without saying another word, she launched her body into

his and celebrated her freedom by placing kisses on his forehead, his cheeks, his ears, his eyebrows and finally his lips.

He claimed her waist with his hands, pulled her close and drank in her joy.

Terrwyn took the key from his hand and prayed it worked for the manacle around his ankle. She winced when she felt the heat coming from the skin around the wound. The blanket strips placed earlier had helped, but now there was swelling. Each step must have been taken in agony. Her heart twisted, feeling the pain he kept in silence.

"A kiss for luck?" he jested.

"Aye. One now." She tenderly placed a kiss on the corner of his mouth. "Another after you are free."

The lock was slow to release. Terrwyn argued with it, twisting and jiggling the key until the manacle finally gave way.

A deep sigh slid out from James as he tipped backward. He carried Terrwyn with him, cushioning her head on his chest. They lay where they fell, watching the stars in the sky, listening to each other's heartbeats.

Sometime during the night, they fell into an exhausted sleep. Terrwyn awoke to find her head cradled in James's arms. Their shared warmth kept the desire to linger alive. She knew she could not. Nor could she ignore the dream that shook her awake.

Now, finally free from the chains, she could move without him knowing. She felt a bit wobbly without James by her side. She had come to depend on him too much. It was best that she regain her balance and manage on her own. She would need to have her feet planted firmly underneath her when they parted ways. Although their parting would mean she had found Drem, the thought of leaving James did not appeal to her at all.

Her night visions had returned. She must make haste if she intended to change the fates this time. She gathered her bow and quiver and headed toward the inn.

Chapter Twenty-Two

The hammer and chisel gripped to her chest, Terrwyn lifted the latch on the shed door. She slipped inside. The light in the lantern had long since blown out.

She grabbed a bucket of grain and fed it to the horses kept in the stalls. They paid little attention to her movements while they filled their empty stomachs.

Aware that her time was limited, she hurried to put the tools back where they'd found them. She meant what she had told James. She was no thief. The innkeeper and his family needed those smithing tools to keep themselves in business. An inn incapable of making repairs would lose a great deal of profit. Coin was difficult to come by. She would not be the cause of their empty bellies.

However, an extra pair of boots would not make a difference to anyone's belly. Those skilled in repairing horse tack often carried that skill over to footwear. She began her search in the stack of leather goods piled in one corner. Halters and bridles hung on a rack awaiting repair.

A rooster crowed. Pieces of the night vision that had shaken her awake returned. They needed to be free of this place and flee to England. The heaviness on her chest made it hard to breathe easily.

The rooster crowed again. Twice now. Her heart began to beat faster. She needed to leave before its next call.

From the small window, the first shards of light cut into the darkest hours before dawn. She must return to the glen before

James awoke and noticed she and the tools were gone. He would be unhappy but since the task would have been already completed, his forgiveness should be easily earned.

The promise he'd forced out of her to not stray from their campsite began to nag at her conscience. It was not a verbal agreement. Not a true vow. The words did not cross her lips. She had merely nodded her consent. Besides, once he understood they could ride out immediately, he would forgive her.

She pushed back the dark portions of the dream that woke her up in the first place. She closed her eyes. This time she would use the good in her night vision. Slowing her breathing, she began to see the workroom. There was a small room off the main stalls. A tack room. Benches lined the wall. Under the bench was a pair of leather boots.

Keeping her eyes closed, she retraced her steps in the dream. When she came to the small room, she opened her eyes. It was exactly as she saw it. Confident she would find what she sought, she knelt down. The boots were hidden behind a strip of leather. She scooped the boots up and tucked them inside her jerkin. A leather braided rope hung from a hook on the wall. She belted it around her waist, tying it off in a knot. The boots tucked under her arms made her waistline full as a fat hen.

Sounds of awakening life began to stir outside. Aware of the warning in her dream, she hurried to leave. She stopped long enough to listen for anyone nearby. Her hand on the door latch, she heard the third crow.

Cursing under her breath, she decided there was no turning back. She could not stay inside the shed all day. The good people of the Inn at the Crossroads would eventually notice her presence.

The lever moved in her hand as the innkeeper yanked the stable door open.

Terrwyn stumbled out. The back of her jerkin hung in his great paw.

"What do I have here?" The innkeeper lifted her off the ground and shook her.

A weak yelp escaped. "I can explain," she choked out.

He pulled her close. His face twisted in a snarl as he kept one eye shut and peered at her with the other one. His sour breath stank from the evening's ale. "What are doing in yon stables, boy?"

Struggling to get her feet back under her, she worked to wiggle from his hold. "I didn't think it would hurt much for me to take a wee rest. I'm traveling by my lonesome. There were soldiers about. Have you seen them too? I didn't want them to conscript me into their damned army. I intended to leave real soon, no worse for the wear." Terrwyn produced the best sorrowful expression she ever created.

"Who do you think you're fooling?" He shook her again. "You won't be peddling your tripe to me. No soldiers have come through this way."

Terrwyn felt the knot on the leather belt loosen. The boots began to shift and slide out from under her jerkin. Plop. First one.

"Here now. What's this?" Wide-eyed, he lifted the edge of her leather jerkin and yanked down the other boot. He held it under her nose. "You're a bloody thief."

Terrwyn thought about denying it, but what could she say? The fact that she had brought back his smithy tools did not seem to hold much weight.

He looked back at the stables. Keeping her in his grasp he dragged her toward the door. The horses munched on the grain she had poured out on the floor.

"I'm betting you are a horse thief, too! 'Tis why you were in there."

"Nay, I was looking for a wee drink of water. I didn't think you would mind."

"You didn't think I would mind?" He grabbed a rope from the stall and knotted it around her wrists. "Sit." He pointed to a pile of straw. "Move and I'll end your misery now."

He bellowed for Tilda to come at once. When his wife did not make an appearance, he marched off, yelling for her to make haste and bring his blade.

Terrwyn had ideas other than waiting for him to run her through. She slowly inched her way up the wall.

She jumped when an angry voice said, "Woman, are you crazed? Move your arse up and out of there before he comes back with reinforcements."

"James." Her heart tapped out a relieved beat until she realized he might wish to do her harm himself.

Cursing under his breath as he slid around the corner, he untied the rope and grabbed her hand. "Let's go. I think he is still looking for his Tilda."

"Wait!" Terrwyn skidded to a stop. "Boots. I found boots for your feet."

"You returned the tools but thought nothing of stealing a pair of boots?"

Ignoring the tirade she feared was on its way, she knelt on the floor, sweeping the straw out of her way. "He tossed them over here."

"Come," he said, his tone softened from before. "We'll find another pair. They aren't worth your life."

Terrwyn rose, the boots held tightly in her arms. "They are castoffs. You cannot steal castoffs. Besides," she sniffed, "they are for you."

Resigned to her stubbornness, James nodded and held out his hand. "My thanks, sweeting. I will try them on when we are safe. Right now you need to run." He locked his arms with hers, determined to drag her if necessary.

The innkeeper blocked their path. His wife, Tilda, stood behind him. A handprint marred one of her round cheeks. She covered her mouth with trembling fingers.

"You travel by your lonesome, do you, young fellow? Running off like a pack of pulling puppies still hanging onto their momma's teat."

James slipped away from Terrwyn and gave her a shove to go on.

"Please, James," she said, "you don't know how to fight."

James walked back to the innkeeper and withdrew a leather pouch from his belt. "I apologize for your wasted morning. As you can see, we leave on foot, not by horseback. I have my own mount waiting for us over there." He motioned over his shoulder to where Zeus was tethered.

"Who's to say that one is yours?" The innkeeper looked James up and down. "I think you are both thieves and I aim to keep that stallion in protective custody. The bailiff will be around these parts of Wales in a month or two." He moved toward the massive warhorse, a determined look in his eyes.

"You really don't want to do that." James shook his head. "Zeus does not let just anyone handle him. He chooses who he lets take care of him, not the other way around."

"We'll just see about that."

"Mind you, he's maimed others before you."

"Hywel," Tilda whimpered, "why not let them be on their way? We've good paying guests to tend when they awaken."

"Be quiet," Hywel snarled. "Make yourself useful. Keep an eye on them. Don't let them try anything underhanded." He took a riding crop from the stable wall and marched over to the silver-coated stallion.

Zeus glistened under the morning light. Sensing danger, he lifted his head. Nostrils flared, he stamped and pawed the ground with his hooves.

The three onlookers stood together. Tilda looked anxiously over at James.

Terrwyn gripped James's arm. "You cannot let him hurt Zeus."

He chuckled and put an arm around her waist. He turned to Tilda. "Dear woman, I offered your husband a few coins for his time, and I see my young brother wishes to procure a pair of boots. Do you wish to finish the transaction before you have other—" he paused to search for the word, then found it, "—distractions?"

"James," Terrwyn said, "you pay too much."

"Ach, you mind your brother and quiet your tongue while he pays me what's due." Tilda had a sparkle about her that had not been there earlier. She counted aloud with James until there were ten coins in her palm. As they were finalizing the transfer of gold coins, they looked up to see Hywel sailing through the air.

James could tell the innkeeper was still unconvinced, so he

sat on a bench to examine one of the boots Terrwyn had found for him. He wondered if it would slide over the bandages. A small hiss of pain escaped when he managed to work it over the wound.

The woman's eyes shifted from her husband to look at him. "I've clean rooms if you are inclined. A bit of a wash-up would do you some good too."

James smiled amicably. "I will keep that in mind should I travel this way again. For now, I fear we have overstayed our welcome. We'll be on our way soon."

Hywel sailed into the air a second time. A howling yelp erupted with a long string of curses. He rolled over the ground in pain, narrowly missing Zeus's large hooves.

Tilda raced over to her husband. James and Terrwyn followed behind her at a slower pace. Hywel lay gasping for breath and holding his ribs with one hand. He crawled up on all fours and proceeded to retch onto the ground.

Seeing he was bruised but alive, Tilda began to tear into him with a lecture on greed. She paused her tirade long enough to watch James lift Terrwyn onto the stallion's back. "Wait."

Lifting her skirts, Tilda ran back to the shed and returned in a matter of moments. She walked cautiously toward them and thrust a small woolen cap into James's hand. "Your brother will need this to cover his long plait of hair."

James leaned over her reddened hand and brushed a kiss to her work-worn knuckles. Then he climbed up into the saddle and rode over to where Hywel lay. "You should be congratulated."

"Shut your trap, bloody fool," Hywel groused.

"Truly. He usually does not back off until the poor sod is unconscious. He must have taken a liking to you."

The innkeeper pushed up from the earth to sit upright. "You don't say."

James saluted and walked Zeus sedately away from the crossroads. He reached around Terrwyn's waist, the cap in his outstretched fingers. "Here. Put this on."

"James—"

"When you are willing to speak nothing but truth, I'd like to hear your reasons for breaking a promise you gave me less than a few hours ago. Until then, pray keep your silence and I will keep mine."

Chapter Twenty-Three

They rode for half a day without speaking. The imposed silence hung between them like a rough woolen cloak. The weight of it rubbed at raw nerves, bringing their anger to heightened levels. Even Zeus must have felt James's control start to slip. His ears back, the stallion flinched at every little sound.

Terrwyn's guilt over her broken promise dissipated. In its place, irritation bloomed and grew over the wall James was using as punishment. By the time they stopped to break their fast she had endured all the silence she was willing to take.

The Bloated Goat loomed in front of them. Three smaller buildings stood around the tavern's squatty structure. The shed near the smokehouse leaned to one side. It appeared ready to fall down at the next storm, although the barn where they would stable the horse looked sturdy enough. It bustled with morning life.

"Wait," Terrwyn said.

James ignored her plea and lifted her down. He dismounted and released Zeus's reins to the young stable boy. After a few words of instructions to the boy, he turned to lead the way. "Try not to draw their attention," he said in clipped tones.

She followed the direction where he pointed with a jerk of his chin. A few of the men standing on the nearby lane glanced her way. She felt her neck heat up. Reluctant to be put off, she grabbed his sleeve, tugging at the material.

A single raven-colored eyebrow rose over his stern visage. "What troubles you now?"

"How do you know Zeus won't take a bite out of anyone who comes near? He might have a fit and trample everyone in his way. How can you think 'tis safe when he went after the innkeeper?"

"I didn't give him the signal."

"A signal?"

He tapped the end of her chin, lifting it to shut her mouth.

Terrwyn drew back, lifting her face to see if he jested. "You trained him to behave like a raving lunatic?"

"Only when I need him to behave that way. Otherwise he's as gentle as a kitten." He yanked the bill of the cap down to cover more of her features. "Now stay put and stay out of trouble."

Terrwyn watched him enter the tavern. The loss of security struck her hard. She had come to take comfort in his bristly presence. She caught her reflection in the horse trough. Filth coated her face and clothing. She rubbed at a spot on the jerkin. Too late, she realized it looked worse from her efforts.

She heard the scuffle of soles against the drive. Thinking James returned for her, she shifted toward the sound of footfalls. The smile she placed for him slipped when she saw the approaching men. Suspicion coated their eyes until they glittered with animosity.

She gave them the best welcoming grin she could manage. While she nodded in goodwill, she felt for the quiver and arrows hanging from her shoulder.

The men did not seem to approve of her movements. They advanced, keeping their hands close to their weapons.

Terrwyn gripped the rolled edge of the trough. Lifting her chin, she refused to give way to their threats. She caught a few of their stares and held them defiantly. She might be a displaced daughter, but by god she was a Welshman's daughter. And a Welsh lord's, at that.

"You there." A rotund-bellied man evidently deemed he was the spokesman for the group. "Have I seen your face before? What do you want here?"

"To be left alone, you horse's arse." Terrwyn let go of the trough and stepped forward. "Shoo! Be off with yourself and take the other arses with you."

"Arse, is it?" The leader of the band of men closed the space between them.

Her irritation with James ignited. He should have known it was unsafe to leave her exposed to the establishment's riffraff. Her best means of escape was to find Zeus and ride out.

Panic rising, she searched for a path of easy access to the stable. When long tapered fingers wrapped around her shoulder, she nearly leapt out of her boots.

"Come, for once the fates shine on us."

C#SO

To reach the attic they had to walk past three long planked tables, each one littered with food spilled from the night before. The scent of ale and smoked meats filled the air. Terrwyn's stomach growled. It had been too long since they had a decent meal. Maybe she could slip out and find a scrap or two for them to eat.

The narrow stairway leading up to the attic looked as if it were in need of repair. She gripped the railing and prayed they would not fall through the wooden planks. The door to their room was stuck and it took James several shoves to get it open. After the third push with his shoulder, it swung in on squeaking hinges.

James's silence made her nervous. She eyed him warily. She wished he would get on with it and yell out his accusations. Then she could defend her innocence.

He held the door open, motioning her in. Their bodies brushed as she walked through. Terrwyn flinched from his touch. She snuck a glance and knew by the look in his eye that he saw it.

She swallowed the apology that wanted to leap out. She had done nothing wrong. But he looked furious. Sad. It was the sadness that nearly did her in.

Desperate to put space between them, she walked into the room. Dust flew about in the stale warm air. A rickety table stood next to a small cot. Pieces of straw used to stuff the mattress stuck out from the ticking. A thin blanket lay at the foot of the bed.

She pressed her fingers to her mouth. She had never been in a bedchamber with a grown man before. What did he expect from her? What did she expect from him?

The door swung shut. The space between them seemed to shrink into the darkness. Except for the bit of daylight streaming past the shuttered windows the room was cast in shadows.

Surprised to discover she was not raining curses down on his head, James attempted to shake free of the rage. The layers peeled away until only a furious need to grab the troublesome woman to his chest remained.

His shoulder braced against the door, he gripped the wooden latch. His hold loosened and he left the safety of the outside behind him. Indeed, his attraction to her was dangerous.

Terrwyn had not moved from the center of the room. Presented with only her back, he lifted the ugly cap from her head, releasing the braid from its mooring. The cap came to a spinning stop where he tossed it on the rickety table. She turned with a startled look in her eyes.

James opened his arms and let her tumble into his embrace. "Hush now, little one."

With the palm of her hands pressed into his chest, her fingers kneaded the leather panel of his jerkin. She pulled back, her face ashen and pale. "We cannot stay here."

"You don't mean to tell me the great Archer is fearful of a few wagging tongues." He shook his head. "There will be no talk."

"But the way the innkeeper looked at us. I'm certain she has a suspicious heart. She won't leave us be until she unearths the truth."

"'Tis pity that you see." He patted her hand as she continued to worry his clothing. "I spun a tale for Mistress Alice while I procured our rooms. She believes you are my runaway brother. It took great trials and tribulation before I caught up with you. 'Tis an abandoned, broken heart that brought you to heel. Your love was a light-skirt and deserted you because you lacked funds."

A small gasp left Terrwyn's lips as she continued to focus on the center of his chest.

"Here now," James said, affronted by her disapproval. "Her taking pity on your broken heart is probably what saves us from having to bed down in the cow byre."

"I cannot believe you think I would give a faerie's damn what that well-padded woman thinks."

He tilted his head to kiss her ear. The dainty shell pinked from his touch. He pushed the jerkin off her shoulder. Her skin was smooth, her muscles strong and supple. He longed to shove his fingers in her hair and possess her body.

When Terrwyn groaned and leaned into his embrace, James wanted more. When she gripped the back of his neck and reclaimed his lips, he wanted to claim what he knew he had no right to. He should turn himself out. Bed down in the cow byre. Sleep with Zeus.

The leather thong holding her braid in place uncoiled in his hands. He tossed it on the table. Quickly, carefully, he loosened her hair. The rich mahogany flowed down her shoulders in waves.

"Beautiful." He wove his fingers to her scalp. He tilted her face and kissed her forehead, her chin, the slope of her neck. She shivered when he ran his tongue over her skin.

He swore at the knock at the door and smiled when Terrwyn echoed his sentiments with a curse of her own.

"A moment." He picked up the cap and held it out for Terrwyn. He waited until she had shoved her hair in, wondering how they had managed to fool anyone. Were people so blinded by their own misery they did not see what was before them?

He tilted her chin and caught her mouth. "Beautiful," he murmured against her lips.

The knock came again, this time more persistent than the first. "Have the comforts you required."

He opened the door and let the mistress of the tavern in. She carried a tray loaded with a pitcher of ale and a platter of food to break their fast. Two serving wenches followed behind her, their arms full of rags and soap. The stable boy had been recruited to carry several buckets of steaming water.

They followed her brisk orders. "Put that there on that table. Place those here. Tobia, fetch another bucket, but make it a cold one."

The boy nodded and turned to do her bidding. He squeezed by the two serving girls and hurried out the door.

Terrwyn's stomach growled as soon as the scent of warm bread and smoked meat filled in the air.

The portly woman paused at her efforts and turned to stare openly. "You'll feel better once you fill yourself with Mistress Alice's good food."

"Please excuse my brother. He is too distraught for conversation," James said, expecting the woman to draw Terrwyn to her ample breasts.

"He's a quiet one, is he? And small, too, if you don't mind my saying." She turned her attention to Terrwyn. "Lord love you, that heart of yours will mend in no time at all." Her eyes narrowed when Terrwyn only nodded. "Imagine you'll be in want of a clothes washing too. Go ahead and strip them off. Leave them outside the door. Tobia will pick them up when he brings that other bucket of water. He'll brush your leathers while you eat and wash up."

She shooed her staff out the door, then slid her hand down James's sleeve. "You come see me when you are rested and finished here. If you have another need, I'll see to that too."

James lifted her hand and bowed over it. "I knew I would find safety and discretion the first time I visited this fine establishment." His lips bussed lightly over the back of her knuckles. "I shall join you when my brother and I have reached our fill."

Her ample breasts seemed to grow as she leaned forward. "You're certain you don't need someone to wash your back?" Her gaze shifted irritably from his attention. "I believe your brother has choked on a crumb of bread."

"Nay, he is fine." James gently led the tavern mistress to the door and gave a little push. As soon as her backend was through, he kicked the door shut.

Terrwyn's face was reddened but not from choking. He searched the tray and prayed the knife was dull.

"Whoreson cur," she ground out. "You kiss me, then place your lips on her skin?" She threw the rag and soap at his feet.

James bent to retrieve them. "You will keep your voice down." He returned the items on the bed. "From now on, you will trust me and you will not question my actions."

He ripped off a hunk of bread and shoved it in his mouth. His chewing slowed. He tore off another and held it out to Terrwyn. Warm butter dripped off the flaky crust. When she did not take it, he shoved it in his mouth. Ignoring the mugs, he grabbed the pitcher and swallowed deeply.

"Monster." She folded her arms defiantly. "You cannot force someone to trust."

"Shrew." James picked up a chunk of cheese. Instead of slicing it with the knife, he tore it with his teeth.

"Beast!" Her insult was softened by the growling of her empty stomach. Her nostrils flared, daring him to mention the sound.

James pulled his leather jerkin off. The padded gambeson was next. The linen undershirt came with it. The silver band he wore on a leather thong glistened against his skin.

"What do you think you are doing?"

"I intend to eat this food and make use of the hot water I purchased. You think I'm a beast and I aim to show you different." He paused, grabbed a chunk of bread and stuffed it in his mouth. Then sitting down on the bed he struggled to pull off his boots.

"I cannot—" she started.

"You will," he cut in. "Or will you let fear keep you from what you want?"

He untied the string around his waist. The band rolled down to his groin. He slipped out of his leggings and wrapped a bathing sheet around his middle. He padded barefoot to one of the buckets.

Terrwyn drew in a ragged breath. While his back was turned she stole a piece of cheese from the tray and shoved it in her mouth. Her mouth watered from the scents floating up from the table. But now she hungered for more than food. He had called her a shrew. Dared her even. Fear did not keep her away. *Did it?*

Water sluiced into a washing bowl.

Terrwyn swallowed the cheese then gulped down some ale from the pitcher. She wiped her mouth with the back of her hand. Her empty stomach a bit happier, she concentrated on the half-naked man standing before her. She had never seen a man so beautifully made.

His shoulders rippled with every movement. The slope of his chest was sprinkled with coiled black hair. She counted at least six sets of muscles on his flat stomach. The angled plane of his low regions was still hidden by the bath sheet. Curious, she peered intently at the shadowy form underneath. Her knees nearly gave out when he bent to test the water.

"Better hurry, 'tis getting cold." James wetted the soap and rubbed it into the small cloth. A large tub stood in the middle where the servants left it. He paused in front of it. Looking over his shoulder, he cast his silent challenge then let the bath sheet drop to the floor.

Terrwyn took a bite of a green apple. Its sweet tangy flavor filled her mouth. She licked at the juice sticking to her lips.

He stepped into the metal basin and, while standing, rubbed the soapy cloth over his body. He moved to add more soap and his position gave her a side view.

Fascinated, Terrwyn sat on the bed and watched. He raised the bucket and poured its contents over his head. His black hair gleamed. His skin was slick and looked—"Delicious."

"Am I?" He paused in his ablutions.

Did I say that out loud?

A slow, languid smile lifted the corners of his mouth.

Oh, Lord in Heaven! Aye, I did.

He winked at her and soaped his thighs. She moaned in resignation when he lifted his leg to soap the manacle wound around his ankle.

She toed off her leather boots with ease and glanced back. James was watching her, a wicked gleam in his eye.

This is madness.

She lifted the leather jerkin, gambeson and linen shirt as one and swept them over her head. Her arms got stuck, caught in the triple layers of clothing. Exposed and unprotected, she began to panic.

The sound of water sluicing onto the floor came before the muted padding of footfalls over wooden planks. The scent of soap and leather melded together. The warmth of James's freshly bathed body heated her skin.

She sucked in a breath when James touched her stomach. Lifting the hem, he peered into her face. Tiny water droplets clung to his ebony lashes and glittered like stars in the night.

"Let me help." He pulled the offending garment off and tossed it on the waiting pile of clothing.

Terrwyn shivered despite the heat coming from his body. She loved the way he looked at her. Like a child waiting for a sweet confection. She squealed in surprise when he lifted her and buried his face between her breasts. He tongued her skin then planted sweet kisses along her ribcage. He made quick work of untying the ribbon around her waist. The leggings fell to the floor.

James brought her feet back to the floor and released her. "Close your eyes."

Terrwyn complied. His breath brushed her neck. "Stay where you are."

She hugged her body, trembling from his absence. Her head began to clear. "I think 'tis best I—oh." She started to turn.

"Don't." His whisper scraped over her shoulder. He swept her into his arms and carried her to the tub.

The soft rosemary soap perfumed the air as he massaged slow circles over her abdomen until he reached her mons. With his other hand, he trailed a warm soapy cloth over her lower back. He moved slowly, rounding over the curve of her hip, sliding over her buttock, her thighs. A heavy sigh was wrung from her chest as she arched her back. He released a pleasured groan and turned her to draw each nipple into his mouth. His rod vibrated his need.

Terrwyn opened her eyes and met his gaze. She knew she should put a stop to this before it was too late. Her maidenhood remained intact. Yet she could not. All the reasons for turning back dissipated when he touched her.

She grabbed the sides of his head. Drawing him to her, she caught his mouth, tugging his lips with her teeth. Fire swept over her skin. She wrapped her limbs around his waist.

James could barely think beyond his desire. He dipped a finger where her legs were spread. The moist flesh pulsated with passion. His muscles bunched, needing to feel the brush of her skin across the head of his rod. He would go slow, give her time to deny him. Her legs unwound from his waist as he stepped into the tub. The absence of her heat left an ache he had never known.

He stepped back, admiring the tautness of her slender body. The ebbing daylight danced over her skin, rippling it with energy. Joy of life glistened from her head to her toes. Her essence drew him to her as if she cast a spell upon him. She met his gaze, daring him to come to her. He could not turn away.

Growling, he grabbed her buttocks and lifted her from the tub. He backed her to the bed. They fell as one. Hands on flesh. Fingers probing, scraping, soothing. Lips suckling. Tongues licking, tasting. Their breaths came, panting, eager to breathe in the other's scents.

James knelt before her, nudging her legs apart. Her knees moved together.

"Sweeting," he soothed. "I will stop if you demand it."

When she responded with an animalist mixture of a whimper and a moan, he bent over her and laid a gentle kiss across her kneecaps. He nipped at the underside of her knees, licking where his teeth had been. He kept his hands on the mattress, touching only with his mouth. He slid over and placed a kiss on the outside of her smooth thigh. Pushing forward, he made his way until his forehead touched the crest of her hip.

Terrwyn grabbed the back of his head and rolled toward him. James buried his face into the apex of her curls. He made little swirls in the nest, licking along the crease of her inner thigh.

Her legs languid and supple, she opened up to him, giving him access to her inner core.

James groaned into her burgeoning flesh. "God, woman, you have no idea what you do to me."

Terrwyn gave him a wobbly smile. "Aye. It this it then? I would have thought there'd be more to it."

Stunned by her innocent challenge, James shook his head. "Nay, love, we have only just begun."

He stretched out over her body, his tongue playing over her nipples as he wound a leisurely path to her mons. Blowing softly he began to suckle the fevered flesh. His satisfaction came when he had her keening his name. She bucked and rocked against his hands and mouth, coming in a burst.

Her legs apart, she nudged him toward her core. James hesitated. His eyes closed, he strove to calm his body. "Are you certain, love?" He waited, praying she would not turn him away.

She responded by pulling him forward. The back of his neck cupped in her hand, she moved to help him gain entrance.

James lifted her hips and slid into the swollen flesh. His eyes closed as he focused on the passion surrounding him. The barrier was there but her walls were slick and welcoming. He pumped, gently testing the resistance.

"James," Terrwyn whispered. She ran her nails down his back, digging into his buttocks. She met his hips, pulling him tighter, begging him to drive deeper.

He drove in and pulled out, threatening to defy her request. When he broke through the barrier, she bucked against him. His eyes snapped open when he heard her gasp and felt her draw away.

Fear reflected in her eyes. He could not bear to have her look at him in that way. He did everything he could think of to silence the demands of his body. Their bodies slowed to a steady rhythm. He drew her close, whispering endearments along her neck.

Terrwyn no longer felt the searing pain that came when James pushed deep inside. Her heart warmed with every sweet word he spoke. Her flesh heated and the hunger returned. She ran her tongue over his neck, tasting his skin. Her fingers skimmed over his smooth back, and the satiny space where his thigh met his hip. James shuddered under her touch. Emboldened, she slipped her hand between them, sliding along the planes of his stomach and through the curls near his shaft.

The pace of their rocking increased. Groaning, James pulled back, then plunged again and again. Terrwyn gripped his waist, sliding her hands over his hips as their bodies slammed into each other. They came together. Their bodies locked as one, they exploded until they could not catch their breaths.

Chapter Twenty-Four

Terrwyn lay amidst the tangle of legs and thin blanket. She looked up at the angled ceiling of the attic room. The sun had shifted overhead. Afternoon shadows were all that was left of the daylight.

She carefully extricated her limbs from James's and stretched her languid body. She never knew her joints were so limber. It was as if her bones were no longer held together by sinew and ligaments. The scent of their time together was all around them. She hid her face into the crook of her arm.

"Terrwyn?" The straw mattress rustled as James turned. His sigh stirred her hair draped over her arms.

She closed her eyes, feigning sleep. She was not ready to face him. Memories of the things they did to each other took her breath away. Her legs squeezed involuntarily. The rush of pleasure coursed through her veins, awakening some mystical being that must have possessed her senses.

Dear heaven, what had she done? She had given her maidenhood to an Englishman. Willingly! Her stomach clenched. She knew she would have to live with the consequences of her choice, just not so soon. What would those consequences entail? Nothing had changed. She still had to find her brother. The battles she saw in her dreams continued to haunt her. She had to find him in time. Fate would be denied her brother's life.

"Terrwyn." James lifted her curtain of hair. His head slanted, he peered into her face. Compassion darkened the color of his eyes to a predawn blue. He pushed her hair back.

Leaning over her, he rested on his forearms. "Beautiful," he whispered before he kissed her.

Although prepared to deny she wanted any more of his kisses or endearments, she responded by wrapping her arms around his neck and pulling him to her. Scooting closer, she let James tuck her body under his.

He looked down at her. His dark hair fell over his forehead. "I should like to sketch you again. Only this time, I will have my beauty in front of me." He kissed her lips, then trailed down to her collarbone.

She shivered when he lifted his head. "Again? You've drawn me before?"

"From memory." A wolfish smile lifted his mouth. "I will have you with me, and you will pose until I have caught the beauty of my Welsh faerie."

"Will that take long?"

"I think it should take a very long time. Years perhaps. Centuries."

She laughed despite herself. "Why is that? Are you that slow?"

"Inspirational breaks." He wiggled his raven eyebrows.

Terrwyn melted into the mattress, barely noticing the coarse straw padding. His hands were moving hungrily over her stomach, her hips. His mouth sought her breast. Her toes curled when he suckled then scraped his teeth over her nipple. He looked up while he tongued the crest, soothing the tender skin.

He shook his head, denying her access to his body. "'Tis too soon. I would not harm you again." He touched his forehead to hers. "You did not warn me."

"Warn you? 'Twas me that bled."

"You're right, I should have known. I am a beast after all. You draw all sense from my brain. You're so beautiful."

"Stop saying that, you great fool."

"And gentle." He nipped behind her ear.

"I won't be won over so easily next time."

"Ah, see, you already promised a next time. I must add forgiveness to your long list of attributes."

"There won't be a next time." Terrwyn crossed her arms. "You doubted my chastity. You thought me a light-skirt, an easy Welsh wench to tup as soon as you could get my heels above your head."

"Forgive me. I never thought that of you." James stroked her collarbone with his fingertip. "I lose my senses. All I can think of when I am with you is burying myself deep within you. Forget all but you in my arms."

Terrwyn noticed the shift in the air. Something in those last few words changed everything. "Nay, vows and duty cannot be ignored, can they? We come from opposite sides."

"But that's not true. I've told you many times. Though my father is a strong Englishman, it is my brave Welsh mother who taught me courage. I come from both worlds."

From temple to jawline, Terrwyn slid her hand down his cheek. Her fingers trailed to the center of his chest. She paused at the silver ring hanging from the leather thong around his neck. "But in here, your heart beats for your English king." She took his hand and laid it on her breast. "And mine does not."

"Nay, you have it wrong. Remember, I am a man of two worlds. My heart beats for king and for you, love." He answered before she uttered a denial. "Let me show you all the ways you are beautiful." He bent his head to kiss her and whispered, "Beautiful," again and again until every part of her body received his blessing.

Cᴚᴓ

Lazy as a cat, Terrwyn stretched, arching her back. Her thighs were sorer than when she rode on horseback all day. Her breasts were tender to the touch, not from pain, but the simplest of movements brought a sensation singing to her core. Never had she felt so beautiful and wanted. She indeed felt loved. She quickly squashed that thought and added, *loved for an afternoon.*

The tiny room was barren without James to fill it with his great, glorious body. She nearly purred at the thought of his return.

Earlier, he had promised to send up another bucket of

warm water. He would see what he could smuggle up in the way of food or whether it was safe for them to dine in the tavern's main room.

True to his promise, a knock at the door came moments after he left her. Terrwyn opened the door wide enough to drag in an empty bucket for her private needs and a bucket of warm water to wash off. She let the steam warm her face. She tested the water and began to clean herself using the towels and a pot of soap from their earlier bath.

ભૂ

James opened the door to find Terrwyn standing in the tub. The damp bath sheet clung to the curves, dips and valleys of her luscious body. Her eyes flashed in surprise then shuttered behind the shy look he thought they had banished with their love play. The voices from the men who had already begun to fill the tavern rose up the stairway and through the thin walls. "You did not lock the door."

"If I would have locked it, I would have had to leave the bath and drip water all over the floor to let you in."

James closed the space between them. He stroked the moisture dripping from her jaw and ran his hands down her neck. "Promise me you will lock the door behind me. I would not have another see you like you are."

Her eyes sparkled with mirth. "As you say."

Satisfied, he lifted her from the tub. Ignoring the water marks her body left behind, he let her slide down his chest and placed her gently on the floor. "We have a bit of time before our dinner is brought up. 'Tis a pity I don't have my tools. I would sketch your image as you are." When she hesitated, he added, "I'm quite skilled."

Her cheeks pinked to a rosy hue as her understanding grew. "You wish to draw me naked?"

"Aye, 'twould be a sin to cover exquisite loveliness."

"Wait!" Terrwyn pulled away, nearly skipping across the room. She rooted through her quiver, her damp hair draped around her face. She spun around, the charcoal and small whittling knife in hand. "I grabbed them before we left Sir William's tent."

James held out his hand. "My thanks, love. What with all your surprises, I'd find it easy to believe your quiver and arrows are blessed by the faeries. Perhaps you'll unearth some parchment as well."

He waited for her to admit she kept his journal of drawings from him. Instead, Terrwyn brushed off his comment as she walked naked about the room. James found the sight of her distracting and it was hard to keep up with her conversation when she turned the conversation to eating instead of being the subject of his artistic talents.

Terrwyn dropped next to the bundle she carried the night they snuck out of the encampment. "We are not to go down to eat in the tavern? Won't Mistress Alice wonder what you've done with your young brother?"

"She's paid well enough to ignore the extra work of carrying a meal up to the attic." James tossed the leather-bound journal on the bed.

Terrwyn ducked her head, keeping her gaze from his. "How did you get that?"

James rocked on his feet and kept his hands behind his back. He had to stifle the need to cradle her in his arms, comfort her, release her from distress. "Why didn't you tell me you had it? I told you to trust me."

"Oh-ho! Look who is calling the bit of coal black. You went through my things. 'Tis you that didn't trust!"

"You know that is not true. You kept this from me, knowing that I needed it. We wouldn't have had to come here."

"Aye, we would have. You memorize everything you see. I cannot believe you wouldn't have found a way to recreate the drawings. Nay, you needed something more. For the king."

James paused, shuttering his heart. "Aye, for my king. Is that why you kept the truth from me? To stall my information until it was too late to protect the throne?"

"Nay. I needed those drawings to find my brother." She grabbed the journal from the bed.

"Put it down."

"You can run me through with your blade if you like. It doesn't matter to me. I've been haunted by the sight until I cannot sleep."

Their harsh breaths cut through the air. The dry sound of parchment rustled as she flipped through the pages. When she finally found what she searched for, she stopped. The discarded drawings fluttered to the bed.

"Here," she said, holding out the sketch. "This is why I cannot let you have it. Not until you give me your vow to help me find my brother."

"Let me see, my sweet."

Terrwyn stepped back and pressed the drawing to her breasts. "This is the closest I've been since you and your king took him away."

Confused, James drew back. Portions of another afternoon so long ago, so very long ago, flashed in his mind. Henry had been new to his own power. He had not realized the pain his decisions caused to so many. The wariness in her eyes told him his worst fears. She would never forget the part he had played that afternoon. "Why did you not speak of this before?"

"I did try."

"When you were blaming me for something while we were held in Sir William's tent? I didn't understand."

"Aye, the first time I saw the drawings in your journal. 'Twas but a quick peek of the sketch before we were taken to speak with Sir William."

"But you had your suspicions."

Terrwyn nodded. "'Twas when you were lying on your side in the dirt, looking at me with sorrow in your eyes, that I recalled seeing your face."

"And still you held your tongue," he said in wonder. "You kept your secret well."

"It wasn't until after I had the drawings in my possession that I had a better look at them. Still I didn't know for certain that was Drem's face you drew. He's a different age since the last time I saw him."

"I never once intended to cause you harm."

"But you did. You and your king's actions caused pain for

more than just a few. 'Twas my responsibility to keep him safe, and my failure to do so is a thorn that has rubbed me every day since."

"Ah, sweetheart." He stepped forward. When she did not cringe, he held out his hand and motioned her to come to him. Though still wary, she closed the distance. His arms widened and she stepped into his embrace. He did not breathe for a few seconds for fear she would leap away from him.

He tilted her chin so that their eyes met. "We will find your brother." The gentle kiss he placed on her forehead was chaste and nothing that resembled their afternoon of passion. "You have my vow."

The drawing caught between them, Terrwyn turned in his arms and sobbed.

The knocking at the door tore them apart as if they had been splashed with cold water. Terrwyn ran from his arms, wiggled into her leggings and drew on the linen shirt, gambeson and leather jerkin. She was stuffing her feet into Drem's old boots when James opened the door.

Tobia walked in, carrying a tray filled with bread and another pitcher of ale. The scent of stew wafted into the room. The boy motioned for some space to set the tray.

"Here lad, let me give you hand with this." James began clearing the table. He grabbed Terrwyn's cap and tossed it to her.

She caught it and clapped it on her head. While she stuffed her hair into the cap, she listened intently as James and Tobia conversed about the comings and goings of the tavern. It was an unusually busy night at the Bloated Goat.

James followed Tobia to the door and promised to set out the buckets for cleaning before turning in for the evening. He waited until the child made it safely down the stairs before he set the lock.

"Come, love. Sit down and eat." He pushed the trencher filled with stew toward her.

To Terrwyn's mortification, her stomach growled again. She took the food from James and smiled her thanks. "Will you not have a bite?"

He dipped a chunk of crusty bread into the stew. "I'd say that despite her faults Mistress Alice does have a good hand with the spoon."

They ate companionably, sitting beside each other on the small bed until the stew was finished. James poured out the remains of the pitcher into their mugs. Terrwyn's lids grew heavier after every bite.

"Here," he said, clearing off the bed and fluffing the ticking. "Have a bit of a sleep. Rest while you can. Tomorrow, we continue our ride south."

She caught his wrist through a haze of exhaustion. "You will honor your vow to help me find my brother?"

"Aye," he said. "Rest while I take a turn or two around the tavern. Need to check on Zeus, make certain he is well tended."

The smile she gave him was that of a trusting angel. James prayed that one day he would deserve it.

◌◌◌

James sat in the corner of the tavern, keeping his back protected. The serving wench set a pitcher of ale and a mug down in from of him. She leaned in low, giving him a look at what she offered. He imagined her mistress would not care to know that one of her girls intended to earn a few coins on the sly. He shook his head and gave her an extra pence for her efforts.

Nursing the ale in his mug, he watched the comings and goings of the smoke-filled room. Soon the patrons began to drift off. Some found a pallet near the fire. Others, he knew, would find their way home to the nearby village.

James leaned into the corner, letting the shadows cover his actions. According to Tobia, there was to be a meeting tonight. It used to bring more men but one by one their numbers had dwindled to a handful. A few stood out in the boy's mind. One of the men he described sounded like Edgar Poole.

James pulled out his journal and sorted through the parchments. He stopped when he came to a particular drawing and held it under a flickering candle. The other man Tobia had described sounded familiar too.

He feared he was about to hurt Terrwyn again.

Chapter Twenty-Five

The meager candle Mistress Alice sent up was slowly burning out. The sounds of the men visiting the Bloated Goat began to diminish. Impatient to speak with James, Terrwyn paced the wide planks of the attic floor.

The night vision had come to her while she slept. Drem's face was that of a nearly grown man. But unlike the other times, his face was partially blackened, his clothing in tatters. He kept calling her name, over and over again. The weightiness of it made her irritation grow. The night visions might foretell only one version of the future. But what if she could change the fates? It she was correct, then she still might stop the grief and set things right.

The sound of several horses coming into the tavern yard drew her to the window. She opened the shutters and looked out. Worried for James's safety, she gathered her bow and quiver.

Careful of the rickety steps, she crept down the stairs and entered the nearly empty tavern room. No one saw her slip through the back door. The yard was deserted. Several horses stood by an outbuilding she had noticed when they rode in earlier that morning. Once a smokehouse, it was nearly falling down. Probably used as storage now.

She leaned into the shadows of the yard as a few men rode up single file. Their movements were secretive and agitated. It worried her that she had not seen any sign of James for some time. Had they captured him and were now holding him in the shed?

She followed the men, keeping her bow in hand. An arrow was nocked and ready. She peeked around the corner. The moonlight struck across the face of one of the men. His movements stiff, he signaled to the other man to dismount.

Terrwyn's breath caught. Dafydd ap Hew stood outside the door. He kept to the shadows but she knew her father's craggy nose, his high cheekbones. A wave of homesickness washed over her. In the joy of seeing her father's face she almost forgot to keep hidden. The joy was soon forgotten when Edgar Poole stepped up and clapped Dafydd's shoulder as if they were long-lost friends.

Her jaw clenched. Her bones ached from the knowledge that Edgar Poole and her father consorted in the same circles. How could he do this? Echoes of arguments between Mam and her father rang in her head. It pulled the life from her blood until Terrwyn thought her heart would break.

Her life shifted, spinning wildly out of control until she thought she could no longer stand. How could her own father betray her? Mam had warned time and time again that their future lay elsewhere. Owain Glyndwr's time had passed. Yet here her father remained, fighting against English rule.

All she had cast aside to correct her family's plight no longer held strength. What was it the soldier had said as they took Drem away? *You'd have no troubles if not for Owain Glyndwr's band of mischief-makers.* Her stomach rebelled at the realization. It was not just the fates that had known she and her brother rode alone. The soldiers had known exactly where to find them. A band of grown men pitted against two children. They never had a chance against those odds.

Saints above, where was James? She needed him. She needed the strength she gathered when his arms were wrapped around her.

Fearing she was about to lose both father and James in one awful night, she struck out toward the shed. She would face her father's deceit, but she would not face James's death. If she were to lose the battle, she would rather lose a part of her soul while fighting for her love. If she did not fight, her soul was already lost.

She gripped the bow in one hand and the arrow in the

other. With the weapon pressed against the bow's frame, she crept along the shadows. She peered through the crack where the smokehouse door sagged away from the hinge. Candlelight surrounded the few men huddled in the tiny room.

She stood to confront her father and found her back slammed against a solid chest. James's arm wrapped around her and enveloped her in his embrace. "Come," he whispered, drawing her away from the dilapidated building.

Relief of knowing James was safe quickly faded. She shook her head.

James left her no room for argument. He picked her up and carried her to a hedge of juniper bushes lining a low stone retaining wall. Once they were safely secured behind the shrubbery, he set her down. "You cannot charge in there, your arrows flying."

"I have to make my father face the destruction he's causing."

"No good will come of it. I won't let you destroy yourself."

She shivered from the harsh truth. Her father had deceitfully jeopardized the safety of their village and all who lay within.

"Do you not see who is in there? 'Tis my good father," she sneered, disdain dripping from her words. "The man of the village. The one who shall lead us out from under the heel of the English boot. Damn him. And did you see who joins him? That Englishman would enjoy seeing you and me, his cohort's eldest daughter, dead on a spike." She gripped James's jerkin. "I cannot support anything or anyone that Poole is involved with." The air caught in her throat. She choked out the last words. "Even if it means I cannot support my own father."

James pressed her head to his chest. She could hear the cadence beating through his blood. "Hush, love. You cannot shoot the lot of them. We'll bide our time."

They peered through the shrubs and watched the outbuilding. The moon lifted until it hung straight overhead. Then finally, the meeting was over. From their vantage point they could see when Poole rode out. A decision had been made. The riders raced off to their destinations. All but a handful of men remained.

Terrwyn squeezed James's thigh when she felt the presence of another standing behind them. The fine sharp point of a blade poked gently at their backs. The jabs were light so as not to spill unwanted blood. But the warning was clear. They would not move unless directed.

"Come from the shadows, nice and steady." He prodded James's broad back. "'Twould be best if your hand didn't get so close to your weapon."

Terrwyn recognized the voice from her village. "Bran? Is that you lad?"

"Just keep moving toward the smokehouse."

Dafydd strode out of the building and stopped in front of Terrwyn. "So this is where you run off to." His speech was slow. His eyes were dull and without hope. "You've gone and spread your legs for the English, have ye, wench? When I get you alone, you will pray to Almighty God to forgive you. Then you will pray for my forgiveness." He spat on the ground by her feet. "You're no good to me now."

Her heart breaking, Terrwyn realized all she had endured and sacrificed meant nothing. "How could you lie to your family?" she choked out.

"I'm fighting for—for—"

"For no one but yourself. For the power you once had."

Dafydd wiped his sleeve across his mouth. "I'll not live with the English boot on my throat forevermore."

"Mam didn't worry for no reason. She saw in your heart and knew the lies you were telling."

"You won't use her name in my presence. You failed her too. 'Twas your lack of skill that killed your mam."

Terrwyn grabbed James's sleeve, stopping him from stepping forward. "Nay, 'tis the bitterness in his heart talking."

"Ach," Dafydd spat out. "I cannot be expected to sit by, eating hand to mouth, while the English take over my land and my country. I do what I can to protect what is mine. Your mam thought she kept me reined in but I know what I'm about."

"You unite with a selfish madman. He pits one against the other."

"Sir," James interjected, "although Poole sympathizes with

the French who promise to place the crown on a true Welshman, you cannot trust what is said. Once they take control, do you think they will just hand over Wales to you? I promise you they will forget the help you gave them."

"Nay! You know not what you are speaking of."

"Sir, I tell you true, the French don't support their promises. You cannot put your family in the jeopardy you are considering."

Dafydd shoved past them and mounted his Welsh pony. His feet hung pathetically over the pony's short stocky body. He pointed to Terrwyn, jabbing at the air with his finger. "Mount up."

When she did not, his glare shifted to cold disdain. "So that is how it is? You failed me before and you fail me again." He struck the palms of his hands together as if removing dust. "Your choice is made. You're dead to me, girl. You are no longer welcome in our village or in my home."

The proclamation made, he kicked his heels into the pony's sides and wheeled about. "You there, Bran, see to it that they don't stand in my way."

Terrwyn turned into James's arms. The dreams, the night visions, they did not wait for sleep but came at her and demanded to be seen. The darkness closed in, waiting for her to give in and let go.

James slid down the wall with Terrwyn still held within his embrace. She felt the life force, the energy that kept her going, seep out of her bones.

"Terrwyn," he said, "you are not alone. I will help you find your brother."

"'S no use. What would he come back to? A family built on deceit?" She looked up, not bothering to hide her heartache. "Mam knew in her heart that Father was not being truthful but, as strong as she was, could never call him on it. How am I to make a difference?"

James pulled her close. "You keep hoping and trusting the best will outshine the worst."

Bran lowered his blade. He squatted in front of them, his hands braced on the hilt of the sword. Confusion darkened his expression.

Terrwyn looked up into Bran's face. "I know you cannot do this. 'Tis wrong and you know it." When he took a deep breath, considering what she said, she pressed on. "You're a good man. Catrin wouldn't love you otherwise."

Bran rubbed the back of his hand across his mouth. "What are you doing here, Terrwyn? Your sisters are worried sick about you."

"Do I have your word you won't harm us? 'Twould loosen my tongue if you gave it."

The smile and slight nod she had been praying for appeared. "Aye, how could I hold Catrin, all the time knowing I murdered her sister?"

"You remember Sir James?"

"Aye, he was with the Englishmen who were looking for Welsh archers to conscribe into their army." His frown returned. "I recall you disappeared soon after they left."

Seeing Bran's mood change, Terrwyn quickly added, "He saw Drem after they took him. He intends to help me find him."

Bran's eye widened in surprise. "You've seen our Drem?" Distrust shifted and narrowed his gaze. "How do you know you can believe what this man says, Terrwyn?"

"I just do, Bran. You have to trust my wisdom on this." Terrwyn stood without a care for the shadows that she created. "I cannot bring my brother home if there is no village left. What does my father plan with Edgar Poole?"

"That lying bastard?" Bran spit over his shoulder. "Your father has been planning to take over where Owain left off."

James sat up. He gripped Bran's arm. "Tell me what you know."

"Aye," Terrwyn urged. "'Tis the only path that will save us."

Bran shrugged his shoulder to escape James's hold. He looked about, searching the shadows. "'Tis not safe to talk out in the open." He tipped his head toward the smokehouse. "We'll talk in there." Seeing the wary look in their eyes, he added, "I won't harm you."

They stepped into the building and Bran lit the stub of a candle standing on the worktable. The scent of smoked meat permeated the wooden planks. The ages of use had darkened the mortar stuffed between the fieldstones.

The dim light from the candle bounced off Bran's brown hair. His face was pale. The circles under his eyes were deep. He motioned for them to sit down in the chairs circling the table. Weary, he leaned his elbows on the table. He picked at the worn wooden planks with his nail. "A handful of English soldiers returned to our village in search of Edgar Poole."

"And did they ask for us?" James said.

Terrwyn heart raced as they waited for his answer.

"Aye," Bran nodded. "But no one knew anything to tell. There was a man who goes by the name of Simon. He left a message with Catrin. Said to tell her sister the gilly-flower was on its way to their family seat. Said you'd know what it means and offered his thanks. In truth, 'twas a puzzle to us all that they kept their visit short and orderly and didn't seek out Dafydd or our men."

Terrwyn smiled. At least one of her visions had ended well. When she caught the concern written on Bran's eyes she stretched out to grip his hands. "Bran, you have to tell us what worries you."

"I'm doing all I can to tend to your sisters and little Padrig but your father makes it difficult."

Tears formed before Terrwyn could stop them. Her heart ached to see their faces. "How are they?"

"Adain and Glynis ask about you all the time. Catrin wears herself out caring for baby Padrig. She has a good heart. I'd wed her today if your father would allow it. 'Tis why I ride with him. To gain his approval. But his plan is filled with madness." He looked up, his jaw set in determination. "I won't have the children harmed. If I have to take them away from the village, then that is what I'll do. With or without your father's approval."

James stood up from the chair and began to pace the small room. "Come on man. The hour grows late. Daylight approaches. Tell us what Poole and Dafydd have planned."

Terrwyn placed a soothing hand on Bran's shoulder. "We will protect the children from punishment. Won't we, James?"

"Aye," he said.

Bran's head dipped in resolution. "They've sent a message on to detonate the ship that carries the English king before it sets sail for France."

Terrwyn's legs buckled. She caught the chair before she hit the floor. The pieces of the vision swam before her. She could not form the words she wanted to speak. She feared Drem was involved in the mad scheme her father put together.

James sat beside Bran and pulled out the leather journal from his jerkin. After selecting several drawings, he placed them on the table in front of the man.

Bran searched James's face as though he thought he had gone mad as well. "You want me to look at drawings of flowers? Has one of the wheels in your head broken a spoke?"

James tapped the parchment with his finger. "Look closer."

Bran picked up the squat candle and held it near the drawing. Men's faces appeared from the flower petals. Their features blended into the scene unless you stared long enough. Then the scene fell away and all you saw were the men.

Bran swore under his breath. "'Tis sorcery or faerie magic."

James pushed the parchment back to Bran. "Are there any faces you recall seeing before?" He glanced at Terrwyn. Her skin had turned a deathly white. Her eyes were wide and unseeing. She swayed in her chair, her hands clasped tightly in her lap. He rushed to her, Bran and the drawings forgotten. "Sweet love, what ails you?"

When she did not respond, he knelt down beside her. He took her hands in his and rubbed the cold from her flesh. Tears slid down her face but she seemed to not notice. She stared off into a place where he could not reach.

Bran stood behind him, his hand on James's shoulder. "She's gone to one of her night visions. 'Tis odd though. Catrin said they haunt her only when she is asleep at night."

"Night visions? Why did she not speak of this?"

"Mayhap she feared you'd condemn her as others have done. There are those who would easily cast her out as a sorceress or find her filled with demons."

"Not I." James swept Terrwyn into his lap, cradling her in his arms. He pressed kisses to her temples, whispering, "Come back to me, love. Come back to me. Let me help you."

"Mind you, her sister Catrin swore me to secrecy. But Terrwyn cannot hear you when these visions come upon her. You'll have to wait for it to pass." He sat at the table and returned to studying the drawings.

James refused to listen to Bran's advice. He pressed a kiss to Terrwyn's trembling lips while he unwound her braided hair. He buried his hands in her hair. Massaging her scalp, he pleaded with her to return. His heart lurched when he felt a soft sigh brush across his lips.

Pulling away, he saw her eyes were closed as if she slept. The lashes fluttered as she awoke. The smile she gave him cleared the leaden fear that filled his veins.

James dropped his head to press his forehead against hers. "Ah, love, you scared me."

Her smile wobbled before she placed her fingers to his cheek. "'Tis a lovely kisser that you are, James Frost. I cannot like the thought of you learning on other women, but I'm grateful you were a fine student. You near curled my toes."

Bran's bark of laughter brought a healthy pink to her face. James grinned down at her and before she could voice any objections proceeded to curl her toes again. Thoughts of doing more than kiss her thoroughly were interrupted when Bran slammed his fist on the table.

"Enough," Bran said. "'I cannot sit and watch you two anymore."

Startled, they pulled apart as if he had thrown water on them. James glared at Bran for putting the wariness back in Terrwyn's eyes. "'Tis all right, love. Tell me what brings you such great sadness. What did you see with your night vision?"

Terrwyn gasped. Her face blanching, she turned to Bran. "What did you say, you horse's arse?"

"Nothing more than you should have done to begin with."

"You had no right," she whispered, her voice thread-thin.

"The man thought you were dying. I could not stand to see him weep over you."

"Terrwyn," James said, "I don't judge you. My own mother did speak of the gift you have."

"Gift?" She shook her head. "I would call it a curse instead." She gripped James's forearm. "We must make haste to England if we are to stop my father from killing his own son."

Bran bolted up, knocking the chair over in his haste. "Padrig?"

"Nay," Terrwyn said, "Drem."

Chapter Twenty-Six

"We will talk more of this difference of opinion."

"Say what you will, James," Terrwyn argued, "'tis a curse until I cause the fates to turn from what I've seen. Until then, I have no proof that this is a gift."

James sighed into her hair. He would let the stubborn woman have her way for now. Her stubbornness was one of the traits that he admired yet drove him mad at the same time. He would see to it his mother had a chat with her when they met.

Earlier that morning they had waved Bran off as he headed to the village. They had agreed that Bran would inform Dafydd ap Hew that Terrwyn and the Englishman were done away with as ordered.

They had yet to discuss what must be done with her father. James's first priority was to save the king. Armed with dates and names from Bran, he knew he did not have much time. Traveling overland would take too long. He would have to find the means to sail from Bristol to Southampton's port.

"'Tis a grand thing you do," Terrwyn said.

"Aye. What am I doing to gain your favor?"

"Writing Bran a letter of introduction to your mother. My father won't like it when he learns Bran has taken the children." She glanced over her shoulder at him. "Are you certain she won't mind the addition of my sisters and brother?"

"She will embrace them with open arms." James squeezed Terrwyn, pulling her to his chest. "Especially after she's met you." He tightened his embrace to keep her from leaping off Zeus's back.

"Meets me? What are you planning that you deemed unnecessary to discuss with me?"

"We will stop at my mother's home, Mallows Marsh. I don't know if she is in residence. If not, then we will move on as soon as I've arranged transportation to England."

"And how am I to meet your mam, dressed as I am?" She brushed the stained leggings and dusty jerkin. "Meeting me would make matters worse for my sisters. She'd think we were no better than a pack of slattern wenches."

James threw his head back and laughed until tears rolled down his cheeks. Holding her as close as he could manage while on horseback, he said, "She will love you as I do."

⋯

Hours later, Terrwyn was still not convinced traveling to Mallows Marsh was a good plan. She did not like the idea of meeting his mother. There was something in the way James spoke that told her he was keeping something from her.

She may have shared most of her secrets, but she knew he still kept more of his own.

Her concerns were softened when she recalled his words. Did he mean what he said earlier? He had grown quiet as soon as he mentioned his love for her. Although it warmed her own heart, she did not tell him her feelings. She still needed to sort them out.

Thoughts of their afternoon of lovemaking at the Bloated Goat heated her blood. She shifted uncomfortably next to James. Did he recall the thrill of it as well? Her breasts brushed against his forearm. Her nipples hardened, drawing her attention back to the things he had done to her body. She had never felt so alive.

James's hand stole up her ribcage and over her breast. Her breath caught as his fingers teased the raised flesh. He chuckled when she groaned and shifted on Zeus's back. She thought she would go mad when he began to lick at her neck. Frustrated that she could not reach what she wanted, she let out a curse and twisted to gain his lips.

"We have not far to travel. I'll come to you once we are there."

She shivered as his words blew across her damp skin. "Aye. When your mam sets her eyes on me, you'll not get within an inch without her knowing."

James grunted. He hated to admit she was right. His mother would make sure he kept his distance from Terrwyn's skirts. He did not like that idea one bit. Yet there were ways to get around the rules of the keep. He smiled into Terrwyn's hair and turned Zeus into a familiar glen.

Mallows Marsh was over another hill or two. He could not enter through the gates with his arousal pressing through his leggings. One look at him and his mother would set to lecturing him about a man's honor and integrity.

He reigned in near a clearing. It had been several years since he had the opportunity to laze about the pond. The trees he remembered were now taller. The brush he had cleared with his own two hands had returned, determined to take over. But the pond remained. The fresh underground stream kept the water cool and fresh.

Terrwyn leaned forward, gasping at the beauty before her. "'Tis a wondrous sight."

James enjoyed knowing she saw the same beauty that he did. He dismounted and, after seeing she landed safely on her feet, turned her in his arms. Cupping her chin, he lifted her face to catch the afternoon sun. "Beautiful," he whispered before placing his mouth over hers.

⚜

Terrwyn stretched her arms overhead and shivered as a cool late-afternoon breeze brushed her skin. She rose slowly and tested her limbs for soreness. Her stomach growled, announcing it was time to feed again. She picked up her clothes, shaking the bits of grass and dust off. The thought of putting them on her clean body did not appeal.

She stood at the edge of the pond and let her eyes skim over the lovely shape of James's strong thighs, his firmly muscled buttock. He slept upon the thin blanket they'd purchased from the tavern. His forearm covered his face, shielding him from the light.

She grinned, recalling his surprise when she grabbed him and drew him in. She touched her mouth where his lips had sucked and pulled. Her hand stole to her abdomen. The thrilling memory of where he'd placed his mouth and hands was fresh in her mind. When the tender places began to throb at the thought, she knew it would be a sad and lonely life if she never received his caresses again.

The shivers that had woken her from her nap rolled over her skin. Senses heightened from their lovemaking, she tensed to listen to the wind. Zeus lifted his head at the sound of thundering hooves. Terrwyn ran toward James to shake him awake.

He had heard the riders too. He was up and moving before she took two strides. His leggings and jerkin remained where he had impatiently stripped them off. He scooped up the pile of clothing as they ran behind a hedge of bushes. He embraced her to his chest and placed a gentle kiss to her ears and then her lips. "They ride toward Mallows Marsh. If you can manage it, we will take to the more rugged terrain. I would that we reach my mother before they do."

"Who were they?"

"I don't know. Couldn't see their faces or their colors. But anyone riding like they were does not bring goodwill."

രⅇഔ

Terrwyn's backside was sore in more places than she cared to think about for very long. As promised, the terrain they rode over was rugged. The meadows were green as emeralds. Pale slabs of rock stood out of the ground like broken bones. She ached to ask James to let her walk out the cramping in her muscles but did not want be the one to slow him down.

Terrwyn saw the keep as they crested the last hill. Nestled on a cliff overhang, it perched over the water. The white of the stone walls glistened from the spray of the channel of water below. A flag with a red dragon surrounded by a wreath of red roses waved over the highest point of the keep.

The portcullis stood open and unattended. The yards were eerily silent. Wary, they rode Zeus into the bailey.

The mistress of the keep walked out and stood on the top step. The only movement was the hem of the forest green gown rippling under the breeze. Her raven hair remained uncovered by a mantle. It was not held back in a neat hairstyle but hung down to her waist and surrounded a face that was pale and strained.

James lifted his hand in salutation. His breath caught when his mother did not move toward them but gripped the railing for support.

"Stay alert, my love," he whispered as he let Terrwyn down and then dismounted.

Keeping Zeus's reins in his hand and holding Terrwyn's in the other, he walked up to the steps of the keep. "Mother, have I offended you in some way? Do you not offer hospitality to me and my friend?"

A small sound came from his mother before she collapsed to her knees. James and Terrwyn rushed to her side. They knelt and together lifted her into his arms.

"Where is everyone?" Terrwyn asked over his mother's head.

"I don't know but intend to find out. No matter the calamity, the gates should not be left unprotected."

The sound of weeping came through the doorway that led to the main hall. She looked over her shoulder to see the men and women of the keep, leaning on each other in sorrow.

His mother's eyes fluttered open. "Oh." Her lips trembled as tears formed and streamed down her pale cheeks. Her smile deepened as she placed her palm over his heart and held it there. When he covered her fingers with his hand she looked up into his face. "You live! James, my son, you've come back from the dead."

"Nay, mother, I'm as hale and hearty as they come. Soon as you are feeling up to it, I'd like for you to tell me how you heard of my death."

Curiosity turned her attention to Terrwyn. "And who do we have here?"

"Lady Mary Frost of Mallows Marsh, may I introduce Terrwyn."

Lady Mary caught the look between them and smiled again. "She's a pretty maiden. Too pretty to traipse around in men's clothing. We will rectify that as soon as I'm set back on my feet."

With her son's help, she righted herself and hugged him tight. She gripped his arm and strode to the doorway. She stood not much above Terrwyn's own height, but her posture and energy made her appear taller.

"People of Mallows Marsh, behold, our James yet lives!"

A cheer rang out and they rushed through the doorway to pay their respects. Terrwyn shrank back as their joy for the lady's son filled the air. Hearty laughter erupted as they came to give their best wishes to the lady and son of the keep.

When all had settled and the household members had returned to their duties, James turned to his mother. "Come. Let us sit in the alcove. You will tell me what has taken place in my absence. More important, how you came to mourn my death."

Lady Mary held her gaze on James as if he would disappear. "A brawny man of stature and a mane of gold rode in. He stayed only long enough to water his horses and mount up again."

"Did he give his name?"

"Aye, said he's called Simon of Norwich. He had terrible news but felt it necessary 'twas delivered properly. Chose to do it himself."

James leaned forward, clasping her hands. "Did he say anything else?"

Lady Mary shook her head. "I didn't hear much after he said one of my own countrymen ended your life. Dear Lord, but I prayed they were wrong and that your father was here." Life was returning to her bones and sinew. Fear and sorrow faded from her face. "Part of my prayer has been answered. I didn't lose you after all."

"My lady," Terrwyn asked softly, "did he mention where he was headed in such a great hurry?"

"Aye. He and his companions were headed for the water, looking for transportation to take them back to England."

"His companions? Did you recognize them?"

"Nay. I sent them on their way with nary a drink to quench their thirst."

James lifted an expressive eyebrow. "You didn't offer the pinnace for them to sail?"

"And why should I? They had an air about them I didn't like. I knew they'd not treat my ship well. Nor would they sail it back to me intact. I need it for deliveries to the merchant in Cardiff."

"Mother, you are a treat. It tears my heart to know I have to leave you so soon after my resurrection, but I must procure my own transportation to England." He turned to include Terrwyn. "It will take me but a few hours to set our plans in motion. Stay here, rest and keep my mother company while I'm away."

"Oh, I don't think 'tis necessary. We but bathed in the pond a few hours ago." Terrwyn felt her neck redden as soon as the words were out of her mouth.

Lady Mary caught the look between them and smiled brightly. "Come lass. I'm sure you won't want to pass up an opportunity to remove the travel dust and change your clothes. We'll have a wee bite before our supper." She looked over their shoulders, searching the floors. "But where is your luggage?"

Terrwyn was certain her skin was now the color of the salmon running in the stream at spring.

"She hasn't any, mother." At her gasp of surprise, he quickly added, "I'll right it as soon as there is time."

His mother rose to stand over her son. "Do you mean to tell me you brought this wee maiden without a gown? She has nothing to her name?"

Terrwyn wished the faeries would perform their magic and make the floor swallow her up. As well-meaning as his mother's intentions might be, Terrwyn certainly did not need her pity. "I have bow and arrows," she said under her breath.

Lady Mary turned, hearing the pain in Terrwyn's voice. "Ah, my dear, forgive me. 'Tis the thought that he did you wrong that sharpens my tongue."

James pressed a kiss to his mother's forehead. He bowed gallantly over Terrwyn's hand, turned it and placed a lingering kiss to the inside of her wrist. Leaving the two women speechless, he withdrew and nearly ran out the door.

Mortified, Terrwyn cast a furtive look toward the mistress of the keep. "My lady—"

"Come, child, while you bathe you can tell me about your family and how you came to be with my son."

"Please, I don't wish to intrude on your duties."

Lady Mary shook her head and laughed. "'Tis a cause for celebration. A few hours ago, I thought my son was lost to me. Instead, he returns to me with a beautiful woman on his arm."

Lady Mary called out orders to two of the serving girls, who ran off to do their lady's bidding. A flurry of work commenced as the mistress of the keep led the way to a bedchamber. She chattered companionably, informing Terrwyn about the keep's history and the location of each room. The joy pouring from her words was contagious.

"Oh, 'tis lovely, my lady," Terrwyn said, in awe of her surroundings. Someone had arrived ahead of them and pushed the drapes from the windows. The room was set afire with the reddish glow of the setting sun. Although two large chairs sat by the fireplace, it was the bed that held Terrwyn's attention. Thick pelts of fur were mounded at the foot. Overstuffed pillows were propped against the massive ornate headboard.

A small side table held a highly polished plate of metal. She picked up the looking glass and gasped. Saints' bones, she hardly recognized her reflection.

Lady Mary came to stand beside her. The strain of the day was evident in her expressive eyes. "No need to worry about what to wear. I'm sure I've a gown or two that will fit you fine." She patted Terrwyn's hand. "Tell Mille when you are ready for me. I've some tasks to see to."

The mistress of the keep walked out into the passageway and turned to the chambermaid. "Mille, I will be in my private solar. I would have a word with my son. Find him and have him sent to me at once."

Chapter Twenty-Seven

Dread filled her empty belly. Terrwyn did not know whether to beat James about the head or cover him with kisses. The gown his mother sent to her was made of midnight-blue wool and lined with a soft fur. The cuffs of the sleeves were decorated with white brocade lace. She could not ever recall having worn a gown as fine.

Her ablutions completed, she nodded to the chambermaid that she was ready. Mille led the way to the solar and pushed the door open when Lady Mary called for them to enter.

The solar radiated the remaining heat of the day. The heady perfumed air was warm and moist. Flowers filled every corner of the room. Lady Mary motioned for her to sit down by the fire, where a pair of chairs flanked the hearth. Set out on the table beside her were a pitcher of ale, two mugs and a loaf of bread.

Lady Mary filled a mug and held it out.

Terrwyn took a sip of the bitter brew. "Heavenly," she said, licking the ale from her lips.

Lady Mary smiled at her appreciation. "You are welcome to come here anytime you need peace and solace to think."

"Thank you, but I cannot imagine we will be here long enough for me to intrude in your special room."

Lady Mary set her mug of ale down on the table and sat straight-backed in her chair. "Why is that?"

"James and I mean to sail to England as soon as we can."

Lady Mary leaned forward and patted Terrwyn's knee. "My wee dear, didn't my darlin' boy tell you he intends for you to stay at Mallows Marsh until he returns?"

"James left without me? Nay, that is not what was discussed." Terrwyn rose suddenly from her chair. She swept back the ale, drained it dry and slammed it on the table. Fury ate at her bones until she thought she would explode. "He is not my husband to tell me what I can and cannot do."

"Perhaps we can rectify that when he returns. I understand there are to be a few children added to the keep. 'Twould be a lovely time to welcome your sisters and brother."

"You don't mind that they'll invade your home?"

"James told me a bit of the situation before he left."

"My father—"

"Has made poor choices and dangerous alliances," Lady Mary finished for her.

"Some that can never be forgiven."

James's mother motioned for Terrwyn to retake her seat. "Come. We will work through this. For now, take ease in knowing that it pleases me to have young life returning to Mallows Marsh."

"They are good and loving children." She paced the solar, stopping at the hearth to warm her hands. "Though the English king stripped our lands and the power that goes with it, the children were raised properly. They won't disgrace themselves or your home." She could not seem to make those blasted tears go away. She scrubbed at them with her knuckles and still they streamed down her cheeks. "Saints' bones, what you must be thinking."

Lady Mary put a consoling arm around her. "'Tis presumptuous of me to ask, but do you love my son?"

At Terrwyn's jerked nod Lady Mary said, "I know 'tis out of his love for you that he desires your safety. You must stay here until he has set things right for King Henry."

"Your son will be safer with me at his side. Without me to protect him, he is bound to place his hide in danger."

"Indeed." Lady Mary studied Terrwyn, her eyebrow cocked in curiosity. "Although he is often secretive about his travels, I imagine James knows how to wriggle out of any snare set in his path."

"Why did he not bid me farewell?" Terrwyn scrubbed her

hands over the chill growing in her blood. "Where is he now?"

"Trying to convince the captain of my little pinnace that Zeus won't stamp a hole through the wooden hull. It would not do to have our shipments of wool and spice sink to the bottom of the Bristol Channel."

"Then he has not set sail, yet, has he?"

"They may weigh anchor at any moment." She shivered expressively. "'Tis my desire that James does not sway the captain to his plan. The channel can be a dangerous one in daylight. To travel under the dark skies is more treacherous."

"I would have liked an opportunity to say farewell. Do you suppose we can find him so that I might speak with him?"

James's mother patted her shoulder. "It has taken me many years to understand the importance of letting your man go when he already has his mind set. We must follow his wishes. We will try to free our minds from worry by keeping busy with preparations for your wedding."

Terrwyn paced back and forth, her agitation filling the solar. What could she tell his mother that would not cause the woman to send for the parish priest? James said his mother had spoken of dreams and night visions as gifts. She took Lady Mary's hand and braced herself for the worst that might come after her explanation.

"First, I cannot marry your son because he has not asked me. And," she said before Lady Mary could interrupt, "you may not want your son to wed me once you hear of my strange quality." She took a deep breath and began the tale of what disturbed her sleep most every night of her life. "That," she added at the end of her tale, "is why James cannot set sail without me."

She waited in the silence of the room. They had returned to the chairs by the fire, their pitcher and mugs empty of ale, the food brought in by young Mille untouched. The fire in the hearth shimmered in Lady Mary's eyes.

She stood abruptly and held out her hand. "Come child, you've not a moment to waste." Calling out for Mille, she had the servant begin to gather up the food in the tablecloth. Before sending the girl off to do her bidding, she scribbled a note and handed it to her with more instructions. "We've fine baskets woven here in Mallows Marsh, but I fear 'twould be too bulky an item to carry," she muttered to herself.

Terrwyn watched her warily. Did Lady Mary mean to send her out into the wilderness? Perhaps tell James she ran from him? Though she knew she'd taken a chance in revealing her secret, she had not figured to be run off in the middle of the night. The thought of James not in her life wrenched her stomach.

"Come. Come child." Lady Mary motioned with an urgent wave of her hand. She pulled her up the stairs and into her own bedchamber. A great chest stood against the wall. She opened the double doors and peered inside. Her head shoved to the farthest corner of the interior, she dragged out a pair of leggings and an old leather jerkin. The clothing sailed in the air and landed on the master bed.

"I know you cannot want to wear men's apparel already, but they'll be there should you need them." Lady Mary stuck her head back in the chest and came out with a dark brown woolen day-gown. Satisfied with her selection, she flipped it on the bed to join the leggings and jerkin.

"I haven't a gambeson to fit you." She snapped her fingers. "But cotton shirting will make a layer underneath the leather."

Terrwyn blinked. Was his mother now speaking to her instead of to herself? "I have the clothing I came with."

"Oh, well—no, dear, you don't. I cannot lie to you. It stank beyond repair. Fact is, it had to be burned." She tilted her chin, daring Terrwyn to challenge her. "Besides, you would not want to wear it again. Leastwise not in closed confinement. And I don't want my shipment damaged by the stink." She lifted her shoulders expressively. "There you have it."

"Confinement? Do you intend to imprison me?"

Lady Mary stared at her as if she had grown two heads. "Are you daft, my dear? Of course not!"

"Then what is all this?"

"Your travel clothes, my dear. I aim to help you steal aboard my own ship that is sailing for Cardiff within the hour."

Terrwyn squealed and threw herself into Lady Mary's arms.

"There now, child, 'tis best you get a move on."

A knock came at the door. Mille handed her mistress a note and, after bobbing a curtsy, ran off with her lady's response.

"My son is throwing a spanner in our plans. He unwisely wants to set sail while it is still nighttime. I'll stall them as long as I can."

Terrwyn picked up the pair of leggings.

"Nay, don the gown, my dear. If James sees you before you set sail for England, he'll be too busy ogling you to yell overmuch."

A leather satchel lay on the bed. Terrwyn quickly folded and shoved the rest of the clothing inside. James's mother held out a heavy black cloak for her. The interior was lined in a wondrous thick layer of fur.

Lady Mary held a lantern overhead and led her down the stairway to a side door. The stone panel swung in when she lifted a lever beside it.

Encased in darkness, they descended into a tunnel that led them beneath the castle. Lady Mary worked to keep the flame in the lantern from guttering. The sound of dripping water echoed against the moss-covered walls. The cool, damp air made Terrwyn shiver despite the heavy cloak about her shoulders. She was beginning to think she had stepped into a faerie's maze and would never return.

They came to stop at a wide stone slab flooring. Another lever was lifted and the door swung in. A lantern hung from a post at the door. Outside, the moon shone brightly; the stars twinkled over their heads.

Two men were loading a boat with supplies. Though it was smaller than some merchant vessels, the pinnace would do well for the channel's shallower depths. It hung low in the water, loaded with their shipment of goods. The masts stood like two fingers pointing to the heavens above; folded canvas rested neatly at the wrists, waiting to be unfurled once they were underway.

"This is Captain Barragh. He will take good care of you. He knows you are my precious cargo and will transfer you to the larger ship in Cardiff." Lady Mary leaned over and whispered, "I cannot explain it, but I frighten him."

"Welcome aboard," he snapped.

Terrwyn eyed the rotund man. His weathered face did not show any signs of welcome.

Lady Mary kissed Terrwyn's forehead. "Don't be afraid. Your bow and quiver are in the lower deck where you will be hiding. A small packet of food is there as well. Remember, James sails on this ship too. Do not move from your hiding place lest you are discovered."

"This way, my lady," Captain Barragh said.

Onboard, Terrwyn stopped to wave and heard Lady Mary say, "Go with God and return to us soon."

At the sound of James's voice, Terrwyn forgot she was no longer wearing her leggings and turned too quickly. She caught herself before she fell into the dark hole leading to the deck below.

CR&O

They were underway and sailing through the channel's choppy currents. Terrwyn swallowed the building nausea. Terrified from never having sailed in more than a small carroche basket to catch fish on the River Usk, she looked forward to when they pulled into Cardiff's port.

Captain Barragh scowled at her every time he came below deck to check on her. She would be happy to be free of the angry, sun-scarred man. She had a feeling he'd be just as relieved when she stepped off his ship and he handed her over to another.

Soon the rocking began to soothe her weary bones. How long it had been since she slept solidly? She blinked, trying to shake off the heaviness that came with the ship's gentle sway.

She went over Lady Mary's instructions. Captain Barragh would see to her transfer to the *Genoese Queen*. The *Queen* was a large merchant ship, a carrack. She would know it by its four masts standing out from the crowd of smaller ships and fishing boats. It was carrying blue woad dye and other spices to Southampton. James, too, would be on that same ship, but if she kept to herself, she would not be found until they were far enough out of Cardiff's port.

When the door to her cramped quarters opened, Terrwyn stood and grabbed the bow and arrow she kept ready at all times. The captain scowled at the weapon in her hands and shoved an hourglass toward her.

"Be ready when the sand empties."

CƺƧ

Wearing the cloak Captain Barragh demanded she put on, Terrwyn stumbled over ropes and pulleys as she clambered down to the dinghy below. Though she felt like a wraith moving over the water in the dinghy, she surely did not feel graceful.

Why she'd heeded Mary's instructions to wear the confining gown was beyond her understanding. The persuasive woman must have caught her by surprise.

The captain and his shipmates hustled her out of the dinghy and onto the planking leading up to the merchant ship. Terrwyn paused to count the tall masts. One, two, three and four.

"Come on with yerself," Captain Barragh said.

When the bag of gold coins passed between the men, Terrwyn grew anxious. There had been talk in her village that women were sold as slaves—some used for household labor and others as whores until they died. She glanced back at the town of Cardiff. A few buildings still held the scars from Owain Glyndwr's attack on the town. Blackened spires thrusting into the sky were all that remained of the wooden structures. That was in the year 1404, just five years before her brother was abducted. Her stomach twisted at the thought that perhaps her father had been one of his followers. 'Twould explain the king's decision to reduce the family's title and take away their land. She had been a child of eight years. No length of searching would help her remember if her father had gone off to war.

She pulled her shoulders straight. Well not this time. She would stop her father's madness. "Thank you, Captain Barragh. I will certainly inform Lady Mary of your good service." She held out her hand to the gentleman standing beside the captain. "I'm Mistress Terrwyn Frost."

His chest puffed out, making the ruffles on his shirt even fuller. The red satin belt around his middle stretched, threatening to burst from the pressure. He took her fingertips, brushing his lips across her knuckles. "I am Russo, Captain of the *Genoese Queen.*"

Terrwyn peeled her fingers from his grasp. "I understand we will soon set sail for England. If you'll direct me to my cabin, I'll settle in until we are underway."

She lifted the hem of her gown, marched past the two captains and ignored the stares she left in her wake. She stopped only when what appeared to be a first mate or something refused to let her cross onto the deck. Saints' bones, how was she to know whom to turn to? She had never been on a merchant ship before in her life.

Terrwyn jumped when the captain grabbed her elbow. "You will follow my orders and do as I say, when I say. *Sî?*" He led her to the small cabin where she would be staying until they landed and nearly threw her into the cramped quarters.

Terrwyn shoved her hair out of her face. She rubbed her arm, certain a bruise would soon form. "Aye. But I won't be made a prisoner, Captain Russo."

"I cannot guarantee your safety if you do not listen." He pointed his thick callused finger at her. "You will stay in here at all times. Unless you are looking to whore yourself out, you will keep the hood of your cloak over your head. You understand. *Sî?*"

"I cannot go out on the deck?" The dank cabin was the size of a cupboard. A small window no bigger than her fist was shuttered closed. "What if I need to gain a breath of fresh air?"

He waved his hands in the air. "Bah! This does not start well. I can tell you are stubborn donkey. It is madness to keep you on my ship." After searching the folds of his doublet he held out the bag exchanged between captains. "Here. Take the coins and be gone with you. Peace on my ship is too important."

Terrwyn flipped down the hood and took the cloak off. When he saw the bow and quiver strapped to her shoulder, his bushy gray eyebrows rose over cold narrowed eyes.

"Nay. Here I will stay. You won't even know I'm aboard your ship." She dropped her satchel on the little bed and neatly folded her cloak. She turned, arms crossed, and waited. The captain would have to physically pick her up and toss her off his ship. She prayed he would not have to. She now had two men to save.

"Please, *signorina*, you be a good girl. Eh?"

"It is *signora*, Captain Russo. *Signora* Frost."

A look of confusion washed over his face, but he shrugged. "I'll let you out for a breath of air once when we are underway."

He took out a key and before she could object, he closed and locked the door.

The ship pitched and rolled on the currents. She found a small blade James's mother must have tucked in the satchel and used it to pry open one of the shutters. After stacking several boxes on top of each other, she climbed up to look out. A fine mist swirled through the window. Once Captain Russo deemed the conditions were acceptable the ship shuddered and swung about. With the sails set, they were underway.

A few hours later, Terrwyn began to pray that she might die.

Chapter Twenty-Eight

Terrwyn squeezed her eyes shut. She could not believe a ship that heaved itself from one side to the other, then bucked up and down, would survive the weather. She was certain they were all going to die. She wished it would be soon.

"'Tis a coward, that is what you are," she scolded herself.

Oh, if only James were here. He would help keep her mind busy with something else besides the way her stomach churned every time the ship shifted direction. The walls of the exterior shook when wave upon wave slammed into the hull.

"Lord above," she groaned into the slop bucket the shipmate had brought to her after his first visit to her quarters.

He had muttered, *"Verde,"* and shaken his head. He returned with a bucket and wet rag and touched his face. His pity lasted long enough for him to lock the door behind her.

Verde. Aye. She translated the word when Captain Russo came down to see for himself. Evidently she was an unusual shade of green. Another roll of the ship and she swore as her stomach tried to come out through her back. Though this time she noticed he did not lock the door behind him. She would have laughed if she had the strength.

Her cheek pressed to the wooden flooring, she shoved her hair off her face. Cursing under her breath, she prayed for the seas to calm. James was somewhere on the ship and she had to find him before they docked in Southampton.

She released her death grip on the slop jar. Sliding to one hip, she steadied her head and waited for the room to stop tilting.

There were voices outside her door. Captain Russo was lecturing someone in Italian. She did not want to be the deckhand who was getting the verbal thrashing. She lifted her head when the captain's victim responded in English. Dear Lord, the sickness must be making her mad. She recognized that voice.

The door swung open as she grabbed the small bed to drag her body up.

"Woman, are you a raving lunatic? What do you think you are doing here?"

Terrwyn started to defend her actions but felt compelled to wait. At that moment the bucket was more important than her pride.

જ્ઞ

James lifted Terrwyn's hair and bathed her face. The pitching and rolling had subsided as they moved out of the storm. It appeared her attacks of sickness had lessened. Though her skin was pale as cream, it no longer had the greenish tinge of the English moors. Her lashes fluttered against her cheeks.

He worked to support his anger but found it weakened as soon as he saw her wee self tormented by the ship's movement. He supposed it was a good thing he hadn't known she had smuggled onto the ship until after they set sail. His conscience would not have allowed him to set her off alone in Cardiff's port. Nor could he have returned with her to his mother's home. But damn, he would have liked a choice.

"Water," Terrwyn pleaded.

"Nay, I have something better for you." James lifted a flask of wine to her lips. "Captain Russo's compliments to my shy bride."

Terrwyn choked on the wine, then swallowed. The décolletage of her gown twisted as she sat up, exposing flesh that made his mouth water.

"Easy, *Signora* Frost, I would so hate to lose another night of wedded bliss."

"I never told him we were newly wedded." Her face scrunched in concentration, she gripped his arm to keep from falling over as the ship took an unexpected roll to the side.

"He concluded that you are too innocent in the ways between and man and a woman and feared our wedding bed. He is also of the opinion you are spoiled and have a sour temper. He pities me." Grinning despite himself, he laughed at her outrage. He handed her a rag and dried mint to rub across her teeth.

Terrwyn gave her mouth a vigorous scrubbing and spat out the foul taste into the pail. "Suppose he thinks you should beat me?"

"Aye, 'twas his idea at first." He turned his back to dip the bathing cloth in the fresh water. "Changed his mind when he saw you weak as an infant. He fancies the notion that I have not wooed you enough. And beating you would only thicken your hide and harden your heart."

Wringing out the cloth, he moved toward the bed where Terrwyn sat. The color had returned to her face. Her cheeks flushed and her eyes sparkled back at him. He ran his finger over the scooped neckline of her gown.

"'Tis a lovely gown you are wearing. The woodland brown suits you. Though if I were dressing you, I would prefer less material."

"Would you now?" Terrwyn batted at his hand. "I would not have thought you were a man of high fashion." She caught his wrist and pulled him close. "Truth be told, there is a great deal I'm thinking I don't know."

James lifted her hair and let the tresses float through his fingers. "'Tis a pity, your not knowing your husband."

Warming to his game of words, Terrwyn slid over, allowing him room to climb next to her. "Hmm, I cannot even speak of your likes and dislikes."

James stayed his ground and stood in front of her, his thighs braced on either side of her hips. He leaned in and played the warm cloth over her skin. The water streamed from her neck, dipping into her cleavage.

Terrwyn sucked in her breath as he caught her neck with

his teeth. He nipped at the tender place behind her ear. He brushed her lips lightly with his, then urged her to open her mouth. When she complied, he slid his tongue in, sucking and diving in for more. He fondled her over the down-soft woolen dress. Rubbing her nipples in circles, he brushed his nails over her aroused flesh.

Terrwyn moved to help James locate the ribbons that pulled the bodice taut around her ribcage. With a gentle tug the bow untied. The bodice slid off her shoulders and down to her waist.

James released her mouth, slowly trailed kisses down her neck and paused over her collarbone. Terrwyn grabbed the back of his head, urging him to the crest of her breast. She arched her back to receive his full attention. James complied with her urging and sucked, scraping his teeth over her skin. His thumb worked her other breast, rolling over her nipple.

James tipped her backward. Lifting her hips, he slid the gown off of her waist and stripped it away. His legs braced, he knelt and left a trail of kisses along her ribcage. Her body bucked involuntarily when he dipped his fingers into her core. Her muscles contracted from his touch. She pulled him.

"Now," she cried. "Now."

Denying her request, he knelt between her legs and brought his lips to the pink tongue of her apex. His lapped at the dew forming on her nether lips until Terrwyn cried for more.

He released her long enough to strip off his clothing. She smiled up at him and wrapped her thighs around his waist. He lifted her onto his primed flesh and plunged until they could no longer hold control.

CRSO

James awoke with a start. Terrwyn's shoulder quivered against his chest, her breasts brushing his ribcage. "Terrwyn?" His concern mounted when she did not respond but kept her face buried in his neck.

"What is it, love? Are you ill?"

She lifted her head. Her eyes sparking, she grinned and a

chuckle escaped. "Nay, I realized that had we traveled together in the first place, I would not have been sick at all."

James looked at her warily. He glanced at her hands to ensure they did not contain a weapon of some sort. Instead, his silver band lay in her palm. He read the word engraved inside. Brotherhood.

"You don't have to look at me like that." She poked him in the ribs. When his expression did not change she added, "All I mean is that you fill me with more than thoughts of the rocking of the ship. I cannot feel it moving when you are filling me." She licked at the place where she'd poked him. "Have you nothing to say?"

"Aye, I've much to say about you and my mother conspiring against me." He slid his hand over her head, playing with her silken hair. "But I can't speak of my mother while I'm lying here naked. 'Tis not fitting and you are too distracting."

Grinning like a barn cat after a go in the dairy byre, Terrwyn straddled his waist. James grabbed the hair draped over her shoulder, his fingers digging into her scalp as she bent over him. She rubbed her breasts over his chest as she climbed forward. Teasing him, her nipples swung just out of reach of his mouth.

He growled under his breath and brought her near. She chuckled again when he gained access to her nipples. While he suckled her breast, she moved her hand down his flat stomach. His cock bounced as if looking for her. She reached back farther to gather him close. She caressed him, then slid him inside.

"Ah, I love you." She sighed, her head tilted up to the ceiling.

James stilled. His body stiffened and then he grabbed her waist. Terrwyn sat up. Bracing her palms on his chest, she rocked with the ship. Her hips moved in time with each pitch and roll. Their passion continued to climax as wave after wave slammed into the hull.

Spent, Terrwyn collapsed on top of him. He lay within her, never wanting to move.

The storm outside their cabin renewed and they slept through it until a wooden box crashed to the floor.

James sat up and rested his shoulders against the bulkhead. He drew Terrwyn into his arms and held her tenderly. "We must speak."

Terrwyn curled up on her side. "Oh?"

James leaned over and kissed the edge of her exposed breast. "I suppose we should marry as soon as we are able. 'Tis certain my mother and father would want to be there, but I think sooner rather than later is best."

"You suppose, if you have to, that you should wed me in a hurry." Terrwyn rolled over and off the bed. She gathered her gown and slid it over her head. Confused, he watched her. "Aye," she said, "if you have to."

James grinned and sat up. "I knew you'd agree 'tis the right thing to do."

"Nay, James, I won't be a bride that you think of as a millstone around your neck, weighing you down until you cannot breathe."

Frowning, he leaped from the bed. "I didn't say you were."

"But you intimated it. I won't speak of this until you no longer think of me as an obligation." Defiant anger glittered from her eyes. She lifted her bow and arrow and pointed them at him. "When you think of me as friend, wife and helpmate, then and only then will I discuss our marriage."

Speechless, James stared at her, at the weapon gripped in her petite hand. His brain worked feverishly, trying to understand what he had said wrong. He had asked her to become his wife. Who in their right mind would consider it an affront? The more he thought of it the angrier he became.

"Dinner," the first mate yelled, slamming his fist against the outside of the cabin door. They both jumped and Terrwyn's hold slipped. The arrow went sizzling through the air and impaled the wooden panel of the door.

James shoved his feet through his leggings, then bowed in Terrwyn's direction. "Does this mean our moment for marital bliss is over?" He drew the jerkin over his head, tugging on the hem to straighten it. "Come in," he shouted at the first mate and yanked the door open.

The first mate's knowing leer slipped as he entered and saw

the still-quivering arrow. He quickly placed the simple fare on the side table. Bobbing his head, he mumbled that he thought he heard Captain Russo yelling for him and slipped out as if fire was on his tail.

"Now look what you've done," Terrwyn said. "He won't be able to look me in the face for the rest of the journey."

"Sit down and calm yourself."

Terrwyn flounced over and plopped down on the bed. She folded her arms and glared.

James held out a thick crust of bread, loaded with creamy butter. He lifted a bottle of wine and poured healthy portions of the red nectar into the two mugs. "Peace, my love. Come keep me company. We've a bit longer before we dock in Southampton."

When Terrwyn licked her lips, he knew she'd forgiven him for being a horse's arse. He should have asked her to wed him when he was inside her. He held out a mug and watched her drain it dry. He raised an eyebrow when she motioned for him to refill it.

He realized their situation remained unresolved. He had to protect Henry and stop the threat against the throne. How was he to do that without losing his woman in the process? He feared his heart could not take the loss of her love.

Terrwyn ran her fingernail over the rim of her mug. She stuck her finger in her mouth to suck it off. "You haven't asked me how I came to be here."

"Ah." James opened his arms wide, giving her a space to sit upon his lap. "I'm all ears."

CRISO

Terrwyn held the same position for what seemed like an eternity. Not that the view was lacking. She just would rather have been close enough to touch him now and again. She realized her impatience must have been easy for James to read.

"Just a moment longer, my love." He sighed and put down the charcoal. "Pouting will not help."

"What will you do, Sir Knight? Thrash my backside?" She

shifted so that her form was more exposed.

"I surrender," James said. "You may have your break."

Leaping up from the bed, she ran to him and draped her arms around his shoulders. "Do you think ill of me?" She fluttered her lashes at him. "'Tis certain my heart would break if you did so."

He laughed at her jest and pulled her into his lap.

She laid her head upon his shoulder and stroked sweeping circles over his chest with her fingertips. She paused over the ring he kept hidden under his jerkin. "Tell me something about yourself that I do not know."

James stiffened under her hand. "What more do you need to know?"

She released the breath she held and shut her eyes. "Did your mother tell you nighttime stories to get you to bed?"

His chuckle reverberated under her palm. "Aye, she had a tale to suit most any reason. She loved to tell us of faeries and the like."

She smiled into his neck. "And what was your favorite?"

"Dragons. I especially liked to pretend I was a dragon tamer."

She lifted her head to look at him. "Tamer? Don't you mean slayer?"

"Never. I wanted to fly across the sky on their backs. Train them to eat out of my hand."

"And why would you do that?"

There was wicked gleam in his gaze. "To rescue the damsel from the evil tyrant."

"Aye, of course. And what would you do with her then?"

James ran his hand up the length of her ribcage, cupped her breast. "I'd make love to her until all the bad memories were replaced with good ones."

"Ah," she sighed into his neck. "A true knight indeed. I believe you should have an emblem to show your allegiance." She touched the circle of silver lying over his heart. "Like this."

James trapped her hand with his. He shifted so that her face was in clear view. "What are you about, my love?"

"We have shared so much together. Yet you keep secrets from me even now. I am not blind. I see that a swan is engraved on the outside. More than once, I've read what is engraved on the inside of your ring. 'Tis a beautiful ring, yet you keep it hidden. I ask only that you trust me enough to explain it." She took a deep breath. "Does it belong to someone who has your heart? If so, I would know her name so that my aim is sure and true when I let the arrow fly."

Incredulous, his eyes widened. Then he erupted into a chuckle.

Heat rose to her cheeks. "'Tis not funny." She tried to pull away and found he would not let her go.

"Nay, my love, 'tis not another woman."

Life ebbed back into her heart. Then her breath caught. "I don't understand. It cannot be a man who—"

Anger slowly bubbled as she waited for his laughter to subside. It was only when he wrapped his arms around her middle that she allowed her back to lean against him. Her anger dissipated when he finally caught his breath, turned her and pressed his forehead to her cheek.

"I think 'tis time for a bedtime tale," he said into her temple. "When I am through, you are to remember that it is nothing more than a boy's dream to be a knight, train dragons and protect their king."

"The swan and the brotherhood," Terrwyn urged impatiently.

He kissed her temple. The caress of his hand against her ribcage and across her belly followed the rhythm of his words. "A long time ago, a mother wished to see her young son safe from evildoers. She gathered his young playmates together and asked for their vow of protection. In so doing, she created a secret brotherhood she named the Knights of the Swan. To this day, they watch over her son."

Terrwyn sighed, melting into his touch. "And you are one of those...knights?"

"Aye, whether I may agree or at times disagree with my friend's decisions, it is always my duty to see him safe."

She stroked his jaw to soothe the tension in his face. "You

do this in secret? Without recognition?"

James turned his head to press a kiss into her palm. His gaze caught and held hers. "I will do all that I must to protect my friend and liege. Even if it requires my life."

"You are a dragon slayer? I thought you wished to save the damsel?"

"I've decided I must love her body until only good memories are present." Grinning, he captured her lips and plundered her mouth with his tongue.

Pliant, breathless, she nodded in understanding. "I will not share your secret with anyone. However, to keep my mind clear of worry for your safety, you shall have to kiss me like this on a daily basis."

"Oh, I vow to do much more."

⚜

Terrwyn stood beside the table built into the cabin wall and fingered through the parchments spread out on the wooden planks. She singled one out. "Where did you draw this?"

James examined the drawing she tapped. "A meeting. Why do you ask?"

"I believe that is my brother. He's older here. Older than the first drawing I saw of him."

James reared back in the chair.

"You knew all this time where to find him?" Terrwyn stared into his face, searching for the answer she desperately did not want to hear. "Why didn't you tell me?"

"You know there are things I cannot and will not discuss." James lifted her hand and licked the palm, nipping at the tender flesh between thumb and index. His hand stole up on her breast in an effort to distract her attention. He pulled her to his lap and kissed her neck, nuzzling behind her ear. "Not even with you, my sweet."

"Again you choose your king over me?"

The need to put space between them grew with each heartbeat. She pushed away and stepped out of reach. "What future do we have if we cannot trust each other with our secrets?"

He locked her with a stormy gaze. His chest rose and fell, shuddering with emotions he would not reveal. He touched the silver band hanging on the leather thong around his neck.

Terrwyn knew its significance, what it represented. It mocked their love. James's loyalty to King Henry would come before her. Mayhap it would forever be a wall between them.

Without a word, he gathered his drawings, stuffing them back into the leather pouch. He hesitated before opening the door. "We will dock soon. I'll send word when it is time for us to disembark."

Terrwyn did not notice when the ship rolled and shuddered underfoot. She hugged herself tight, her arms empty of James's heat. Through the porthole she watched England's shoreline draw nearer and did her best to ignore the heartache threatening to swallow her whole. Her mind raced to recall all the sketches laid out on the table. Visions danced and wove their way through her blood. By the time Captain Russo gave the order to drop anchor, her plan to follow James was in place.

Chapter Twenty-Nine

James walked down the plank, leaving Terrwyn and the *Genoese Queen* behind. He searched the docks and made a point to avoid touching the note hidden in the folds of his cloak. The means of delivery was suspect. The brotherhood made every effort to avoid putting anything in writing. Mayhap it was best hidden in plain sight. He nodded at Captain Russo.

"Ah, *Signore* Frost, where is your bride?"

James held out his hand, passing him a small bag of coins. "I trust you will keep an eye on my wife while I arrange safe passage to our lodging."

He ignored the questioning look the captain sent him and tipped his cap before setting off to the row of buildings lining the port. The tightening in his chest caused him to glance back. Captain Russo stood where he left him, staring at something he held in both hands.

James attempted to shrug off the gnawing tension. He hoped that when he completed his mission Terrwyn would forgive his ill treatment. Though he did his best to direct his mind on the task at hand, he had to jerk his thoughts from the lady posing as his wife.

Saints' bones! He swore he saw her reflection everywhere he went. There was even a time or two he felt her nearby, heard her voice. Even the memory of her scent distracted him.

The suspicion that he had not gone mad after all began to grow. He dodged into an alley filled with refuse. His hand shot out, grabbing the front of his stalker's jerkin. A surprised yelp followed.

He spun, slamming mouth on mouth, chest to chest, against the building. Feeling her resistance in the kiss, he lifted his head. Anger and relief boiled into a heady stew.

"I should beat you as the captain suggested." He kissed the corner of her mouth, dodging her threatening teeth. "But I have the good sense to know it wouldn't do a whit of good. Will it?"

"You won't lay a hand on me again, English."

James raised her off the ground when she kicked out at his shins. "Have we returned to that again?" He shook his head.

"You are not true to your word! You left me to fend for myself."

"I paid Captain Russo good coin to care for you."

"Aye, well he's been paid doubly well. Even offered to set me off in the direction you took."

James released his hold. "Probably feared I meant to burden him with your care forever."

Terrwyn gripped his arm. "I don't forgive you for lying, but I will protect you."

Resigned to her presence, he stepped back and started for the lane leading down to the shadier side of the docks.

"Do you intend to make me follow you all day and night?" Terrwyn called out.

James jerked her to his side. "I had my reasons to leave you at the ship. If there were time, I would return you there myself. You will keep silent and stay out of the way. Do you understand?"

CRSO

James sat at the trestle table in one of Southampton's more questionable taverns. He watched as he always did, but this time he could not seem to manage the skill of remaining unnoticed. At least that was what he feared. Even though Terrwyn was dressed in men's leggings and jerkin, her presence was not easily ignored.

Twice now the serving wench had delivered their ale and trenches. Twice she had propositioned Terrwyn for a tryst in the back rooms. The girl promised the pretty young man she would give him a turn he would forever remember.

James pushed Terrwyn's wrist under the table. "Put that away."

"She'll mind her words when next time I flash my blade in her face. Did you hear that last one?"

He squelched the sudden urge to try some of the serving wench's ideas. He leaned into her, the sudden need to kiss her foremost on his mind. "Aye, she has a streak of imagination."

Thunderstruck, Terrwyn pulled away. "Imagination be damned. Even if she is a whore, I'm certain most of those feats are impossible."

James fingered his mug of ale. Thanks to Terrwyn's indignation, the nearest tavern patrons were casting covert glances in their direction. He wondered how he would get them out of the backstreet establishment without altercation. The docks were always a dangerous place. With the king's army gathering for war, there were more than a few souls looking for a drunken fool to roll free of his coin. Robbery, assault and the business of whoring all could be found in a single night. He did not want to experience any of those this evening.

A tall, mountainous man stumbled through the door. Obviously almost too drunk to stand up, he knocked into tables and chairs, ricocheting off angry patrons' backs. Shoved by a man dressed all in black, he fell onto the table where James and Terrwyn sat.

Before James could tell the drunken sot to shove off, Terrwyn stabbed her blade into the wooden planks of the table. It struck close to the odiferous stranger's eyes.

"You'll take your mangy cur hide and leave before I carve a hole in your head where your brains ought to be," she said.

"Beg your pardon, young gosling." The drunkard burped loudly. He winked then shoved his filthy body off the table. Saluting the duo, he made a wobbly bow and headed out into the night.

James slammed down enough coins to cover the cost of their bill. He groaned out loud when the apple-cheeked serving wench trotted up to them.

"Coo, that was amazing, my lad." She rubbed her hand up

and down Terrwyn's sleeve. "I'd be 'appy to thank you proper like for ridding our fine establishment of that oaf."

Terrwyn jerked her arm out of the maiden's grasp and trotted after James. "Was that Drem?"

A group of men pushed past them. The apparent bulges at their waists announced the presence of clubs and dirks tucked within easy reach. A reveler, his steps heavy with drink, stumbled out of the passage between the two buildings. He yanked at the cords holding his hose up and drifted toward the tavern lights.

"Was it?" Terrwyn demanded.

James stopped and pulled her into the dark alleyway. The stench of waste assailed their noses as they moved deeper into the shadows. He unlaced his leggings and pretended to relieve himself against the wall of the tavern.

"You cannot speak so loud," he said under his breath.

"Would you tell me if you knew?" she pressed.

"There are more lives at stake than ours or your brother's. He knows we are here and will reveal himself when he knows it is safe. Do you understand?"

"Aye," she whispered, apprehension filling her gaze.

A horse-drawn cart rolled by the alley. James hooked his arm through Terrwyn's and strolled behind it. He whistled a jaunty tune until the cart was well ahead of them.

They walked in and out of the misty shadows. He led her to a small cottage hidden in the gloomy night. A small wooden sign with a faded emblem of a swan swimming in a sea of ivy swayed in the sea breeze. He lifted a rock and pulled out a key to the gate. Despite the unkempt, dilapidated look about the cottage, the gate swung open on well-oiled hinges. He lit the lantern hanging on a fence post and then blew the flame out.

The door opened after he rapped out a cadence. Terrwyn waited for James to motion that it was safe to enter. He nodded at her caution and led the way.

Hushed voices paused in mid-speech. Though the lights were dimmed, the darkness about the place was due largely to the heavy furs covering shuttered windows.

Terrwyn moved closer to James's side and found his hand. He gave her fingers a gentle squeeze and started to lead her away from the door.

A large redheaded man stepped up. He held a candle aloft and peered at them. His eyes glowed with the most astonishing green Terrwyn had ever seen. It reminded her of the first shoots of grass after a winter. She supposed her mam would call it meadow green.

"Frost," he said, "I cannot believe you enter as you do."

James looked at the ham-sized palm pushing his chest and then looked up at the man. "What's the meaning of this, Nathan? You've known me most of your life."

"Aye, I thought I did until word came of the danger you pose to the king."

James released Terrwyn and nudged her to step aside.

"Nay," she hissed.

Nathan took notice and pointed at her with his chin. "Said that you'd be traveling with another." He shoved James's chest with the flat of his hand. "Though no one would believe you'd bring a stranger here."

Though the man called Nathan was taller by a foot, James stood his ground. "Who delivered this message? How long ago did you receive it?"

"I tell you that you've been named a traitor and that is all you want to know?"

When the great paw did not ease off his chest James added, "Sir Nathan Staves, you know me well enough to let me speak."

"Aye," a voice over Terrwyn's shoulder rumbled. "I would hear of his tale before we run him through." He pushed past Nathan. His dark head came closer in height to James's but his shoulders were wide and powerful under his leather jerkin and doublet. He pointed his blade to the table where three other men sat.

"My thanks, Sir Darrick," James said. "I'd as well tell it once and be done with it."

"Aye? No promises here. You'll tell it until we're satisfied."

James smiled at the menacing faces. Each kept to the shadows, but Terrwyn knew that any one of them would gut them from throat to hip. She winced when Sir Darrick caught the back of her neck and pushed her to the table.

James nodded at Terrwyn and spoke slowly out the corner of his mouth. "'Tis okay, love. They're a good lot of men once we get past this formality."

Nathan drew back. "Love? Dear God, man, have you lost your senses completely?"

James shook his arms free. Before he could make another move, heavy hands pushed his shoulders down, forcing him to sit at the table. He pulled Terrwyn to his lap when the drunkard from the tavern broke through the door.

The man sat next to them and leaned in, his words clear of liquor. "They may hesitate, but I won't have trouble running you through if you don't take your hands from my sister."

Terrwyn searched his face. Under the dirt and stink of his disguise was the man in her dreams. The same man who broke her nights with the visions. The little boy she knew six years ago no longer lived. In his place was this tall brawny man. He had the same high cheekbones as their father's. His nose was similar too. But his eyes, now those were the same golden-flecked shade as their mam.

"Drem," she whispered. "'Tis really you." She touched his cheek with trembling fingertips. "You're alive."

He caught her hand to his face. "I should pray so. Though when our mam and father learn you've run away, 'tis certain they'll skin the both of us."

Terrwyn slid from James's lap and fell into Drem's embrace. "I fear we have so much to discuss," she said, her voice breaking as she swiped at the tears streaming down her face. She lifted her gaze to James then looked at the rest of the men in the room. "With all of you."

CRBO

A few hours later, a handful of men, brothers of the Knights of the Swan, rode off in the middle of the night. Armed with their instructions they would find the two men who had brought the false message that accused James and the archer of deceit. Aided by Bran's information, they knew which tavern to search for Simon of Norwich and Edgar Poole.

CR8O

Word came to the cottage in the wee hours of dawn that the brotherhood had found their prey.

Tasked with protecting the king's ship, James and Drem sat at the long plank table. Though not a Knight of the Swan, Drem was one of King Henry's personal guards. James listened to his observations and advice on protecting their king.

Heads together, they discussed Henry's plans for taking France by storm. He intended to reclaim what he deemed should have been England's prize all along. Surprise and perseverance were his battle cries.

"And a great number of men," Drem jested. "Ever hear the tale of a Welshman called the Archer? Said to be on his way. Can bring down a bird in the air, blindfolded."

Terrwyn lay on the rug in front of the hearth. She turned on her side and watched the two men she loved dearly. She knew when James broke the news of her history as the famed archer. Drem's stunned silence ended with a string of curses.

Lifting the blanket to her chin, she listened to them talk throughout the night. Despite the pain he caused her by his lack of trust, James had delivered on his vow to find her brother. After all this time, she could not believe she found Drem only to learn he prepared to go to war with his king. At least the night visions would not come to her tonight. Her eyelids began to drift shut. This time sleep would indeed be restful.

Startled by the silence, Terrwyn awoke to an empty room.

Sweat-soaked, she shoved back her damp hair. A note lay on the table. Recognizing James's hand, she picked it up and read his cryptic letter.

My love,

Received word Simon and Edgar Poole slipped through our fingers yet again. Your brother and I are off to slay this dragon once and for all. Stay put until our return.

Yours,
James

Terrwyn lifted the fur and stared out the window, searching for answers. No matter her efforts, the chill in her bones lingered. She could not make sense out of the dream's return. Although Drem's face remained blackened, a new element had been added. Blood. Blood on her hands. More worrying were the thick rivers of blood on James.

The recent dream coupled with James's note told her she should not stay, idly waiting for the vision's fulfillment. She tossed the parchment on the table and hurried to dress for the day.

After donning the woolen gown Lady Mary sent with her, Terrwyn tucked a blade in her boot. She lifted the skirt and strapped another blade to her thigh. Her hair hung down her back in a single thick braid.

As the door slowly swung open, she turned, feigning surprise.

"I told ye I'd make ye pay for yer interference," Edgar Poole said.

"My father—"

"Yer father's a foolish man. I knew better than to believe that tale young Bran brought back. Didn't have the heart for spilling a little blood."

Though Terrwyn knew from the dream that she must go with him, she struggled to break free when he grabbed her and threw a bag over her head. He looped a rope over the sack and knotted it around her waist.

"Not like I do," he said as he hoisted her over his shoulder. "Don't mind me a little blood now and then."

With every step, Terrwyn's head bobbed against his back. She fought to drag in a breath and ignore the rising nausea. She kicked out as panic began to swell. Her muffled shouts for freedom continued until he dumped her into the back of a cart. Her head hit the wooden slats so hard that she thought she might lose her morning meal.

"Don't ye worry none. Yer two men are anxious to see ye. They be waiting for ye to join 'em."

Terrwyn strained to see through the bag over her head. The coarse grain sack allowed bits of light to filter in. She could tell by the salty mist in the air that they were drawing closer to the harbor. She rolled to her side when he brought the cart to a sudden halt. The bag had inched up until she could stick her fingers out and grab the folds of her skirt.

Poole lifted her out of the cart before she could gain access to the blade in her boot. Once again slung over his shoulder, she focused on the sounds around her. The lonely call of a seagull rose over the sound of his hobnailed boots striking the cobblestones.

He opened a door. "Damn Simon's black-hearted soul. What's the impatient fool gone and done now?" Poole dropped her off his shoulder, unknotted the rope around her middle and shoved her into a room. "Appears yer man left without ye. Now don't ye fret. When I come back for ye, we'll have a right cozy talk."

"Go to the devil," Terrwyn shouted.

"Mind yer tongue, ye spiteful wench." Poole slammed the door and the lock clicked into place.

Terrwyn wiggled the bag off her head and made a quick search of the room. The brick walls looked solid and strong. Large iron hinges held the heavy oak door in place. A rustic bench, the only piece of furniture, stood against the wall. The only light came from a small window, no bigger than the one on the *Genoese Queen,* which overlooked the waterfront. A fleet of ships floated in the harbor. Their tall masts rose into the gray sky.

Her hands no longer confined, she dug into her boot and pulled out the blade.

She sat on the bench to recall where she had seen James and her brother in her dream. The pain in her head grew as she tried to force out the details. She pressed her temples. It was difficult to focus on the background and not on their faces.

They were not alone. Someone else stood nearby. The small room was dark, deep in shadows. Much like Captain Russo's tiny cabin. Then it went to black. Nothing. The dream evaporated into the mists.

Opening her eyes, she saw the sun had begun its descent. Her patience worn, she knelt down to examine the flooring for loose boards. Her hand swept over the floor and under the bench. A silver ring emblazoned with a swan rolled out. She picked it up, cradling it in the palm of her hand. She read the word engraved inside. *Brotherhood.*

"James," she whispered. She kissed it, knowing he'd left it there for her to find. He meant to return for her and for the ring. Her thoughts turned to their talk of marriage. Surely one of her dreams would come true. She recalled the happy faces of children running and laughing in a meadow. The sun was shining on their faces. Faces that looked like James.

The explosion rocked Terrwyn to her knees. It sucked the breath from her lungs. Gripping the edge of the bench, she dragged herself off the floor. She ran to the small window and peered out.

Smoke billowed from one of the tall masts. A tongue of fire flickered from the porthole of one of the ships. Bran's message returned to her. The treacherous men had succeeded in igniting a ship.

A shadow of movement caught her attention. Her stomach clenched and she turned to confront the rat-faced man running through the door. Edgar Poole came toward her, a wicked gleam in his eye.

"What a sight to behold! I daresay there's nothing much left of them now." He rubbed his hands together. "Went off a bit sooner than I planned, but I know how to make a nasty situation better."

"Who?" Terrwyn cried. Flashes of her night vision exploded in her head. *The blood. Dear God, do not let it be James and Drem.* "What did you do?"

"Told them yer man was never a match for me. Too bad yer father wasn't here to see it." He reached out to stroke her head. "Though, like I said, I don't think he woulda' had the stomach for it either. Not in the long run."

Terrwyn jerked her head out of reach. She felt the comfort of the blade strapped to her thigh. She gripped the other blade she kept hidden in her skirts.

"Yer a pretty wench, aren't ye? I cannot see why Dafydd wished ye dead. Maybe ye gave him too much trouble." He snatched her braid and gave it a yank. "Ye need a firm hand is all ye need."

He drew her close enough for her to smell his sour breath. "You are no man for me, Edgar Poole. You won't have me, nor will you have your victory."

Poole pressed her to his chest. "Plenty of men of station are willing to pay me good coin to rid Lancaster blood from the throne. 'Tis Henry's ship that is aflame. He bedded there last eve. And he met his death by noon." He lowered his head to gain access. "Ye are me added prize."

Air sucked through the gap in his teeth. His eyes widened in shock. He let go of her head and stared down at his stomach.

Terrwyn's blade, struck through to the hilt, impaled his body. Furious, he pulled it out and stumbled back. Armed with her own weapon, he staggered toward her.

She flipped up the hem of her skirt and withdrew the blade strapped to her thigh.

Poole fell to the floor. His eyes glazed, he struggled to breathe.

She did not wait for him to draw his last breath but ran out the door.

Chapter Thirty

Her feet flew over the cobblestones and toward the docks where the fire raged. The harbor was alive with soldiers and common folk running to put out the flames on the ship. A water brigade had been set up. Townspeople and soldiers handed off bucket after bucket.

The ring gripped in her hand, Terrwyn searched for familiar faces. Two men stumbled past, one with blood streaming down his face, the other one blackened from soot. She ran to them. They looked beyond her, their eyes marred from shock.

She turned to scan the harbor, searching the waves lapping at the shore. They had to be alive. She would not believe otherwise. Caught in the swell of locals who did not want the fire to reach beyond the bay, she pushed closer to the king's ship.

Captain Russo stood in the water brigade line. He had removed the brocade coat and rolled up his sleeves to pass the buckets, one after the other.

"*Signora* Frost," he said over the roar of the crowd. "Where is your husband?"

Terrwyn blinked, pushing through the terror of life without James. "Have you seen him, Captain?"

A deep frown furrowed his bushy brows. "*Sí*, but that was before the explosion. Is possible he has returned to your lodgings?"

She shook her head. "Nay, I—I believe he and my brother are still here somewhere. Mayhap near the king's ship."

Captain Russo motioned one of his men to take his place

and stepped out of the line. "This is not a place for you. The docks surrounding the ship have been cleared. The only ones there are the wounded and the dead."

"Captain, you know how stubborn I can be. You know me. I will stay by your side until I get my answers." Seeing his wariness, she tried a different tack. "Please."

"You stay," he said. "I will see what more I can learn."

Terrwyn nodded and watched him walk into the bank of smoke. She jumped out of the way when the soldiers came out with the first stretcher. She peered closely and offered a prayer of thanksgiving that it was not James or Drem. Only one came out covered in canvas sheeting.

The shuddering of her bones built as the waiting continued. By the time Captain Russo returned, she feared his answer.

He gripped his hat under his arm. Blackened from the smoke, his countenance seemed grimmer than when he entered.

"Good news, *signora*." His teeth flashed in contrast with his soot-coated face. "Though many are injured, only one is with mortal injuries. Burned beyond recognition, but I do not believe it is your man. Is as I said earlier. He is probably waiting for you at your lodgings."

Hope swelled and nearly knocked her to her knees. The captain grabbed her elbow and steered her past the brigade. He motioned for one of his men to help the mistress get to the lodging safely.

Ensconced in the cart, they rattled off to the cottage by the harbor. Her heart filled with joy. She would apologize to James for losing her temper and promise never to lose it again. She would smother him with kisses, tell him of her love.

"Stop here," she called out.

The ship's mate reined the horses in and helped her out. Terrwyn waited for him to drive out of sight before heading to the cottage. She recalled the cadence of knocks. When no one responded she tested the door and found it unlocked.

Wearily she sat at the table. The empty cottage grew grimmer as the day wore on. Her hopes plummeted. The captain was wrong. James was not here. Nor was Drem. The loneliness without James was unbearable. Tears began to fall. She feared she'd made a terrible mistake in leaving the harbor fire.

Panic began to build. She would make her way back to the ship. Mayhap more news would be available.

The door secured behind her, she slipped out of the gate and walked swiftly down the road. Memories of the nights with James filtered into her thoughts. Each memory gave her strength to move on. She searched the buildings, the people passing by, praying she would see his wonderful smile, his stormy eyes. With every person she passed, the fear she would never see him again burrowed into her hope. What if that lone soul they pulled from the fire was James?

Following the sounds, Terrwyn entered the tavern nearest the ship. Conscripted to house the injured, the building was filled with both common men and soldiers. Their thirsts quenched, the burns bandaged, they sat at a table, their faces gaunt with fatigue.

Terrwyn pushed her way through, all the while scanning the room for those she loved. She scoured the faces of everyone in the room. The stench of sweat and smoke pulled at the breath in her lungs. Her eyes stung.

She approached a familiar-looking man sitting at the table who had bandages covering most of his head. A young serving wench appeared none too happy with him.

"Lord love you, Millie, I'm fine," Drem said over the din. "Just a bump on my noggin and a burn here and there. There's others hurt worse than me."

"I'll be the judge of that," the young miss said sternly. "Just look at your poor hands."

The words lodged in Terrwyn's throat. She tried again. Her mouth moved, but nothing came.

The grimness in his face intensified. "God's bones, Terrwyn—" He started to rise and Millie brusquely pushed him back in the chair.

Terrwyn rushed to her brother. "I feared I lost you." She brushed her lips on an undamaged portion of his cheek.

"Here, miss," Millie said, pulling out a bench. "You need to sit down before you fall over."

Her brother held out his bandaged hand. "Aye, sit, sit." Assured the blood was not her own, he settled back in his chair. "Thank God, you are all right. Poole—"

"James," Terrwyn said, fighting back the tears. "Where is he?"

Drem wiped his mouth with his sleeve before meeting her gaze. "I don't know."

Her heart pitched. "But you were with him—"

He shook his head slowly. "He left with Simon."

"Simon?" Her heart pitched again.

"Then the explosion—"

"Explosion." Terrwyn leaned forward, gripping her brother's forearm. "You and James were on the ship?"

"Aye. And Simon." He took a pull of the ale in his mug. "The lad confessed he found himself in too deep with Poole. Convinced James he desired to set matters right and could lead him to where they intended to set the fire." Emotion choked his next words. "Led him off like a sheep to the wolves."

The room blurred. Terrwyn swiped at the burning in her eyes.

He covered her head with his bandaged hand. "God's blood, Terrwyn, I should have demanded to stay with him. But your James would hear none of it. Said 'twas my responsibility to protect the king if they did not get there in time. And I knew he was right."

"But you didn't see him? You haven't seen him since?" Terrwyn asked, determined to cling to hope.

He winced where her fingers dug into his wrist. They both ignored Millie's clucking concern. "'Tis true I haven't seen him since. The explosion ripped through the deck below Henry's chamber. It knocked me to my knees. Poole caught me off guard when he ran by, cracking me on the head with his cudgel." His eyes lit. "The cottage. I wager he returned to the Swans' cottage and is waiting for you there."

Despite the trembling quakes running through her body, she shook her head, her voice barely discernable. "I've already been."

"Aw, Terrwyn, I cannot tell you how saddened I am."

"Nay." The single word came out in defiance. "It cannot be as you say."

She turned, mindless of the feet she stepped on, the injuries she bumped, and ran out of the tavern.

⊂�⊃

Once again, Terrwyn stood at the docks. The fire out, repairs had already begun on the ship anchored in the harbor. Her steps faltered as she drew nearer to the destruction. The wooden planks were littered with soot and bloodied bandages. Two soldiers guarded a lone body covered in the portion of a canvas sail. James's vow to his liege echoed in her ears. He would protect the king or die trying.

She shivered and took a step toward the soldiers. "Please. I would see the soul you have there."

"Halt." Their pikestaffs blocked her path.

"Please, can you at least tell me his name?"

"By order of King Henry, we are not to let anyone near."

"But I would know this man under yon canvas," she pleaded.

One of the soldiers shifted forward, giving her false hope that he might let her draw near. "Then I suggest you take up your grievance with the king. 'Tis certain he would be curious about your interest in this man."

At a loss, she turned to look over the buildings' roofs, wondering which one held Edgar Poole's lifeless and decaying body. Mayhap James had gone to retrieve her and the ring. The slightest glimmer of hope began to build, scorching out despair.

She searched the skyline of Southampton, recalling the path she ran to reach the harbor. She marched forward, toward the building where she was certain she'd left Poole. Night was moving in, but she did not care. Finding James was all that mattered.

She pulled the cloak close as a man stumbled down the road. He was covered in soot. Her stomach knotted when he redirected his path. She braced for his assault, suddenly aware she had forgotten to tuck her knife into her belt.

"Terrwyn," he bellowed in her ear. "Through God's blood, you are alive."

"Sir Nathan..." She hugged him tight, thankful he was well. She gripped his sleeve, fearing the knight's answer. "James? Have you seen him?"

He pointed toward a cobblestone path that led to a small shed.

She heart lurched as she ran toward the shed. "James!" she cried. "James!"

The most wonderful sight she had ever seen stepped to the doorway. The light behind shone around him in a halo.

"Terrwyn," he called. He met her in the middle of the path. Lifting her into his arms, he held her as if he would never let her go. He buried his face into her shoulder and wept. "Ah, God's mercies! I didn't know what to think, my love. There's so much blood."

"And I feared you dead." Breathless, she pulled away. "And Simon? What of him?"

James cupped the back of her head. "You were right, you know. Deep down, he had a good heart. He could not live with the disgrace to his family and gave his life so that Henry might escape the ship. Said he did it for Gilly's. He did not want his greed to tarnish his niece's future. Terrwyn, your father—"

"Dead?" she whispered. Though it pained her to think of him no longer in her life, she'd come to accept that was the way it must be.

"Nay, 'tis said that he hides with Owain Glyndwr."

"How long will his luck continue?"

James kissed her forehead. "The man no longer has the love and respect of his family. If you ask me, his luck already left him."

Terrwyn nodded and gently caressed his cheek. Burn marks littered the heavy leather gambeson, one hole exceedingly too close to his heart. A film of smoke and dried blood coated his hair. "You're hurt."

"'Tis only a scratch, my love. I'll heal faster with you in my arms."

Aware of how close she had come to losing him, Terrwyn covered his mouth with hers and drank of the life flowing through his veins.

Knowing his injuries caused him more pain than he let on, she lifted his arm and gently placed it on her shoulder for him to lean on. "Let's go home, James, my love." She looked up at the gray sky. "'Tis certain to be a bright and lovely tomorrow."

James stopped and turned her to face him. His lips lingered over her mouth before he lifted his head. "Now, will you be mine and marry me?"

"I've always been yours. I just didn't know it."

∙≈∙

Shouts of good cheer rang out in the dingy cottage by the seaside. Soon the fleet of ships would be sailing to France. Word had come that Simon of Norwich had given his life while trying to stop the fire. Although Edgar Poole succumbed to his mortal injuries, the Knights of the Swan continued their search for the others who had plotted against the throne.

Young King Henry tipped his glass to the band of men he trusted to keep him alive and his throne safe. He looked at the couple kneeling before him. "Rise. I give you a toast to carry with you." Lifting his mug high overhead, he said, "May there be someone to hold 'til the wee hours of the morn. Someone to love us despite our faults. Someone to care whether we live or die. And may that someone be ours to love throughout eternity."

James folded Terrwyn in his embrace and she knew that, aye, her life was blessed with love. As her lips touched his, she saw their laughing children and knew her vision was a gift indeed.

About the Author

Growing up on a farm in the Midwest, I learned to escape the never-ending chores by storytelling. I'd slip off to the barn or the fields and settle into a book that would take me away. Before long, I started creating my own stories to keep myself entertained. Eventually, adult responsibilities took over and I put away my storytelling, but never my love for reading.

One year, during an exceptionally long Wisconsin winter, my fascination with historical romance blossomed from reading them to needing to write them. I just couldn't get the dream out of my head. I had to write. I began the arduous task of learning all I could about writing a story. Those lessons continue every day.

I believe there are wonderful courageous characters waiting for someone to tell their story. When I write, my goal is to capture a moment in time, where the threads of history, adventure, hope, passion and love, sweep the reader away.

To learn more about C.C. Wiley, please visit www.ccwiley.com.

LaVergne, TN USA
26 August 2010
194797LV00003B/56/P